WHERE TRUST BEGINS

SONIA HARTS

CONTENTS

CHAPTER 1

My plane lands in nowhere suburbia at noon. Passengers rise to gather their luggage from the overhead compartments and line up to leave before the doors have opened. I can't even muster the energy to sit up straight in my seat.

When Mr. Banks suggested I take some time off, I wanted to refuse. My father would've wanted me to push through my grief for the greater good of Seidel Computers, but he's not here to see how I'm coping. Maybe it's a blessing in disguise that he's not around to see what a failure his daughter turned out to be.

Five months of pretending I was fine passed, and then last week happened. I can't even think about it without cringing, but I also can't force the incident from my mind. Even looking down at myself reminds me why I'm here. In the office I wear power suits - high-waisted slacks and blouses with lace detailing to soften the edge of a bold blazer on top. An entire row of blazers in varying styles and colors occupies space in my closet, each one a week's worth of an assistant's salary. If I ever have children, they'll have my suits to compete with for my love.

Now, I'm practically unrecognizable in leggings and an over-sized Chicago Bears hoodie, my dark hair tied back in a messy braid. I didn't bother changing out of the clothes I slept in last night because that's how low I've sunken. It's only once I exit the terminal that I remember it's the start of summer and Texas is bound to be ninety degrees outside. I blow out a breath between my teeth. Just perfect.

After searching the carousel for my checked bag, I find Chastity and Christian Barrera waiting for me outside at pickup. My best friend is leaning against her brother's Mustang and smiles brightly when she spots me heading towards them.

"Dacia! Over here!" Chastity waves her arms over her head, jumping up and down as if she's not noticeable enough in her bright coral dress and wedged heels. Figures she would dress up just to pick me up from the airport. I rush forward, not even the wheels of my suitcase catching on dips in the gravel able to stop me. When I reach her, I throw down my bags and wrap my arms around her in a tight hug. Four and a half months have passed since I've seen my best friend in person. With my brother at NYU and my cousin occupied with work in California, I turned to Chastity for sanctuary in my time of need. Ever since we finished undergrad and moved to different cities, we can only manage to see each other for no more than a week at a time. If I can take one good thing away from this forced time off, it's that I can spend the entire summer with her.

"Oh, don't mind where you put your bags. I've got them." A sarcastic voice to my right says, but Chastity and I don't so much as look up. I watch over Chastity's shoulder as Christian picks up my suitcase and tote bag and places them in the trunk of his car. "And by the way, I'm still waiting on my hug."

"One more minute," I tell him, squeezing Chastity's shoulders. "I swear, I'm almost done."

Chastity laughs before pulling away. "I knew you missed me too much to avoid Texas forever. I'm just sorry it has to be in San Antonio."

"When you said your parents were expanding the restaurant, I was hoping they'd start with Austin. But I'm biased." Despite being an avid Texas-hater, I was actually born and raised in Austin before moving to Chicago after middle school. I only come down once or twice a year to visit my grandmother, but usually I prefer when she comes up to visit me. The same goes for Chastity and Christian, though they have even less reason to visit Illinois than my grandmother.

"Austin is too hip for our parents." Christian says, stepping forward to hug me. It doesn't last half as long as my hug with his sister. "They don't understand millennials, and they're not trying to."

"Plus, their Hispanic demographic doesn't even compare to the one here." Chastity says. "They keep saying Austin doesn't have the appreciation for true, authentic Mexican food that San Antonio does, and they're not wrong."

Chastity and Christian could be twins for how much they look alike. They both have dark hair, high cheek bones, one dimple on the right sides of their cheeks, and dark brown eyes. The only differences are in their skin tones and body build; Chastity's skin is two shades deeper than Christian's. He could almost pass for white, but the Barrera family is all Mexican (and the overtly religious kind, if their first name's are any indication). Even I'm darker than him and I'm not fully Mexican. And while Christian is built like an athlete, lean and muscular, Chastity is all soft curves. A size twenty with all the confidence of a size two, as she often says on her channel.

"Well, your parents are the experts." I climb into the backseat as Christian walks around to the driver's side. Five whole minutes standing outside and the heat is already seeping in through my thick hoodie. I can't remember the last time I've looked forward to a car's AC this badly. Chastity slides in beside me, much to her brother's irritation.

"What am I, your chauffeur? Someone better get in the passenger seat right now if y'all want to get out of here." Chastity scowls before switching seats and I let out a laugh. "Much better." Chastity flips her brother off as he puts the car in drive.

"So, when are we moving into the apartment again?" I ask them. Their parents bought a house on the north side of town, but Christian found a three-month lease on a villa in midtown for the three of us.

"Not until the first." Chastity says. Three days from now. "But until then, we do have a wedding to look forward to tomorrow night."

Shit. I knew I was forgetting about something. "Right. Your cousin is getting married to that finance guy."

"God, can you believe we're at an age where wedding and baby shower announcements are normal?" Chastity mimes her head exploding. "I swear, in my head I'm still seventeen and not almost twenty-six." She gasps suddenly, putting a hand to her mouth. "I'm almost ten years older than I think I am!"

"Maybe that's because you spend way too much time on the internet." Christian says. "Half your subscribers are teenage girls. I think it's warping your sense of self."

"I can't help that I appeal to a younger audience." Chastity pushes her hair back off her shoulders. "I like to think that I'm teaching the youth valuable life lessons about confidence and accepting yourself for who you are." As a plus-sized Beauty Vlogger with almost a million subscribers on YouTube, I have to agree with her. She's attained so much in her time on the internet, from multiple paid promotions to companies sending free stuff at her door, but more than that it's given her the confidence to stand out. I met Chastity when her online journey began our freshman year of college, and she was already ten times more confident than I was. We didn't get along at first, but by the end of our first year we were inseparable.

"Don't let the hater in the driver's seat get you down." I say, and she turns around to high five me. Christian rolls his eyes at us through the rear view mirror.

We arrive at their parents house twenty minutes later. Two U-Hauls are parked in the driveway, but there are no other cars to be seen. Their parents must not be home. Christian helps me bring in my bags, and Chastity gives me the grand tour of the mostly-empty house before showing me to the guest bedroom where I'll be staying. When she closes the door behind her, I know I'm in for a talk I'm not ready to have.

"How are you feeling, by the way?" She sits down on the perfectly made bed, patting the space next to her for me to sit. I give a heavy sigh as I do. "We didn't have much time to talk after the funeral."

"As well as can be expected." I look down at my scuffed sneakers. They look so out of place in this pristine bedroom.

"Cut the bullshit. After seven years, we're passed all that." I force myself to look at her. "You wouldn't be here right now - in the heart of Texas of all places - if you were okay."

"You have a point." I admit, albeit begrudgingly. "I'm not anywhere near okay, and it took me a hell of a lot longer than it should have to realize. I just..." I trail off. Chastity is silent as she watches me gather my thoughts. Talking about my emotions isn't something that comes easily to me. "I still can't shake this fear that I'm not good enough to fill my father's shoes. Nana didn't even think he was good enough to fill her shoes, so how the hell am I supposed to?"

Seidel Computers has always been a point of pride and contention in my family. But for me, it's consumed my entire life knowing that one day I'll own it all. Every ounce of effort I've put in since interning at sixteen has been in pursuit of the top position. I just never counted on that day to arrive before I was ready.

"I still have to prove to the board that my father didn't make a mistake choosing me to succeed him as CEO." I tell Chastity. "I can't do that if I'm here."

"You also can't do that while you're grieving." She says softly. The problem is I don't want to grieve. I want to throw myself into work so I don't have to think about how I've been made an orphan at twenty-five.

"But-"

"Dacia, you had a screaming match with your boss in the middle of a presentation and then ran out into the street during rush hour." Damn my cousin and her annoying habit of oversharing. Amelia is the only one who could've filled Chastity in on the details I'm trying so hard to repress. "You were almost hit by five different cars. You're lucky no one had you committed."

I wouldn't call a broken five-year streak of no panic attacks in the middle of a work meeting "lucky".

"It was a mistake." I straighten my shoulders. "I was under a lot of pressure to adjust to certain changes I have no intention of making, and Mr. Banks had it coming when he interrupted me mid-sentence to suggest I use a less robotic tone of voice." The panic attack isn't even what I'm most ashamed of. Weeks of compromising to appease board members, weeks of "yes, sir"'s and "no problem at all, sir"'s, and then they have the nerve to request that I change the most important thing about myself.

My name.

I don't know why I didn't see it coming. The request shouldn't have blindsided me the way it did, not when they asked my father to do the very same thing before he became CEO. Seidel is a family name - my grandmother's name before she married my grandfather. There's as much power in sharing a name with a corporate legacy as there is in being the face of one. But it wasn't just my surname they were asking me to change.

"Dacia," The name - my name - was said with as much distaste as I have for the man who said it. James Felding, Seidel's most demanding shareholder. "How many people can actually pronounce it, anyway? And it's not a very American name, either. It doesn't reflect the values of Seidel."

As if Seidel, the incredibly German name of my incredibly German grandmother, could ever be considered an "American" name.

I had the retort ready at the tip of my tongue when our COO (standing CEO until the board decides I'm finally "ready", whatever the hell that means) stepped in and actually told me to consider Mr. Felding's point before outright refusing. That had been the tipping point in my sanity, and if I could go back and redo that moment, I wouldn't have screamed at Mr. Banks the way I did. Instead, I would have snatched the hair piece right off his head and shoved it so far up his-

"It's obvious to everyone but you that you're in desperate need of a vacation." Chastity says, snapping me back to reality. "Which is exactly why you're here! We'll start with the wedding tomorrow-"

"Lord help me."

"We'll get a little drunk, get a little jiggy with it," I mime gagging, but Chastity is not one to be deterred. "And then we'll finally snap you out of this funk!" She grabs my shoulders and shakes me until my head is bobbing up and down. "Yes! I see you nodding!"

"Because you're shaking me." Each word is punctuated by a head bob.

"I fail to see your point." She stops harassing me for the moment and I regain my equilibrium. "You need to blow off some steam, Dacia. Especially after everything you went through with your dad and at work. When was the last time you had some fun, huh?"

I think for a moment. "I did some light reading on the plane."

Chastity is not pleased. "That is unacceptable."

"But you know I hate big events like these." I tell her. "I'd feel better if you didn't have a habit of ditching me multiple times in one night." I'm referring to the last wedding we went to together, where I stood in a corner all night reading an ebook on my phone. Come to think of it, I actually didn't mind being ditched all that much.

"Hey, I had to pee."

I give her a pointed look. "You spent half an hour flirting with a bridesmaid."

"She was cute and I totally would've set you up with a grooms-man! Come on, Dacia. You need this." I in no way need this, actually. Chastity makes everything look effortless, which is why she's less understanding of people like me, who dodge invita-tions to hang out like they're bullets and make up excuses week after week for why they can't leave the house. There are only so many flus a person can acceptably have in one year without drawing suspicion. This is how I know there's no way Chastity is letting me get out of this wedding.

My shoulders slump as I accept defeat. "Fine. But only be-cause there's an open bar."

"Yes!" She fist-pumps the air, a wide grin taking over her face. I can't help but return it. Chastity's smiles have always been infectious. "Who knows. You might enjoy it. I may even make good on my promise to set you up with a groomsman, unless there's something going on in Chicago I should know about." She gives me a pointed look.

"Like what?" I scoff.

"Oh, you know, like any clandestine affairs or potential romantic dalliances you've been hiding from me?" She smiles slyly.

"When have you ever known me to 'dally'?"

"Then it's official. I'm making it my mission to find you a summer fling." I'm already shaking my head before the words are out of her mouth. "This is happening."

"I sincerely doubt it. The only reason I'm going to this thing is to get as drunk as socially acceptable."

She slings an arm around my shoulders. "We'll see about that, Dacia. We'll see."

CHAPTER 2

At the reception, Chastity finds a fling for herself before she can think to find one for me. Not that I mind in the least. I'm sitting at the open bar, nursing a rum and coke. My plan for the night is twofold: avoid talking to people and get completely shit-faced on free drinks. I think I deserve it, given all the crap I've been through in the past year. And to think it's only halfway over.

Chastity and I are different people. Her idea of a good time is going out and making friends at every turn. People love her instantly because she has the kind of bubbly, outgoing personality you can't ignore. That's part of what makes our friendship work so well: she's not afraid to force me out of my comfort zone, and I'm not afraid to tell her like it is. On any other night, I'd try harder for her benefit. Maybe I'd even be out on the dance floor with her if I wasn't at such a low point right now. Chastity means well, but this is the last place I want to be.

I watch her from the sidelines as I sip my drink. She's dancing with a pretty girl in a red halter dress, one hand on her waist and the other tangled in the girl's short brown hair.

"It took what, half an hour for my sister to find a hook up?" Christian appears from behind and takes the drink from my hand, sipping as we watch his sister from afar. We've known each other for years, so I don't mind sharing germs with him. There was a time when I thought something more might happen between us, but our timing has always been off. Chastity was more bummed about it than I was.

"Two minutes flat." I take my drink back. "You didn't see? They locked eyes across the room and Chastity walked over, whispered something in her ear and they've been dancing ever since."

"At least someone's having a good time. I swear to god, if I hear one more screaming child I'm calling an Uber the fuck out of here."

"I'm right there with you, buddy." I pat him on the shoulder. "It looks like everyone's doing great without us, anyway."

"Dacia García!" I flinch at the voice. When I turn around, Chastity is facing us, hands on both hips and a pout on her lips. "How long have you been over here for?"

"Long enough to finish three rum and cokes, but you'd know if you hadn't left me the second we walked into the ballroom." I down the rest of my drink. "Actually, make that four." I'm two drinks past my limit and the second I stand up from this barstool, everyone else will know it, too.

"I can't help it." She wraps her arms around my shoulders, her scowl already melting into a dreamy smile. "I'm in love."

"Shut the fuck up, Chas. You say that every time you meet a pretty face." I peel her arms off of me. The booze is making me sweat enough as it is, and her body heat isn't helping.

Chastity ignores me, latching on to my upper arm to drag me off my seat. When I somehow manage to hold my ground, she pouts further. "Come on! You need to have some fun, and I know just the way." Her smile turns sly.

"I don't even want to know what you mean by that."

"I'll introduce you to Jane's brothers." She tells me anyway. "You've got plenty of options to choose from. One of them was even in the wedding party! We both know I've always wanted to set you up with a groomsman."

I'm already shaking my head. "Thanks, but I'll pass. Christian and I were planning on getting out of here."

"Nooooo," Chastity whines. "You guys can't go! We just got here!"

I glance at Christian, who lets out a long sigh and shrugs as he relents to his sister's plea. He always chooses to be unhelpful at the most inconvenient times for me. Now, I have no choice but to relent as well.

"Come on!" Chastity pulls me off the barstool and doesn't so much as bat an eye as I stumble against her back. We head to a middle table, where I spot exactly zero familiar faces sitting around it. Chastity plops down next to a girl with short hair and wide brown eyes. "Jane, this is my best friend, Dacia." She pulls me down into the seat next to her. There are no more available chairs, so Christian idles behind us. "And that's my brother, Christian."

"Nice to meet you both." The girl takes my hand, and then Christian's. "I'm Jane Galindo."

"I was hoping you could introduce one of your many handsome brothers to my straight and very available friend here."

She slings an arm around my shoulders. There's no hiding my scowl. I've never been good at hiding my discomfort, and I'm even worse at it when I'm drunk. Jane gives me a weird look and it takes every ounce of willpower my drunk ass still possesses to resist an eye roll.

"That's not necessary. Truly." I wave my hand in a dismissive way. "You guys keep having fun. I'm just here for the open bar." I snap my fingers and point to where the drinks live. But when I start to rise from my seat, Chastity reaches for my arm and pushes me right back down.

"Why? We just met and you already think you're too good for us?" Jane smiles teasingly. There's no ire in her tone, but her words still irk me. She turns to the side, where two boys are approaching the table. "Marcus, Luke! Come meet some new friends of mine!"

The boys are dressed in twin maroon oxford shirts and black dress pants. From afar their shirts look similar, but up close I notice they're actually different shades of red. The shorter one has his hands in his pockets, a bored expression on his face. He looks young, maybe fifteen or sixteen. The taller one has his sleeves rolled at his elbows and a button or two undone at the collar. He has a boutonniere pinned to the pocket of his shirt, marking him as the groomsman. His head of curls is artfully disheveled, only a shade or two darker than his skin. Anyone with eyes can see how gorgeous he is. Goddamnit. I need a good excuse to get out of this setup, and fast.

Jane indicates the younger boy as Luke and the undeniably gorgeous man as Marcus. Introductions are exchanged awkwardly, or maybe I'm the awkward one. I resist the urge to immediately excuse myself to the bathroom.

"So, this is the girl that whisked you away for the first song." Marcus says as he shakes Chastity's hand. "Nice work. My sister can be shy about meeting new people."

"What can I say?" Chastity brushes her hair back from her shoulder. "I saw her and just had to shoot my shot." She winks at Jane, who turns three shades of red. But she looks pleased nonetheless. "So I know your lovely sister is an aspiring singer. What about you?"

"I work at a daycare part time while in school." Marcus says. "It's taking me awhile 'cuz FAFSA is a joke and my parents have five mouths to feed, but this will be my last semester before I graduate."

"What are you studying?" I ask to appease Chastity after she nudges me with an elbow. Then I shoot her a look as if to say, There. Happy?

"Education." He looks between us with a quizzical expression.

"Tell them what you wanna be when you grow up." Luke says with a shit-eating grin, prodding the older boy's shoulder. Marcus rolls his eyes and his smile becomes strained.

"Our brothers give him crap because he wants to teach first grade." Jane interjects.

"God bless you." Chastity puts a hand to her heart. "You're either a saint or a masochist. I don't know you well enough yet to guess which."

Jane says "saint" at the same time Luke says "masochist".

"Probably both." Marcus shrugs. "What about you guys?"

"I'm a YouTuber, but I'm also helping my parents open their restaurant." Chastity says.

"Oh, hey! Jane's on YouTube too!" Luke exclaims. Jane sinks lower in her chair in embarrassment, but Luke seems not to notice or care. "She just started in January and already has three thousand subscribers. How many do you have?"

"I have a good amount, if I do say so myself," Chastity says slyly. "But I've also been making videos for seven years, so I've definitely put in the time."

"Oh my god, that's incredible." Jane says, brightening with interest.

"Please," Chastity tosses her hair off a shoulder. "It's just me talking to a camera for a couple of hours. It's not like I'm a singer, or, oh, I don't know," She shoots me a teasing grin. "The CEO of Seidel Computers or anything."

Everyone is staring at me, and it's all Chastity's fault.

"Wait a second." Luke says, pointing a finger at me. "You're not actually saying she owns Seidel. What's your name again?"

"Hey man, don't be rude." Marcus chides his brother before facing me. "Is that true, though? We all use Seidel computers. That's pretty amazing!"

"I'm not-"

"Well, she's technically not CEO yet." Chastity says for me. "But her grandmother was the founder, and her father was the CEO after her and now she's taking his place soon."

"Chas-" Christian attempts to stop his sister, but she keeps going. My heart is beating double time in my chest and I suddenly feel like I can't breathe. I have to shut my eyes against all the eyes on me. Chastity continues to brag about me, but I don't register a word of it. I'm an imposter. The person Chastity is describing doesn't feel like me at all. I'm a failure. I'm so much of a failure, Mr. Banks had to put me on sabbatical.

Now everyone is raving and asking question after question that I can't answer, because I can't give them the short, perfunctory answers they want. All I have is my misery and self-doubt, and absolutely no one wants to hear about my depressingly long list of problems at a wedding. Chastity and Christian save me from answering their questions, and I barely hear how over the roar in my ears.

"Excuse me." I rise abruptly and bump into no more than twenty people on my way to the women's restroom.

It wasn't a shock when my father died. My brother and I knew it was coming, but nothing ever prepares you for losing the only parent you have left. He cared more about the company than his own life. In his last days, my father worked more with his business team preparing for his death than he did with his family. Not that I ever expected him to prioritize my brother and I. The company never would have gone as far as it has if he were that kind of father. Even my own worries in his last days revolved around whether I was ready to succeed him. If I was really cut out for all that was to come.

I never had a second to breathe when the inevitable happened. My one week off work was spent planning the funeral, taking care of my brother and accepting empty condolences from virtually everyone I know. I only allowed myself one day to let all my tears out. One day to mope around the house feeling sorry for myself. One day to hate my father for continuously choosing work over family, and then feel unbelievably guilty over that hate. It's a wonder I lasted as long as I did without having a complete mental breakdown, but that's not even what I'm most ashamed of.

No one, not Chastity or even Amelia, knows about the resignation email sitting at the top of my drafts folder. I'm never going to send it. At least, that's what I tell myself. That I've worked too hard to throw it all away now. I'll be playing right into the board's hands if I quit, and I've sacrificed too much already to let them win. But the temptation remains, just a few clicks away.

But no. No. I may have as many cracks in my sanity as I do in my heart, but even after all I've been through there's still no cracking my pride. Mr. Banks will have to fire me himself if he wants me to walk away from Seidel. Even then, I won't let him. I won't.

I take in a deep breath as I kick off my heels and lean against the cool tiled wall. I'm not angry or sad anymore. Just tired. Now that the initial anxiety has passed and I lay slumped over on the grimy public restroom floor, embarrassment is the next feeling quick to follow. For fuck's sake, I'm a grown adult and I can't even make normal conversation with strangers.

Chastity finds me ten minutes later, a sad smile on her lips. It never takes her long, not when I really need her. She slumps down on the tile next to me, kicking off her shoes with a relieved sigh.

"Good god. Breaking in new shoes is the worst." She rubs her feet before turning to me. "How ya doing, Dacia?"

"Oh, fine. You haven't truly lived until you've had an existential crisis or two on a public restroom floor." I shoot her a sly smirk. "It's practically my brand after twenty-five years."

"No kidding." She laughs. We're silent for the longest time before she finally asks, "Wanna talk about it?"

I shrug. "Nothing to talk about. Just me on my social anxiety bullshit again."

"It's not bullshit." Chastity says, and I hate how grateful I feel for her saying it. "I forget other people find it hard because it's not something I've ever had to deal with. And I knew better than to brag about you like that when you're struggling at work. I shouldn't have put you in that position."

"Don't worry about it. Really." I bring my knees up to my chest. "Mr. Banks gave me this time off to clear my head, so that's exactly what I'm going to do."

"I think you definitely deserve it." Chastity says. "You worked your ass off for months, all while your dad..." She shakes her head, unable to say it.

"Yeah." I clear my throat of the emotion threatening to overtake me all over again. "He's been telling me to take one for weeks. It still feels like admitting defeat, though."

"There's nothing wrong with taking a step back."

I'm already shaking my head. I can't help the tears filling my eyes this time. "What if they don't let me come back?"

"Oh, Dacia. They will." She puts a comforting arm around my shoulders. "Get some rest. Christian won't stop complaining, so you can go back to the house with him. I'll Uber home later. We'll start fresh tomorrow."

"Thank you." I shoot her a watery smile. She helps me off the floor and we put our shoes back on and adjust our dresses before leaving the bathroom.

"I'll set you up with a brother next time." She holds the bathroom door open for me and we step outside. "You did notice how unbelievably hot Marcus is, didn't you?"

Here it comes. "Please." I roll my eyes.

"Come on, you can't even deny it. He's so your type." She bumps my shoulder with hers. "Plus, Jane tells me he's bookish. I know you love your men well-read."

"A teacher who still lives with his parents? Sign me up." Chastity's face falls at my sarcastic tone.

"Hey!" Her frown makes me feel guilty, but I don't stop there.

"Oh, sorry. Daycare worker. You're right, that's much better." I'm being harsher than I need to be, but there's no way I'm letting Chastity so much as entertain the idea of setting me up with someone this summer. If I'm being forced on this vacation, I'm going to spend it reading the days away. Alone.

"I know you've had a hard night, so I'm going to let that one slide." Chastity says as we reach the ballroom's open double doors. She hugs me goodbye before we part ways. "Go get some rest. Lord knows you need it."

I stick out my tongue at her before turning down the hallway. The elevator comes sooner than I expect and once inside, I aggressively press the button to close the doors until they slide shut and I'm carried down to my freedom. I find Christian already waiting for me in the lobby, hands in the pockets of his dress pants.

"You ready to get out of here?"

I let out a sigh. "Fuck yes."

CHAPTER 3

We move into the apartment on Monday, and the next week is spent unpacking and decorating. Chastity is adamant about decorating the place from head to toe so she can document the process in a new video. Christian spends most days complaining about how much stuff his sister brought for such a short stay. Between the constant bickering and close quarters, the two are inescapable and I'm beginning to regret agreeing to stay with them for a full three months. Only half the reason is that I've started smoking again and living with them makes it harder to hide. I wake up at five in the morning every day just to bum half a pack in peace out on the balcony. I'm well aware it's a filthy habit, but dammit if it isn't a hard one to kick. Amidst the wreckage my life has become since my dad died, it's the only thing that calms me down.

But it doesn't last very long. Chastity catches me in the act early Wednesday morning. She rolls her eyes before confiscating my pack of Marlboro's.

"Is this why you've been waking up at the ass-crack of dawn every day this week?"

"No, I do it for the sunrise." I deadpan, holding out my arm to the gray, sunless sky. My sarcasm isn't usually this obvious, but it's five in the morning and I'm extra cranky.

"Three years, down the drain." There's no worse look Chastity can give you than when she's disappointed in you. She crosses her arms and frowns at me like I'm a puppy who tore up her favorite shoes. It's not a look I appreciate this early in the day. "Come on, Dacia. No one wants to see you die of lung cancer. Least of all me."

"It was actually just one and a half." I confess, and she slaps my arm. "Ow! You see? This is exactly why I don't tell you when I slip up. I can't take the abuse."

"Look, I get it. You've had a tough year, but I'm officially cutting you off. I'm gonna set you up with some nice nicotine patches and we're gonna talk through your feelings." Chastity might be my best friend, but she's not the easiest person for me to open up to. She either has Amelia do all of her recon or forces me to talk no matter how much I don't want to. Since we're in close proximity, she's chosen the latter this time.

"Oh, come on. You know I hate that."

"Too bad. I'm not letting you waste away in San Antonio of all places. I think subconsciously you came down here because you know I'm the only one who can save you from yourself. Now, come on." She's not wrong, not that I'd ever admit it. After a trip to CVS, we return to the apartment and Chastity sticks a patch on my upper arm like I can't do the most basic of things by myself. "There. Now tell me what's going on."

"What do you want me to say that you don't already know?"

"How bad is your anxiety getting?" I look away, crossing my arms over my chest. "Dacia, you can't ignore this forever. There's a deeper reason behind what happened to you in that board room-"

"I'm never telling Amelia anything ever again."

"But you did." Chastity counters. "When was the last time you renewed your prescription?"

"Two weeks ago. I saw my doctor before I left Chicago." I tell her. "You don't need to worry about me. Cigarettes aside, I'm taking care of myself."

"Okay, good." She wraps an arm around my shoulders. "I just want to make sure you're okay, and that you know I'm here for you."

"I know. And I do." I lean my head on her shoulder. When I'm away from Chastity for so long, I forget how caring she can be. But now, I find my eyes stinging at Chastity's words. My chest feels full knowing I finally have someone on my side when for months its seemed like everyone I work with is against me. Half the board doesn't think I deserve my position. The only reason I'm about to become CEO is because my family founded the company. It's not hard to understand why they see me as nothing more than an entitled brat, but I've earned my keep. I might be young, but I've worked at Seidel for nine years. I wasn't ready for my dad to die, but in spite of everything I am ready to be CEO. I just have to show them I'm ready.

I'm crankier than usual for the next few days, even with the nicotine patches. Unpacking proves to be just as unhelpful as you'd think in lifting my mood, and now I'm kicking myself for bringing so much shit with me. And I'm not the only one annoyed with my life choices. Friday morning, Christian bumps into three of my boxes stacked haphazardly on top of each other in the hallway.

"This is a quarter of the books you own?" He slides the stack out of his way to meet me in the living room. "How many is this?"

"About a hundred, give or take." I slice open the first of seven boxes with a kitchen knife. Christian looks at me like I've lost my mind. "I probably should've brought a second bookcase."

"Already ahead of you." Chastity says, emerging from her bedroom. "The bathroom is in dire need of an upgrade, so I'm thinking a day trip do Ikea is in order."

"What do you mean 'day trip'?" Christian asks. "I told you I'm not spending an entire day of my life at that place ever again."

"Yes, I haven't forgotten." She rolls her eyes. "I meant that the closest one is almost an hour away."

I shake my head, cutting open another box. "I don't know if I have the energy for all that. I spent all of yesterday unpacking my room, and the entire morning unpacking the kitchen. We also need a spatula and mixing bowls, by the way."

"See? This is why we need to go to Ikea. We all need stuff! Go get ready!" With that, she turns on her heel and back into her bedroom. I let out a groan before falling back on the carpet. I'm exhausted, craving a smoke, and in dire need of a nap. But Christian nudges my leg with a toe and gives me a look that says, If I can't get out of this, neither can you. I let out another groan as he helps me up and go to my bedroom to change.

We're out for nearly seven hours before we return back to the apartment. Christian helps me set up the new bookcase I bought and Chastity goes straight to the bathroom to decorate. We're halfway done building when Chastity emerges holding up her phone, a sly smirk on her face.

"Guess who just texted me?" We don't need to. The answer is written all over her face.

"You gettin' ready to ditch us for your boo of two minutes?" Christian teases.

Chastity's smile falters before shifting gears. "Not at all. In fact, I'm inviting you guys out to a cool bar downtown." Her smile returns, brighter than ever. "Jane's family comes as a package deal. She and Marcus are as close as siblings can be, just like me and Christian!" She pulls him off the floor and pushes him into the direction of his bedroom. "We leave in thirty, so be ready!" Once he's gone, she turns to me with an expectant look.

"Was bringing me to Texas secretly a plot to kill me?"

"Just give it a try. If you hate it after an hour, you have my permission to fake an illness and call an uber back here."

I give her a once-over, judging her seriousness. "You must really like this girl if you're okay with me leaving early. Are you hoping everyone else will too?" I wink and her cheeks turn a shade redder.

"Don't be crass!" She swats at my arm. "I really like her, and it's been awhile since I really liked someone. You know more than anyone how hard it is for me to find someone I click with." Chastity has a point. Despite the fact that it's easy for her to fall in love, it also doesn't happen very often. "I just want to see where this goes. So yes, you've pegged my intentions remarkably well."

"To be fair, it wasn't at all hard to do."

"Now, I need a favor-"

"Right on schedule."

"Can you and Christian please distract Marcus while I get to know Jane?" She folds her hands in prayer to show her desperation. "And their friend Jesse? As psyched as I usually am about group hangouts, I was really hoping it would just be the two of us tonight. I think she's nervous, so I'm going to try to put her at ease as much as I can."

"Fine." I say with a sigh. I hold out my hand, and she lets out a squeal as she takes it. "I've got your back, but don't let this one break your heart."

The St. Mary's Strip is a haze of neon lights and drunken debauchery. The line to get into The Paper Tiger wraps around the block. I'm glad we're not meeting there, but I am curious to know what event so many people would willingly wait in that long of a line for. A fight breaks out in front of a bar next door, and I have to drag Chastity back to stop her from stepping forward for a closer look. We head to The Brass Monkey to wait in a respectively short line outside.

"I think we're the first one's here." Chastity says, looking down at her phone. "Is that good or bad?"

"I'd say good, considering you're usually late to everything." Christian says.

"Am I trying too hard?" She looks to me, eyes wide with panic. I resist a laugh, if only because she's not one to freak out over social engagements of any kind. She's dressed in a floral print dress that stops mid-thigh and ankle boots, her hair styled in loose curls that fall over her shoulders.

"When have you ever asked that question in your life?" Chastity's not one to freak out over the people she dates. I can only hope Jane sees what she's about to get and doesn't take her for granted.

Chastity rolls her eyes just as her phone beeps. "Oh! They're already inside."

"I knew we couldn't be early." I roll my eyes. "Some things never change."

Fifteen minutes pass before we're let into the bar. We spot Jane and Marcus sitting at a bench in the outdoor portion of the bar, both nursing drinks. Jane jumps up from her seat to pull Chastity into a hug. We all exchange greetings, and when my eyes lock with Marcus's I freeze. He's openly glaring at me. When I blink twice the look is gone, an easy grin on his lips. I shake my head, thinking I must be losing it.

"This place looks amazing." Chastity says, looking around. String lights are hung above us and wrapped around tall, oak trees. A band is set up at a small stage a few feet from us, playing a country song. Good lord, my ears are bleeding already. The bar is set up on the right, where a large crowd has gathered to order.

"I'll get you guys caught up." Jesse, a short Black girl with her hair in twists, says. I don't recognize her from the wedding, but she could've been there for all I know. "Tonight all shots are a dollar, so I finally get to say this: first round's on me!"

Everyone laughs as Jesse leaves to get the drinks before I can tell her I don't do shots. Not after Chastity dragged me to a Game of Thrones themed pub crawl last year in Chicago. I was hungover for three straight days afterward.

"I'm gonna go order some sodas. Wouldn't hurt to have some chasers handy." Christian shoots me a smile, and I give him a relieved one back. He knows me well. And then there were four. Jane and Chastity are locked in conversation at the other end of the table, leaving me with Marcus. Make that two.

"So. First grade, huh?" God, I hate small talk. I hate everything about making small talk. The awkwardness, coming up with questions to ask when you could care less about the answers, the fake smiles. But I also hate awkward silences even more, which is the only reason I'm attempting conversation now.

"Yup." He nods, taking a sip of his drink. "Lifelong dream."

"Wow. Not a lot of people say that about teaching elementary schoolers." I can't hide my surprise, even though I'm not particularly interested in learning more about him. Chastity was right about him being cute, but that doesn't make him interesting. And if Marcus's body language is any indication, he's far from willing to get to know me better, too. He turns his head away, and even in the dim lighting I swear I see him roll his eyes. What the hell is up with him? I'm at peak politeness and he's acting like a complete dick. Maybe I can hide in the bathroom for a few minutes until Christian and Jesse return with the drinks.

Before I get the chance to, Chastity and Jane rise from their seats. I reach for Chastity before she leaves the table (because I'm apparently that desperate not to be left alone with this guy), and Marcus eyes my hand on her arm with a raised brow. A flush of embarrassment heats my skin at the instinctive reflex, but I train my eyes on Chastity in a look that I hope says, please don't leave me.

"We'll be right back. Bathroom break." She squeezes my hand before leaving, an act that makes me feel small and childish. I'm sure I must look childish to Marcus. God, why do I even care? I don't know the guy, and I don't even want to. I straighten my shoulders before turning back to my remaining table companion. He smirks into his drink, and the urge to slap it out of his hand is overwhelming.

I drum my fingers on the table, racking my brain for another conversation starter. I'll give this guy one more chance, for Chastity's sake, before cashing in on her promise to let me leave early. "When did-"

"Listen, we don't need to fill these silences." His tone is easy-going, but his eyes are hard. "I know you don't care about what I do. Let's just let everyone have a good time, okay?"

My brows furrow. "I'm sorry?"

"You should be. Not that I'd dare expect an apology for failing so miserably to reach your dating standards."

For a full beat, his words don't make sense to me. Then dread sinks in as I finally realize what he's talking about. Shit. He must've somehow overheard what I said to Chastity before I left the wedding reception. That's why he's been rude to me all night, because I was rude to him first. Of course he'd want nothing to do with me after that. My eyes shut tight. I can't bear to look him in the face. It's too mortifying.

"You weren't supposed to hear that."

He scoffs, shaking his head. "Wow. That's the best you can do?"

"I doubt saying I'm sorry would help. It would just sound like I'm sorry I got caught, which I am." I shake my head, knowing full well I'm botching this explanation. "I was drunk and having a bad night. I know those are lame excuses, but it's all I've got."

I dare to meet his gaze, but it does nothing to help my nerves. He tries to keep his expression blank, but his clenched jaw gives him away. "Is that your idea of an apology?"

"It's not an apology." I shrug. "It's just the truth."

He scoffs again. "You're really something else, aren't you?"

Jesse and Christian return with drinks before I can think of a reply, though I have no idea what I'd say in response. They apologize for the hold-up, accounting it for an apparently hilarious mix-up at the bar. Jesse launches into the details, but I'm barely listening. My eyes train on Marcus, but he doesn't look back at me. He looks like he's trying not to.

This is far from the first time I've turned people off of me, but I have to say it's one of the quickest instances in a while. It's almost impressive. I've sworn them off, but suddenly the shots of vodka have never looked better. I throw two back in quick succession, relishing the burn at the back of my throat as they go down. I even snatch one out of Christian's hand as he raises it to his mouth. He laughs it off, failing to sense my mood.

But Marcus doesn't. I catch his glance from the corner of my eye, his mouth turned down in a frown. Once I've drained my coke, I get up to order round two for the table. Christian catches my arm as I stumble out of my seat, attempting to straighten me, and I guess I know where my tolerance level is at. Three shots in and I'm ready to face-plant on the concrete. I force my way through the crowd of sweaty bodies to the bar.

"Six shots of vodka." The bartender nods and turns to make them. Someone touches my shoulder from behind and I flinch.

"Whoa, sorry, I didn't mean to scare you." Marcus comes into full view when I turn. "See? That's how you say you're sorry." He smiles wryly.

I cross my arms over my chest. "Did you really follow me over here to demonstrate how an apology works?"

"No." Something like guilt flashes across his features and the look softens me. I'm the one who should feel guilty here. He rakes a hand through his longish, dark hair. My eyes catch a rogue curl resting above his brow, and part of me wants to reach up and push it back. I swallow back the urge, keeping my hands firmly planted at my sides, because that definitely won't go over well. Why does my drunk brain need me to touch his hair?

"I came for this." He holds out his hand, and my eyes fall to it. "Truce?"

"Do I look that pathetic?" He resists an eye roll. I know because I've done it enough times to tell. Sarcasm is my default tone, but what's worse is that most of the time it comes out cutting, even when I don't mean it to. I could never quite pull off sarcastic teasing for some reason, and if Marcus's expression is any indication, I definitely still can't.

"No." His jaw clenches, and I can tell he's working hard to be civil. "Look, I have a feeling we'll be seeing a lot of each other, so it wouldn't hurt if we could get along." He gestures behind me and I turn. Chastity and Jane are at a corner table by themselves, hands intertwined, gazing at each other like no one else in the bar exists. I let out a sigh that's almost a groan before turning back to him.

I get it. Marcus is a far better person than I am. He's willing to put aside our differences (that were my fault to begin with, no less) for my friend and his sister's sake. I should swallow my pride and do the same, but somehow I know that won't be the end of it. But I could at least try for Chastity.

"Fine." I say, taking his hand. "Truce."

"That's the spirit." Marcus says faux-cheerily as he shakes my hand, his mouth turned up into a sly grin. He's one who can pull off sarcastic teasing. The bartender chooses this moment to deposit six shots in front of us. Marcus slides one my way and takes another for himself. "Cheers."

We clink glasses and throw them back. If Marcus is anything like me, my first blunder is far from forgotten. My father once told me that you can't truly forgive without first forgetting, and I never forget anything. I'm always waiting for the next time someone crosses me, because, in my experience, there's always a next time.

I have a philosophy of my own: never forgive, and never apologize. They're just arbitrary niceties we use to assuage our guilt and hide our true feelings. I'd much rather be honest than polite, which is half the reason I suck at socializing. This is where my pride and my anxiety disagree. Not everyone understands why I am the way I am, but pride tells me they don't have to. I shouldn't have to change who I am for anyone else's benefit. Anxiety visits later to tell me this is why I can't make friends, and why I'll eventually drive away the two remaining ones I have and end up all alone.

Anxiety hasn't won, yet.

Despite our truce, there's a knowing glint in his eye that tells me from this moment on he'll be watching me. I return his gaze tenfold. I'll be watching Marcus, too.

Chapter 4

My feet pound the pavement as the dusky sky above turns pink. A nicotine patch covers my upper arm, but it's not enough, which is why I've been opting for early morning runs in lieu of the early morning smokes I've been craving. I round the corner back to my apartment complex as I close on the third mile. Sweat beads down my face and all of the muscles in my body ache, but it's a good ache. I don't run as often as I should, but this morning is a reminder of how great I feel afterward. The looming doubts circling my mind quiet as I put all my focus on getting air to my lungs, the pain in my muscles, and the distance still left to complete.

I hate running, but (meds notwithstanding) it's the best thing I've ever done for my anxiety. Over the years, I've tried pretty much everything. Meditation makes me antsy. Chamomile has no effect whatsoever. There's not a single therapist I've met that I imagined I could grow to trust. It took twenty-three doctor visits over seven years to figure out what medication works best for me, and in the meantime I've had to find other coping mechanisms.

Not all of them are good for me.

Smoking and running. What kind of criminal was I in my last life to be cursed like this? I'm constantly swapping between the two, because I can never manage both at the same time (for obvious reasons). The day I swap smoking for running is always hell on my lungs, but worth every ounce of pain. I could only run a quarter mile last week, and now I'm practically Forrest Gump.

An hour later, Chastity and Christian wake as I finish making breakfast. Chastity eyes the display of food on the counter with suspicion before turning her narrowed eyes on me. A glorious sizzle sounds as I flip the final chocolate-chip pancake with perfect precision. The level of satisfaction is unparalleled in my eyes.

"Coffee's ready." I tell them as I transfer the pancake onto a fluffy, drool-inducing stack. "And we've got scrambled eggs, toast and jelly, and plain pancakes. These are mine." I indicate my chocolate-chip pancakes before turning to the fridge for whipped cream and strawberries.

"Wow. This is quite the display." She says. "Wait a sec, I need to get my-"

I hold up the nozzle and aim straight for her face. A line of whipped cream shoots out and hits her square on the nose. "No cameras! Live in the moment!"

Chastity chuckles before lapping up the whipped cream with a finger and licking it off. "Looks like somebody's meds finally kicked in this morning. I take it you're feeling better?"

"Mildly." I shrug. It's an understatement, but I'm not willing to jinx my change in mood. This is the first morning I'm actually glad to be on vacation. I dowse my pancakes in whipped cream before turning to cut the strawberries in half. "What time do you guys go in today?"

"Nine AM sharp." Christian says between mouthfuls of scrambled egg. After a hard swallow, he adds, "You burned the blancios." I glare, not deigning to answer.

"You should come with us! The restaurant's looking great." Chastity tells me. "You don't want to be stuck in here all day. Which reminds me, are you planning to get a rental while you're here?"

"Nah. I'm going to spend my days locked in my room reading. You did see the thousands of books I brought with me, right?"

Chastity rolls her eyes. "Fine. Bring one with you to the restaurant. We'll only be there for a few hours anyway."

I agree with a shrug of my shoulders.

The Barrera's restaurant is as colorful on the inside as it is on the outside. It's lime green paint stands out garishly compared to the red brick storefronts surrounding the restaurant. Inside, colored lights hang on the walls and mariachi music plays over-head. The scent of delicious, fried food wafts towards us and even though I just finished devouring a whole stack of pancakes, my stomach grumbles in response.

"Wow. This place is amazing." I tell them.

They give me the grand tour before leaving me on the patio of the upstairs dining area. I settle into a wooden table with a copy of Daisy Jones and The Six. Nine chapters pass peacefully when a waiter arrives to drop off a piña colada in a glass bigger than my head. "Compliments of the owners."

"Thank you." I say, staring at the drink as if it could sprout wings and fly away at any moment. I might actually prefer that to drinking it. The piña colada sits untouched as I return to my book, but it isn't long before Chastity comes to interrupt my reading time. "Let me guess. The drink was really for you."

"Busted." Chastity smirks before taking a sip from the gigantic glass. "We might not have to be here for much longer. Christian's wrapping up his pitch and then we can head out."

"His pitch?"

"To make the restaurant trendier." She rolls her eyes. "I don't why he bothers. They're too set in tradition. Being semi-accepting of their bisexual daughter is about as modern as my parents can get."

"That's the trouble with working with family. Their vision doesn't always align with yours." I had this problem with my dad over the years. Even my grandmother couldn't stand the changes he made to the company during his time as CEO. Between Seidel's flop at going international to my father accepting deals from shady shareholders, they weren't even on speaking terms until my father was diagnosed with cancer.

I loved my father. Truly. I just never respected him.

Just as I'm about to return to my book, a flash of copper-colored hair catches my eye from the stair landing. I don't know when it happened – when I somehow managed to memorize the back of his head is beyond me, but it's so clearly Marcus. He turns around and our eyes lock, recognition flashing through his from ten feet away. Marcus makes his way toward our table. I nudge Chastity's arm and gesture toward him.

"Oh, hey! You made it!" She exclaims, waving him over. I give her a quizzical look, but she ignores it. Had I known she'd be inviting Marcus along, I would've...what? Not come? Internally prepared myself for his arrival? Somewhere between those two seems right, not that it matters now.

"I wasn't sure where to drop this off." He hands her a single sheet of paper from a folder. When I look over Chastity's shoulder (but not before catching Marcus's grimace), I see it's a resume. "Is there any chance I could get an interview today? I'm still fulltime at the daycare until next week so it might be difficult to schedule one 'till then."

"Sure." Chastity folds her hands on the table. "Do you have any previous experience waiting tables?" He nods. "How good is your Spanish?"

"It's my first language, so it better be good." He smiles wryly.

"Fair enough." She hands him back his resume. "You're hired. I'll talk to the manager and he'll get in contact with you about scheduling."

Marcus smiles, but it doesn't quite reach his eyes. I clap my hands over-enthusiastically before turning in my chair to face Chastity. "Now do me!"

"Oh!" She clears her throat and grabs Marcus's folder to use as a prop, pretending to look inside as she says, "Miss Dacia, please describe your qualifications for the position."

"Qualifications? What are those?" I widen my eyes in faux-terror, turning over to Marcus with a gasp. He's looking between the two of us with a stunned expression that quickly softens into amusement.

"And how about the language requirement?" Chastity feigns pushing up the reading glasses she's not wearing higher on her face. "How is your Spanish?"

"I know just enough to tell when the staff is talking shit about my waitressing skills."

"You have no waitressing experience, you don't speak Spanish, and yesterday you gave Christian the cup of coffee I asked for." Chastity shakes her head with disappointment. "Consider yourself fired." She bops me on the head with Marcus's folder.

"Oh well." I shrug and lean back in my chair. "At least I have Seidel to fall back on."

But do I? I try to shake away the thought, but I can't quite manage it.

Marcus claps his hands with the faux-enthusiasm I used earlier, and I give a small bow in my chair. He smiles, and though it's an exasperated one, it's a real one this time, too.

He's a vision when he smiles, the mid-morning sun casting him in a golden glow. I wish I could somehow not notice how attractive he is, especially since the other night. My stomach sinks just thinking about it, and then further as he raises himself from his seat and waves goodbye.

Stupid. I could slap myself for how stupid these thoughts are, in the grand scheme of things. We'll be strangers again in a few month's time, and then I'll never think of him again.

Christian meets us almost twenty minutes later, exhausted but happy. "Sorry about the wait. It took awhile, but I think I finally wore them down. They asked for a full business proposal of my plan."

"Damn. I'm impressed." Chastity says. "I didn't think they'd cave."

"They still might not, which is why I have to make it good." We get to the car, and I settle in the backseat with my book. But it's not long when Chastity's phone dings and she let's out a loud squeal, interrupting my concentration.

"Yes! She said yes!"

"What are you talking about?" Christian asks.

"I mentioned to Jane that I wanted to host a dinner party to get to know her family more. She just replied that everyone will be free on Saturday!" She squeals again. "Now I have a new video plan and a date to get to know Jane better."

"Uh, don't you think it's a little soon to meet her whole family?" Christian asks the exact question I'm thinking. I snap the book shut and sit up straighter in my seat. "Let alone invite them over and cook for them? We both know that isn't exactly your area of expertise."

"I told y'all before: Jane and her family come as a package deal. If I want to be good with her, I have to be good with her family first."

"That seems a little backwards. But then again I am an orphan now, so what do I know?" Chastity turns around in her seat and rests a hand on my knee. She doesn't have to say anything for me to know she sees through my self deprecating humor. Christian, however, isn't done with this conversation yet.

"You're about to put in a lot of effort over nothing. You know that right?"

I wince before Chastity goes off. She snaps her head around to glare at her brother. "Excuse me?"

"Did you suddenly forget we're only staying here for three months? I don't think it's wise-"

"Then you don't have to come!"

"Fine." Christian bites out. "Maybe I won't."

The rest of the car ride devolves into tense silent. I'm probably a shitty person for taking advantage of it to finish the chapter I'm in the middle of, but this isn't the first time I've witnessed a Chastity-Christian fight. They'll avoid each other for a couple days, then circle each other and make passive aggressive comments until one of them (historically Christian) breaks and apologizes to the other with food. But for now, the jury is out on if it'll happen before or after the dinner party. Preferably before, so the job of cooking and cleaning isn't up to me and Chastity alone.

By Saturday morning, Chastity and Christian are still on the outs and I have my answer. I wake to my bed shaking and my eyes snap open to see the cause. Chastity has plopped herself beside me, fully dressed for the day. Even her hair and makeup is perfectly done.

"Dacia, wake up! We've got a full day ahead of ourselves!"

I groan and lift the blanket over my head, but it does me no good. She immediately wrenches the fabric from my hands and throws it to the floor. I let out a groan, knowing when I've been defeated. Ten minutes later, I'm dressed in flip flops, cutoff shorts and an oversized tee, just to show her what I think of being woken up at seven AM on a weekend. My hair is even pulled up in a sloppy bun at the top of my head.

If only the board members could see me now...

Chastity shakes her head when I finally emerge from my bedroom. "It's like I haven't taught you anything."

"I am not dressing up for Trader Joe's. If you won't take me as I am, I'll just go back to sleep."

"Have I told you yet how lovely you look this morning?" She changes her tone immediately, wrapping an arm around my shoulders. I let out a groan as she pulls me out the door.

We return to the apartment two hours later carting four full-to-the-brim brown bags of groceries. I have no idea what this dinner is going to look like because she didn't even bring a list. Her parents might be proud owners of a restaurant with rave reviews across every local publication, but Chastity is no chef.

"What are we making again?"

"It's this stuffed pasta recipe I found on Pinterest." She says as she unpacks the first bag. Then she pulls out her phone and says, "Here, I'll show you."

I watch as her fingers tap the screen. A beat passes and her brows knit together. "What's wrong?"

"Nothing." But her lips purse, telling me otherwise. Finally, she admits, "I can't find it."

"Did you save the recipe in a screenshot?"

"No. I had it pinned to my Foodie board. At least, I thought I did." She looks down at her phone again, her index finger scrolling furiously. "Oh, here it is!" She clicks on the image, which redirects her to a food blog. "Whoa, okay, this actually looks way harder than it did yesterday."

I squint down at the screen. "Wait, go up again. What does it say about soaking the cashews?"

"'Soak cashews in water overnight'...oops." She shrugs. "We just won't do that part."

"We still kinda have time. What's the harm in starting now?"

Christian emerges through the front door just as we've soaked the cashews. He takes one look at us in the kitchen before turning on his heel and locking himself in his bedroom. Chastity scowls to herself before asking what I want for lunch.

We start preparing for dinner two hours before Jane's family is set to arrive, and everything that could possibly go wrong does. Chastity boils a full bag of shell pasta in a medium-sized saucepan, so when the noodles are fully cooked, they've also expanded and caused water to boil over onto the stovetop. The shells have also stuck together, so Chastity and I have to be extra careful not to tear the noodles when we separate them from each other. Chastity realizes we have all the ingredients for homemade pesto, but no blender to mix them. When she returns from her second trip to the store, I realize we also don't have ricotta cheese. We make due with shredded mozzarella, and by six o'clock the dish is in the oven. It seems like we've jumped all the hurdles, until -

I sniff the air and turn to Chastity. "Do you smell something burning?"

"Shit." She runs into the kitchen and pulls out the dish. The entire top layer is charred over and black. "What the hell? Why did the cheese burn?"

"You're the one with chef parents. Shouldn't you know?"

"Dammit, Dacia, what are we gonna do?" Chastity's voice goes an octave higher as tears fill her eyes. "We only have an hour before everyone gets here. What's that enough time for?"

"Takeout." I pull out my phone and look up the closest Italian restaurant.

By the time our dinner guests arrive, we've transferred the pasta dishes onto ceramic plates and gotten rid of the brown-bagged evidence. Now, the Galindo's are seated at the dining room table Chastity got from Pottery Barn and complimenting us on our "cooking".

"This pasta smells delicious!" Mrs. Galindo says. She switches to Spanish as easily as breathing, and by the time I translate in my head what she's asking, Chastity is already answering her in English.

"Shrimp scampi with a lemon garlic sauce." Chastity smiles, ever the gracious party host. "You'll have to forgive me, my Spanish is severely out of practice. I'd hate to embarrass myself stumbling over a response." She flashes a nervous smile that somehow also manages to be charming.

"Ah, no worries, chiquita." Mrs. Galindo assures her before turning to me. "Y tu? Tu no hablas Español?"

I shake my head, guilt building in the pit of my stomach. She smiles and touches my shoulder before turning away, but not before her eyes lose their light and I'm reminded of my own mother's disappointment.

"Don't feel bad." Oddly enough, this response comes from the youngest Galindo. Luke appears at my shoulder with a plate as he makes his way to the dining table. "I can't speak Spanish either. Jane and Marcus can, but our parents neglected to teach the rest of us."

Mr. Galindo mutters under his breath. When Luke takes a seat by Marcus, his older brother leans in to whisper something the rest of us don't catch. Chastity and I exchange a look, but we don't say a word. The tension passes as we settle down to eat, but a new one arises when Luke speaks again.

"You know, it's funny, this almost tastes like the shrimp scampi from Margianno's." Luke says. Chastity's eyes go wide. "We passed by it on our way here, didn't we?" He nudges Marcus with an elbow.

"What a coincidence." I take a sip of my water to avoid eye contact as Chastity stuffs her mouth with pasta to avoid speaking. Luke's eyes narrow in suspicion at us. The little brat. I shoot him an icy smile and he quickly looks away.

"You're so great to invite us over." Jane tells Chastity, who beams at the compliment. "You really didn't have to go through all this trouble."

"Oh, it was no trouble at all! Plus, I thought it'd be a great way to get to know your family. I know how close you are with them."

"We appreciate your hospitality." Mr. Galindo says. "The meal was delicious."

"Are we allowed seconds?" Isaac, the second youngest brother, asks. "That spaghetti with meat sauce sounds good."

"Oh, me too!" David, the middle child, says. Jane gives him a pointed look, and he adds, "If it's no trouble, that is."

"No trouble at all." Chastity gets up from her chair. "Dacia, can you help me in the kitchen?"

"Oh, I can-" Jane starts to get up from her seat, but Chastity stops her in her tracks with a panicked expression. I save her by assuring Jane that it would be rude of us to let our dinner guests help out in the kitchen before dragging Chastity away by her arm.

"Chas, you have got to calm down." I tell her once we reach the kitchen. "There's no reason to freak out. Everyone's having a good time."

"But Luke's onto us." She says, looking over my shoulder to the dining table five feet away. "He knows we got the food from a restaurant. I feel like such a fraud."

"Chas, no one cares where the food came from." I take out the black takeout container from the fridge and shovel the contents onto two dinner plates. "They're getting a free meal out of us, and we get to give away all the extra food you bought. I swear, it's like you have no concept of-"

I pause as Marcus comes around the counter and spots me with a takeout container in hand. Despite my assurance to Chastity, I feel like I've been caught doing something illegal. Chastity covers her mouth before she can let out a whimper, but he gives her a sympathetic look.

"I didn't see a thing. I just came in looking for water."

Chastity opens the fridge and hands him a water bottle with a sigh of relief. Marcus nods covertly at us before returning to the dining table.

"We're saved." Chastity says as I place the food in the microwave. "You don't think he'll spill the beans after everyone leaves, will he?"

"Not if he knows what's good for him." We return to the table, and I hand Isaac and David their plates of spaghetti. "Would anyone like anything else while I'm up?" If running Seidel doesn't work out, at least I know I have waitressing to fall back on.

"Oh no, you've done enough for us, chiquita." Mrs. Galindo says, reaching up to clutch my arm in what I'm sure is an appreciative gesture. But because I don't see it coming, I flinch. My expression must giveaway my discomfort, because after one look at my face she quickly removes her hand and turns away.

I return to my seat next to Chastity, almost wishing Christian were here so I'd have someone to talk to. Three different conversations are happening all around me, but I'm not engaged in a single one. Chastity, Jane and Mrs. Galindo are talking about their time spent on YouTube. I turn their direction to listen, hoping I won't have to contribute much myself.

"...Just worried it won't turn out the way my daughter is hoping." I catch the last half of what Mrs. Galindo is saying to Chastity. "How did you do it? My daughter says you have a million people watching your videos, which is crazy to me!"

"There's really no secret but to stay consistent." Chastity answers. "I started when I was eighteen, and I've stuck with it ever since."

"Ma, stop hounding her for advice." Jane says, her cheeks turning pink. She explains to Chastity, "I just reached monetization last month, and she's been eager to help in anyway she can."

"I don't blame her. You're really talented. I've been binge watching your videos since the wedding." Jane lets out an embarrassed groan, and Chastity comforts her with a hand on her shoulder. "Seriously, you're so good! You're gonna blow up before you know it. I can even help with that."

Jane shakes her head, but her mother pipes up. "Really? You can help her?"

"Sure." Chastity shrugs. "I have a lot of followers, I could tell them to check out her channel."

Her mom cheers, but I don't get a chance to hear what Jane says in response. Someone taps my shoulder, and I turn around to face Luke sitting at my other side. "I have a big idea for Seidel Computers. Should I submit it in writing, or can I give you my pitch here and now?"

Here we go. Shutting him down would be probably be rude, so I relent for Chastity's sake.

"What's your idea?"

"Luke, don't bother her, man." Marcus says, but his brother ignores him.

"A kill switch for the webcam." Luke says. "That way no one has to worry about creepers peeping in on them when their laptops are open anymore! As an owner of a Seidel computer, this is extremely important to me." As was it extremely important to Seidel when hundreds of our consumers had their webcams hacked, and were finding proof in screenshots of strangers saved to their desktop and in one case, blackmailed for extortion. The story reached every high profile news outlet days after my father's death and HQ was a mess for weeks trying to account for the source and ultimately save face.

"I can assure you that as long as you have the updated protection software installed on your computer, your webcam is safe." I tell him.

"But I think people would feel safer if-"

"People are safe." I tell him. "Those cases you're referring to were targeted because their systems were years out of date, which made their computers vulnerable to creeps with nothing better to do with their time." That was along the lines of what the official report told the press. The truth is, those computers were susceptible to hacks because they were blocked from installing all old updates while we were getting ready to launch the newest update, which was delayed because of my father's passing. Not that I'm about to tell Luke that.

"You could always stick a post-it note over your webcam." Marcus says with a shrug. "That's what I do."

"Does the future CEO of Seidel do that, too?" Luke asks. "And if so, can I quote you for future reference?"

I take a swig of water, thinking of the Batman bandaid taped over mine. "No comment."

"So, about the kill switch-"

"Luke, I think your glass could use a refill. I saw some soda left in the fridge, why don't you go get another?" Marcus asks him. Luke rolls his eyes before snatching his glass and leaving the table. "Sorry about that. Luke got a bit overexcited when he found out what you do. He hasn't been able to stop talking about pitching you the perfect idea since the wedding."

"Well, if he tries it again I'll tell him Seidel isn't taking unsolicited ideas at the moment."

"Think you can let him down easy?" He asks. "As a favor to a friend?"

"Since when are we friends?" My brows furrow. His face stiffens with surprise, but before he can answer Luke returns with a pack of breadstick, the Margianno's label printed on the side. He holds it up as if fist-pumping the air.

"I knew it!" He proclaims. "They did go to Margianno's!"

Chastity's mouth falls open in embarrassment. I rub my forehead with a rough hand, wishing this dinner would end already. This is why I hate teenagers. I watch from the corner of my vision as Jane puts an arm around Chastity to comfort her, but my eyes are trained on Luke in a glare. He cowers at my expression and quickly drops the breadsticks on the counter.

This night has lasted far too long for my liking, and the Galindo's have only been here for two hours. How am I going to last an entire summer in this town?

CHAPTER 5

Once the Galindo's leave, I help Chastity clean up in the kitchen. Mr. and Mrs. Galindo assured her they didn't care where the food came from, but she still expressed her embarrassment over the whole situation and insisted the family come over again for a do-over soon. Christian is still nowhere to be found, but that's to be expected. He'll be back soon to make up with his sister now that the dinner party is over and he didn't have to help cook, clean, or host.

"Well, that could've gone a lot worse, right?" Chastity asks over the rush of running water from the sink. She's never washed a dish in her life. I eye her process as I wipe down the kitchen counters, sighing to myself as she places each clean dish in the dishwasher to dry. Guess that dishwashing liquid below the sink will start gathering dust soon. "Other than Luke blabbing, I think everyone had a good time!"

"Sure." I say. "Like I said, no one really cared where the food came from."

"I guess that turned out to be a good thing in the end. Such a shame I didn't inherit the chef gene, though." She laughs.

"I'll have to do my homework before I'm ready to plan the second dinner party. Maybe I should ask my mom to teach me a few of her recipes when she's not so busy with the restaurant. Christian is clearly no help."

"It's too bad Amelia's still in California, or you could pass off her cooking as your own." My cousin actually considered culinary school before following her mother's footsteps in computer engineering. "Or you could start with something simple, and nothing from scratch."

"I got a little ahead of myself." She smiles sheepishly before turning back to the dishes. Once she's finished, she turns around and asks, "Do you think he's right?"

"Who?"

"Christian." She clarifies. "Am I annoying for falling for people too fast?"

"It doesn't happen often enough to be annoying. Christian's just being a dick 'cuz he doesn't want to cook for strangers if he's not being paid to."

"Thanks." She laughs. "So you don't think it's a bad that I'm already falling for her?"

I pause. "Those are strong words to use for someone you just met." She gives me a pointed look, sensing what I'm holding back. "Okay, here's what concerns me. It's been two weeks and you're already diving into the deep end with this girl. You're meeting her friends and family and trying to impress them with your nonexistent cooking skills. As much as I hate to agree with your brother, it wouldn't hurt to take things slower."

"Believe it or not, but we actually are taking things slow. We haven't gone on a single one-on-one date yet. I only invited her family over because I know how much she cares about them, and I wanted to do something nice. Jane doesn't think we should take things too fast, either."

"Oh." I feel my brows crease as I take in Chastity's point. "I guess I see where you're coming from, then."

"See? I know what I'm doing. I'm not running away with my feelings this time."

Before I can reply, the front door opens and Christian emerges from the other side. He gives us a cautious wave before stepping into the kitchen. Chastity rolls her eyes, but her smile tells me its in good nature.

"I'm sorry I stepped out on dinner. That wasn't cool of me." He holds up a box with a gorgeous chocolate cupcake inside to his sister. "Forgive me?"

Chastity snatches the box from him. "I love when you apologize with gifts."

"Hey, I stepped up when you walked out. Where's my cupcake?"

"I'll show you the place tomorrow. You'll love it." He tells me before turning to his sister. "So, we're good?"

Chastity grins. "We're good. If," She steps forward, holding a finger up before divulging her one condition. "You come with me and Dacia to Jesse's birthday party."

I groan before Christian can answer. "Another party? Don't these people ever rest?"

"You know there's a difference between weddings and parties, right?" Christian laughs before agreeing to go, and Chastity squeals.

"Tomorrow night at seven. Casual dress." I don't have time to ask who the hell throws a party on a Sunday night before Chastity gives me a pointed look and turns into her room. Guess I'm out of luck once again.

The next day, my phone chimes with a message as I'm getting ready for Jesse's party. I groan when I see the name. Alex Henderson is someone I haven't heard from in almost two years, and that's purposeful on my part. But according to this text, I'll be seeing her tonight.

Hey, Dacia! Long time no see, huh? LOL. But thankfully that's about to change! I hear we have a mutual friend in Miss Jessica Brooks, and will both be attending her birthday party this evening. Looking forward to catching up soon!!!

As if I'm not dreading this night enough already. I burst into Chastity's room and throw myself on her bed. When she asks me what's wrong, I hold up my phone. I don't lift my head until I hear her raucous laugh echo off the walls.

"It's not funny! You know how hard I work to avoid this girl." I don't care if our families have been friends for decades. Nothing is worth putting up with a lifetime of Alex Henderson.

"I know, you're right. It's just funny how she always manages to find you wherever you go."

"How the hell does she even know these people? I thought she was still in California." That's where she went for undergrad, anyway. I have no idea what she's been up to since she graduated. Clearly.

"You'd know exactly how if you bothered to check your socials every once in awhile. She's starting her Masters program at Texas State in the Fall." Chastity and Alex have met exactly two times, yet they follow each other on every social media platform possible. It's almost as if Alex knows how hard I work to escape her, and has taken every preventive measure there is to thwart me. The real kicker is now she has fate on her side.

"And so is Jesse." I remember Christian mentioning it to me when we left The Brass Monkey. "Fuck."

"You're shit out of luck, my friend. At least you'll have someone to talk to when I ditch you for Jane tonight." She smiles slyly.

"Have I told you how great of a friend you've been to me lately? No? Good." I shove her shoulder playfully and she grins. "Come on. Let's get this night over with."

Jesse's off-campus apartment is a small two-bedroom cramped wall to wall with guests. I'm standing in a corner with Christian, red solo cup in hand, eyeing the crowd with narrowed eyes. I've already spotted Alex twice, stopping just short of ducking and rolling to keep her from spotting me back. Both times Marcus saw my weird attempts at avoiding her, his eyes inscrutable as he wondered what the fuck I was doing, no doubt.

I don't know why he bothers me so much. Maybe it's just that I don't like the taste of my own medicine. He called me out on my bullshit immediately, and as much as I hate admitting so, it stung. And as it turns out, I was right to think he'd be keeping an eye on me because now there's no hiding from him.

"He's been staring at you all night." Christian says near my ear. I shudder at his beer breath and wonder how many drinks he's had tonight.

"What are you talking about?"

"Marcus." He says. "I can tell him you're not interested, if you want."

I scoff. "You're delusional."

"You're pleased." There's a note of surprise in his voice as he looks at me, no doubt seeing what he wants to in my face. There's nothing in my expression that says I want Marcus's attention. How could I want what I've been trying to avoid all night?

"And you're drunk." I take the cup from his hand, trying not to spill the contents on myself as he fights me for it. "Maybe we should get you a glass of water."

"No chance, Dacia." He snatches his drink back from me, sloshing beer over the rim and soaking my shoes. I step out of the puddle with a scowl. "Don't be such a buzzkill. You don't see me trying to stop you from living your life. But then again, that's 'cuz you've already stopped yourself."

"What the hell is that supposed to mean?" At my tone, a drunken laugh dies in his throat. The question is rhetorical. I know exactly what he means. It's no secret that I'm a reserved person. I'd much rather be back at the apartment by myself than here at a party, keeping strangers and cheap liquor for company. I've never seen it as a bad thing.

Christian seems to realize what he's said and backtracks. "I'm just messing around! Dacia, you know what happens when I'm this wasted. None of the shit I say means anything." He downs the remaining contents in his cup and I look away. When he starts to wrap an arm around my shoulder, I shove him off me. He stumbles into the edge of the couch, recovering himself before he can topple to the floor. Christian scowls at me before disappearing into the crowd of guests.

Alone, at last. I pull out my phone and look for an ebook to start. While my iBooks library isn't nearly as extensive as my physical one, I have to make sure I always have options easily at hand (especially when visiting Chastity, who's known to drag me all over town).

There are no available spots to sit at on the couch, so this corner will have to do. I've managed with worse. But as I read the first sentence of chapter one, I find I can't concentrate. There's too much going on around me. Too many bodies. Too much noise. And underneath it all, I can't get Christian's words out of my head. You've already stopped yourself. Is there a chance he's right?

My eyes find Marcus in the crowd immediately, and I'm not sure what to think of that. He's wearing a simple white button down tucked into dark wash jeans, sleeves rolled to his elbows. His curls flop in his face when he laughs at whatever remark Jesse says. He rakes his hair back with his fingers, exposing the veins running down the inside of his arm. I can't hear the sound of his laugh over the general noise of people, but his smile is more infectious than it has a right to be.

He's so unlike me. Not the center of attention like Chastity, but he makes everything I hate about socializing seem so effort-less. His easy grin. His relaxed shoulders. The way he laughs with his whole body, his smile so wide he has to close his eyes from the force of it. The way he talks with his hands constantly in motion. No one in his circle of company can seem to stop smiling as he tells some apparently hilarious story. Meanwhile, I'm wishing I could sink into the wall behind me and disappear completely.

His head turns toward me like he can sense my stare. Our eyes meet and lock for a whole beat before I have the good sense to look away. Shit, why is my heart racing? When I glance up again, Marcus is excusing himself from his group and walking towards me. I don't know what to do, so I avoid his eyes and look down at the chapter on my screen without reading a single word. Maybe it's not me he's headed to. Why would he be? We don't even like each other. But two paces later, he's standing right in front of me.

"You're reading." He notes. "While a party rages on around you."

I shrug easily, or at least I try to. Every muscle in my body is tense. "It's what I'd rather be doing at home, but Chastity insisted I make an appearance. Besides, this is hardly the weirdest place I've been caught reading."

"Oh yeah?" He asks. "What's the weirdest?"

"My college graduation." I say. "They had to call my name three times before I heard it and stepped forward onstage. The dean gave me the nastiest look as he handed me my diploma."

"You're kidding." He guffaws.

"Actually, I am." I say, and Marcus let's out a surprised laugh. "There's no way I could've done that. I was nervous enough about trying not to trip onstage. I just read while I was seated."

"But you actually did read at your own graduation?" When I nod, he says, "That's still pretty weird."

"Those things are three hours long. I had to do something to pass the time."

"I'll take your word for it." He says unbelievingly. "So, where's your crew tonight?"

"Chastity is with Jane on the balcony, and Christian's around somewhere." I cross my arms over my chest. "This isn't really my scene, to be honest."

"That's fair." Marcus says. "This must seem so juvenile to you. Clearly we haven't grown out of our college days yet."

"I wouldn't know. I never grew into them to begin with." Though it wasn't for a lack of trying on Chastity's part. She dragged me to every school function there was, and safe to say I went kicking and screaming. Now that we're reunited, we've fallen back into old patterns. Some things never change, I guess.

"Right." He chuckles, but it sounds hollow. His mouth forms a frown, and I can't help but wonder if I'm the one to put it there. "Actually, I came over to let you know there's someone looking for you." He doesn't have to say her name for me to know it's Alex.

"Where?" I look back and forth, but don't spot her anywhere.

"I think I saw her go into the bathroom a moment ago."

"Thanks." I step aside and head toward the kitchen. He calls my name, probably to let me know I'm walking in the wrong direction, but I don't stop.

Liquor bottles, liters of soda and paper cups litter every inch of space on the counters. I find the coke and start to pour myself a new drink when a tap on my shoulder makes me flinch and spill half the bottle on the floor. Before I can fully turn around, Alex is pulling me into her arms for a hug.

"There you are! I've been looking for you everywhere!" She exclaims right into my ear. I wince, but she doesn't notice. "Good thing your friend helped me track you down." I notice Marcus standing behind her, shooting me a quizzical look. I avoid his eyes and work to keep the fake smile plastered to my face.

"What a helpful person you found." My sarcasm goes unnoticed by Alex.

Even though I haven't seen her in two years, she looks exactly the same. Her blonde hair is cut into a short bob stopping at her chin, and she's wearing the same purple frames she wore in high school. Freckles scatter along her cheeks, nose, and forehead, so I can properly assume she's been in the sun a lot this summer. When our families took us out on a beach trip in sixth grade (not my idea), we both broke out head to toe in freckles. From then on, she had the nerve to call us "freckle buddies". That's when I knew we could never be friends.

"Just thought it'd be the kind thing to do." Marcus says with a pointed look.

"Oh my gosh, can you believe we're finally in the same city again?" Alex asks, practically jumping up and down in excitement. "That hasn't happened since we both went away for undergrad. I was so sorry to hear about your dad by the way, that must've sucked. I'm sorry I couldn't make it up to Chicago, I was swamped with applications. But I did send a nice floral arrangement with lots of roses. Did you see it?" I give a noncommittal gesture, looking over her shoulder for any out I can find. All I find is Marcus, and he's already made it clear how helpful he'll be to me. "How does it feel to run the empire? You must be so excited! Did they make you a big shot CEO yet?"

This is exactly why I've been avoiding her all night. There isn't a tactful bone in this imbecile's body. As if what happened to my dad simply "sucked". As if I don't care because I get to be a "big shot" at work now. As if I'm actually succeeding at work and not about to run Seidel into the ground where my father was just buried.

I clear my throat and take a sip from my drink to buy enough time to come up with a proper response. Ignoring everything that came out of her mouth seems like the only viable option. I muster my best fake-polite voice and reply with: "And I hear you're starting Texas State in the Fall. You must be so excited." There. That almost sounded civil.

"Oh, I am!" She exclaims, oblivious to the torment she's causing me. "Jesse's going to be my roommate. I contacted her as soon as I got the confirmation email. How sweet was it of her to invite me to her birthday party?"

"And how lucky that you were in the area." Sarcasm leaks into my tone once more, but Alex hardly notices. "Why are you in the area, again?"

"I'm staying with my aunt and uncle for the summer until I can move to San Marcos." Damn the Henderson's extended family. Alex's mom has more siblings than the Galindo's. "That's the other piece of news I waited to share. We'll be in the city all summer together!"

"Hur-fucking-ray!" She pulls me into another hug, and I take the chance to roll my eyes while she can't see. Marcus, who's still standing with us, notices and shoots me yet another pointed look. Why the hell is he still here?

"Well, I'm glad we finally got to catch up! We'll have to do it properly soon with a lunch date." She squeezes my hand, and I squeeze hers back hard enough for her to wince.

"No chance. I'm super busy." I shoot her an icy smile.

"Oh, I'm sure you can find the time! Amelia told me you're on vacation." She says brightly. "Firm handshake as always. I'm gonna go find Jesse."

"You do that." I let out a sigh of relief when she's out of eye-shot. Marcus steps forward to take her place, his face unreadable. I roll my eyes again. It seems my night of torture isn't over yet. "What?"

"I didn't say anything."

I walk past him. "You didn't have to."

I need air, but that requires walking past tens of sweaty bodies to the front door. Yet another obstacle to my freedom, but it'll be worth it. When I reach the hallway outside the front door, I'm flooded with the overwhelming relief of it. I decide I'll call Chastity and Christian later to tell them I bailed and call an uber home. The app is searching for rides when the door cracks open behind me and Marcus emerges.

"I just can't get rid of you tonight, can I?"

"Most people call it socializing, but I guess you're not into that sort of thing." He says evenly. I don't look up from my phone, but I can feel his eyes on me.

"Not really. Not with people I don't know, anyway." I admit. "Plus, I'm extremely bad at it, as you can probably tell."

"You're not that bad." I look up and narrow my eyes at him. He relents immediately. "Okay, you're right. You really suck at talking to people." I can't help the laugh that escapes my throat. His eyes widen just slightly in surprise before his mouth quirks up in the barest hint of a smile. "Small talk is overrated, anyway. Everyone knows that."

"Then why do we continue to do it?"

"Because there's no way around it. You just have to try a little more, you know? You can't stand in the corner all night reading and call it a solid effort."

"I can and I will. Besides, I was trying to lay low tonight. You threw a wrench in my plans bringing Alex over to me."

"I thought you guys were friends, but my mistake. Is that why you were so mean to her?"

"She is not my friend, not that that's ever stopped her from trying. A real friend wouldn't say the death of your father 'must have sucked'." I imitate her tone.

"Oh." His mouth moves as if to say something else, but nothing comes out. I watch on in amusement at having rendered him speechless, hoping I can find a way to replicate it in the future. If he's going to continue checking up on me like this, I may need to.

"Yeah." I laugh humorlessly. "You don't need to say anything. I've had quite enough of the useless, obligatory condolences. They don't mean anything."

"I get it. I mean, I don't really, but-" He lets out a breath, flustered. If his complexion were fairer, I bet he'd be one of those guys who flush pink when they're nervous, from his cheeks down to his neck. He takes a steadying breath and tries again. "It must've been hard."

I don't say anything. It was hard. When I was younger, I used to think losing a parent as an adult wouldn't be nearly as hard as losing one when you're still a kid. My mother passed right before I started high school, and back then I thought I'd seen the peak of grief. Turns out nothing hits harder than the knowledge that you're now parentless, adult or not.

There must be something pitiful in my expression, because Marcus asks, "Can I give you a ride home?"

I keep my gaze trained down at my phone, the wheel still spinning. "You don't need to do that."

"I know. Come on." He steps out into the hallway and closes the door behind him, leaving me no choice but to follow him. We stop when we reach a silver Honda Civic parked right outside Jesse's building. He slides into the driver's seat as I settle into the passenger. "Let's see, I think I still have your address saved in my GPS."

"Not creepy at all."

"Right? I mean, we hardly know each other. I could be a total psycho, waiting for the perfect opportunity to get my revenge for that teacher-who-still-lives-with-his-parents comment." He teases. At least, I hope he's teasing. But the way he says this with a smile is more unnerving than him saying it at all. I shiver when he flashes his teeth.

"You know I have to sleep tonight, right?" I'm not Catholic anymore, but I make the sign of the cross on myself just in case. "I'll start keeping a kitchen knife under my bed. A big one."

"Alright, sorry." But he's grinning like he's not sorry at all. "Just think happy thoughts, Dacia. Butterflies. Rainbows. Ice cream sandwiches falling from the sky." This might be the first time I've heard him call me by my name. I can't help the rush of surprise that goes through me, or how much I like the sound of it on his tongue.

His brows furrow at my expression, and heat floods through my chest as if he can read my mind. To distract him and myself, I say, "I hate ice cream sandwiches." He lets out a dramatic gasp.

"Oh, come on!" He exclaims. "Alright, alright fine. Books falling from the sky. That better?"

"And have them fall on my head and kill me? Doubtful." I counter. Then as I realize something, it's my turn to gasp faux-dramatically. "Wow, first you threaten to kill me in the middle of the night and now this. You're trying real hard to get rid of me, aren't you, Marcus?" My mouth forms his name easily, wrapping around the syllables like I say his name all the time.

"Who, me? Never." He smirks and my heart stutters.

"I don't know about that." I say. "Now I know better than to drunkenly insult people I just meet. I better watch out for myself around you." I shoot him what I hope is a sly grin.

"I just can't win with you. It's impossible." His tone is teasing, but I think back to what he said that night at the bar. You're really something else, aren't you? It had been an insult then, so I'm not sure why I'm remembering it now.

"Well, they do say I'm something else."

He turns into the first entrance, and I direct him to my building. We're silent for awhile until he pulls into an empty parking space. The tension is so palpable, I begin to fear I've said the wrong thing again. Or maybe it's just me that's tense. I can never be sure where long silences are concerned. They never feel comfortable to me.

"Thanks for the ride." I tell him. "Sorry you had to miss out on the last half of the party."

"It kinda sucked anyway." He shrugs easily.

"I thought you liked that sort of thing." I say. "Why'd it suck for you?"

He gives a humorless laugh. "It's stupid. You're gonna laugh."

"I could use a good laugh. Tell me."

His mouth curls up at the side in a grin. "Well, I was kinda hoping this girl would show up, but she didn't. She didn't say she would for sure, but you know. I held out hope and got shot down."

"Bummer." I say. He laughs again, but it's a real one this time. My brows furrow in confusion. "Why is my lack of pity funny to you?"

"Because it's the kick in the ass I need." He says. "I just met this girl and I'm already wallowing over her. It's pathetic."

"Yeah, sounds like it." I agree, if only to keep being the kick in the ass he needs. "Is this really helping you?"

"Yes, and I'll tell you why. I like to think I'm one of the nicest guys out there, you know?" I roll my eyes. "You're keeping me humble, Dacia. I like it. But anyway, I'd like for it to be true. I don't ever want to be the fake nice guy who expects the girl to fall for him because he's been there for her all along and gets mad when she doesn't."

"You can't pat yourself on the back for thinking that about yourself. Your words mean nothing to me because they're just words. I have no idea if they're actually true." Because I don't know him. Not yet, anyway. But his expression is earnest and open in a way I rarely see in other people, and it makes me think he actually does mean what he's saying.

"You're exactly right. Actions speak louder than words, and I can only prove that I'm not that guy by not being that guy. And the way not to be that guy is to find out what she wants first. It's just hard because everything in the beginning is all mind games, and you might think you have all the answers, but you could be wrong." He shakes his head. "You could be so wrong it's not even funny."

I nod sagely. "I know about being wrong."

"Yeah?"

"Yup." I say, voice dripping sarcasm. "Like when I asked why the party sucked for you? I could already be in bed sleeping if I hadn't, and now I'm regretting the ten minutes you just wasted for me."

The car is silent for a full beat, and I start to wonder if I was too harsh with him. Then, he surprises me again when he bursts out into laughter. His eyes crinkle shut in the stomach-clenching kind of laugh you can't hold in. The sound is contagious, and I find myself laughing with him.

"Yeah, you really are something else, Dacia." He says, grinning. "Sorry to just unload on you like that. You're probably tired of me by now."

"Does that mean I'm free to go?"

"Yeah, get out of here." He unlocks the passenger door from his side. "I'll see you around."

I watch his car drive off from the porch before I head in to shower and get ready for bed. When I check my phone, I have three missed calls and two texts from Christian apologizing for what he said and asking where I am. I text that I'm back at the apartment and safe without acknowledging his apology. It's not even midnight yet, so I'm sure he and Chastity will be out for awhile longer. I pick up Daisy Jones, but I only get four pages in before I fall asleep.

CHAPTER 6

You're something else, aren't you?

I let out a groan, feeling his hands everywhere. On my waist, traveling slowly down my hips. I feel him grin against my neck, his breath hot on my flushed skin. His weight presses me into the mattress, pinning me in place. The scent of his cologne - all spice and musk - envelops me, intoxicating. My eyes stay shut, for fear of this being reality or a dream, I'm not sure. If I think about it too much, I'll ruin the moment. I should want to ruin the moment, a distant thought from the lucid, logical part of my brain tells me. But his touch feels too good, and I'm tired of thinking so damn much all the time.

So I let my thoughts quiet and allow myself to be taken over by the dream playing out in front of me. My hands find his hair, his curls soft to the touch. He parts my legs with a knee. My breaths come in shallow spurts of air I can barely drag into my lungs. I pull at the wavy strands of hair and I'm rewarded with an illicit groan in my ear. His hand reaches lower, sliding up the inside of my thigh, right where I want him -

I jerk awake, a moan caught in my throat. Shit. Shit. I throw myself back down on the bed, my skin heating from a mixture of shame, embarrassment, and desire burning in the pit of my stomach. Please tell me I did not just have a sex dream about Marcus. I can't catch my breath, so I wait until it regulates before bringing the comforter up to my eyes, as if hiding from my own thoughts. I'm just being ridiculous. It's clearly been way too long since I've had sex, so of course my brain would conjure the first attractive man I met since breaking up with Anthony.

Of course! That has to be it. I haven't dated in...over a year? That can't be right. I do the math in my head, flashing back to Anthony's condo in Boston. We'd been together for four years, two of those years long distance. It was the first time we'd seen each other face to face in months. My father had just gotten his diagnosis, and Anthony was worried about breaking up with so many changes going on in my life. But I couldn't ignore the truth any longer. That was exactly one year and two months ago.

An entire year, and I only just realized it. That says more about our relationship than it should.

A knock at my door startles me from my thoughts. Chastity comes in wearing a giddy smile and the same outfit from yesterday. My brows furrow as she plops down at the foot of my bed.

"Guess what I did last night."

"No, Chastity!" I burst up from my cocoon of blankets. "What happened to taking things slow?"

"We are, and we did!" She exclaims. "Jane and I stayed up all night talking. Oh my god, I can't even remember the last time I did that with someone. It was amazing, Dacia. This girl is just..." She shakes her head, words failing her.

"Something else?" The words come unbidden. I slap a hand over my mouth as soon as they're out.

"Yes." She points a finger at my face. "That is exactly what she is. I know what you and Christian think, but there's just something about this girl. I can already see myself starting a life with her. Is that crazy?"

"Yeah." She swats at my arm. "But we're different. And if you want to put yourself out there, then as your best friend I have no choice but to support you."

She squeals before pulling me into a hug. "Dacia García, has anyone ever told you that you're the best friend a girl could have?"

"Can't say they have." I hold onto her back. When we pull away, I say, "Well? Tell me everything!"

For the next hour and a half, I forget all confusing thoughts of Marcus and Anthony and focus on Chastity's love life. It's a nice change of pace for the morning, but somehow I know it won't last for long.

For the next few days, Chastity doesn't ask Christian and I to hang out with Jane and her friends. Part of me is relieved, because I'm not ready to face Marcus after that god-awful (not-at-all-awful, actually) sex dream I'm still working on repressing. But surprisingly, I find I'm also...disappointed. The apartment is peaceful and quiet, just like I wanted, but it doesn't sit well with me. I finish Daisy Jones and three other books in the amount of time I have to myself, but as the hours wear on I find myself growing restless. Especially after Chastity and

Christian come back from the restaurant on Thursday and tell me that a few of the Galindo's stopped by for a visit.

"And they brought a friend we've never met before." Chastity says conspiratorially. "Sarah something? She's actually from Chicago! I asked where she went to college, but she said she moved after high school."

A Sarah from Chicago? Goosebumps rise on my arms. She can't be talking about her. Chicago's a big city, with lots of girls named Sarah who leave after high school. I tamp down the fear rising in my gut and clear my throat.

"Small world." My voice manages to come out steadier than I feel.

"She's also gorgeous. Christian kept staring at her from across the room."

"I was not." He says, but he can't meet either of our eyes.

"So, who is this mysterious girl?" I ask, feigning casualty.

"One of Marcus's friends. She was just hired at the daycare he works at." Chastity says. "She seems really sweet, but a lot to take in. Very talkative, very energetic."

"Sounds familiar." I tease, but I'm still on edge. Too familiar.

Chastity scoffs. "Not fair. You didn't meet this girl. She's in a whole other ballpark. Christian knows, he'll tell you."

I turn to her brother in the kitchen. He looks up from a plate of food. "I didn't meet her either, to be honest. I was actually busy working."

"You can crunch numbers any time and you know it. You should've sat down with us. Marcus already thinks you don't like them."

"Well, I don't like him, so he's half right."

"Since when do you not like Marcus?" I shouldn't ask, but I'm curious. I'm not even sure I like him. Really. "Are you sick of working with him already?" Christian's eyes narrow in a quizzical look, but Chastity interrupts before he can reply.

"We're getting off topic here. Can I just vent about this girl for a sec?"

"I thought you liked her. What do you need to vent about?"

"I do like her, but there are some..."red flag" seems like a strong term, but I'm not sure how else to put it." She turns back to her brother. "You saw how she was all over Jane's brothers, right? She was practically sitting in Isaac's lap and he's barely seventeen."

"Isaac didn't seem to mind." Christian smirks suggestively, and even I have to scoff at that.

"Wait, how old is she again?"

"She's our age!" Chastity gives a full-body shudder.

"Yeah, that's real weird." I say. To some people, it's nothing. There are plenty of relationships out there with eight year age gaps. But when a minor's involved, there's a power imbalance that can too easily be abused. I'd know. I've seen it myself.

"That wasn't the only thing." Chastity adds. "She kept going on about how other girls hate her, and how she has such a hard time making girl friends because we're all apparently so catty and judgmental." She rolls her eyes. "I don't know, Jane seemed to sympathize with her so maybe I'm being too harsh. Jane seems like a good judge of character."

"And you know this after less than a month?" Christian's tone isn't harsh, but a flicker of emotion passes over Chastity's face.

It only lasts a second before she schools her expression to one of indifference and shrugs.

"Whatever." Chastity says. "The point is I'm not writing this girl off or anything, but I'm calling it right now if she turns out to be bad news."

"You don't know this girl's last name?" I ask her.

Chastity cocks her head, thinking. "I know she said it, I just don't remember what it is."

"What does she look like?"

"Why? Do you think you know her?" Chastity leans in curiously. "Are there a lot of cool-girl types named Sarah who flirt with teenage boys in Chicago?"

I open my mouth, but nothing comes out. Then I mash my lips together, thinking. How many coincidences does it take to make a warning sign? This is a story only Amelia knows, because I could only bear to tell it once. Seven years have passed without so much as a peep. I'm being paranoid. I have to be.

"Never mind." I lean back against the couch, letting myself deflate. But it does nothing to quiet the alarm bells ringing in my head. "Just be careful. And make sure Jane and everyone else is being careful around her, too."

"Don't worry about me. I can look out for myself." She smiles reassuringly and Christian rolls his eyes behind her back. Despite their nonchalance, something isn't sitting well with me. For the first time in years, I'd rather be paranoid than right.

A few days later, I finally breakdown and stop by the Barrera's restaurant to visit Chastity on her lunch break. There's no sign of her in the main dining area, so I head upstairs to the patio. Instead of finding Chastity, I find Marcus seated at a far table outside. He's still in uniform, black dress pants and simple white button-up, but his sleeves are rolled up to his elbows and the first few buttons of his shirt are loose, making me think his shift is done. His head is bent down, looking at the phone in his folded hands. I'm not sure what possesses me to take a seat at the table next to his, but I do.

"You waiting on someone, too?" He jumps at my voice, and I stifle a laugh. "Didn't mean to scare you."

"No worries." He shakes his head before giving a tired smile. "I was supposed to meet someone for lunch, but our plans fell through. I think."

"You think?" I tilt my head.

"I never got a text back, so." He shrugs, but his shoulders are tense. "Anyway, what about you? Are you meeting Chastity?"

I nod. "You can join us, if you want. Since your plans fell through." I add quickly. I'm not even sure why I'm inviting him to join us, but the air between us feels different somehow. Like maybe we're finally becoming friends after our rocky start. I'm still surprised when he agrees, getting up from his table to sit in the chair across from me.

We're silent for a full beat, until I decide to ask, "So, any luck with that girl you were telling me about?"

"Oh, god. I'm not gonna live that down, am I?" He rubs his forehead with a hand, cringing as he looks away from me.

"Never." I smirk. "I'm invested now. What excuse did she give you for bailing on the party?"

"She didn't really give one." He scratches the back of his head. "I don't know, when I came into work today she just kinda acted like nothing happened, so..."

"Ouch." I say. Then as something occurs to me, I add, "Wait, were you supposed to meet her here right now?"

His expression is pained as he nods again. "How pathetic am I? I should just give up, since she's clearly not into me."

"At least now you can move on."

"You think so?" His brows crease as he considers me.

"No sense wasting your time, right?"

"Yeah. I don't know. Maybe."

"That was three different answers." I find myself smirking as I watch Marcus squirm. He rests a hand at the back of his neck, looking down at the table as he blows out a nervous breath. It gives me the confidence I so rarely have around him, seeing him vulnerable like this.

"It's just that she keeps sending so many mixed signals, you know? I don't really know what to think." He admits. "What would you do?"

"If I was getting mixed signals from someone I liked?" He nods. "Bash my head in a wall from frustration, probably."

"Thank you. You're a ton of help." His voice is sarcastic, but his lips are pulled up into a crooked grin. I hate to think what that grin is doing to me, given the topic at hand.

"You're welcome."

The silence that follows is more comfortable than ones we've had before, even if it still puts me on edge. I shake my leg under the table as I look around the restaurant, but there's still no sign of Chastity. I'm about to text her when I catch Christian emerging from the backroom. His head is bent over his phone, a scowl marring his mouth as his brows crease. That's not a good sign. When he kicks a chair in his path out of his way with a force that makes me flinch from ten feet away, I know he's pissed. I wonder if it's because his proposal didn't go as planned.

Marcus turns in his seat to see what - who - I'm looking at, and his brows are furrowed with concern when he turns back to me.

"That reminds me, I wanted to ask if you were okay after everything that happened at the party. You know, after what Alex said and what happened with Christian-"

"How do you know what happened with me and Christian?" I look back at him, surprised.

"I don't, really. It just looked like you guys were arguing about something." He says. "And then you seemed upset when he left you alone."

My eyes narrow slightly, but it's not quite a glare. "You notice a lot more than you let on." He shrugs, as if everyone is like this. But no one is like that, quietly noticing things no else does. I cross my arms over my chest as if to stop my rapidly-beating heart from bursting free. "I'm fine, as long as I'm not forced into attending another party for a very long time."

"Isn't Chastity planning one at y'all's apartment?"

Goddammit. "Thanks for the reminder. Now I can kill her as soon as she deigns to show up for lunch."

"Don't tell her I'm the reason." He laughs.

Before I can respond, Christian spots us and comes over to interrupt our conversation. "If you're waiting for Chastity, she left an hour ago."

I let out a dramatic gasp. "She ditched me?"

"Something must be in the air." Marcus says, stifling a laugh.

Christian doesn't even spare him a glance. "Did you Uber here?" I nod, and he says, "Alright, let's go."

He walks away, fully expecting me to follow.

"What about lunch?" I call out, but he doesn't slow down to reply. What the hell? Anger heats my skin. I don't know what kind of mood he's in, but I don't care. I'm starving, already seated at restaurant known for delicious food, and perfectly capable of finding my own ride home. I text Christian some reiteration of this before slamming my phone down and picking up a menu.

"You okay?" Marcus asks.

"No, but I will be after a full plate of chilaquiles." I say. "What about you? Are you ordering?" I don't mean for the question to sound like a challenge. He leans forward, folding his arms over the table. Marcus's expression never gives him away as he considers the unspoken proposition here. A ride home is one thing, but going through a whole meal with someone you don't like is something else entirely. I'm internally preparing myself to watch him walk away when he raises his hand, calling the waiter behind us to our table.

Marcus transitions easily to Spanish as he puts in an order for chilaquiles, crispy tacos and two Mexican cokes. When the waiter asks him if we're on a date, Marcus let's out a choking sound and shakes his head. I look away. Then, Marcus laughs nervously before saying he'll fill him in later.

I shake my head at him when the waiter leaves. "Do you order for all the girls you lunch with?"

"Sorry," He has the good sense to look sheepish. "I figured I'd go ahead since I already knew your order."

"Did you?" I raise a brow and hold up my drink. "What if I wanted something stronger?"

He laughs to himself and says, "Fair enough."

There's an amiable silence between us when our entrees arrive. I'm too preoccupied with eating to notice, but it's nice not to worry what all these silences between us mean for once.

"So, what's your drink of choice?"

I wait until I've swallowed my last bite before answering, "Rum and coke."

Marcus waves over another staff member to fill the order. I don't bother commenting that he did it again (though part of me doesn't mind that he's ordering for me), only hold up the drink to toast with his Mexican coke. It feels like we're on the brink of a reversal of sorts. I'm about to ask if I've made up for that teacher-who-still-lives-with-his-parents comment when the waiter arrives to deliver to the check. Marcus is asking him if he can split the bill when I pull out my credit card from my purse and hand it back to the waiter.

"You didn't have to do that." Marcus says.

I shrug. "I know. Figured it was the least I could do since I need a ride home from you again." Need is a strong word, considering the amount of Rideshare apps on my phone. But it scares me to admit that I want to spend more time with him, because I have no idea what that means. Or rather, I do know. And that's what scares me.

He nods easily, flashing a grin that makes my heart race. "Alright, Dacia. Let's get out of here."

Chastity isn't home when I get back, but Christian is. He's sitting on the couch with his arms crossed over his chest, staring blankly at the TV. The sight of him immediately plummets my good mood. We're more alike than I'm comfortable admitting - when he's annoyed, his words are merely barbs that prick the skin. But when he's angry, his words hit to kill. I still don't know what happened to him today, but I know enough to tell that he's beyond pissed.

I know better than to interact with him when he's like this, but I don't make it to my bedroom door in time before he says, "You could do so much better than him."

"Like you're so much better." The words are mumbled under my breath as my hand reaches the knob.

"What was that?" When I don't answer, he says, "You know he's the main one pining after that girl. Trust me, you don't want to add yourself into that equation." It dawns on me suddenly. The girl Marcus likes is the same girl Chastity and Christian were talking about the other day. I'm not sure why that bothers me more than not knowing who she was before. Hell, I still don't really know who this girl is. At least, I hope I don't.

That's the thing. It's been days, and I still can't quiet the panicked thought screaming that this Sarah is her. Sarah Bailey. The girl who nearly destroyed my family.

It's crazy. I'm crazy. And I can't let myself go there right now.

"Why not?" I turn around to face him. "The equation's still at zero. She doesn't even like him back."

"Dacia, stop fooling around-"

"Who says I'm fooling around?" This is the moment that might come around to bite me on the ass, because the truth is I have no intention of pursuing Marcus. There's just nothing I hate more than someone telling me not to do something I already had no intention of doing. If he calls my bluff later, I have no idea what I'll do in retaliation.

Christian's eyes narrow. "That's who you wanna go for? You're about to become the CEO of one of the biggest tech companies in the country, and you want to date the almost-teacher?"

"You shouldn't talk about him like that. Success isn't the only thing that makes a person." Plus, I've yet to prove myself a successful CEO, but if I say that to Christian he'd just dismiss the idea and say I would eventually. But how could he know that when I don't even know that? I really need to stop thinking about work when I can't be there. All it does is make my head spin in circles. I make a note to go for a run tonight so that doesn't happen.

"I just don't see him with you." Christian says. "You should be dating someone on the same wavelength as you, and Marcus is so far down below you it's not even funny."

"You might think that's true, but that's never mattered to me." I shake my head. "When I said that stuff to Chastity, I was just trying to stop her from setting me up."

"Then what are you saying? Do you actually like this guy now?" That's the last question I want to answer right now. As if he can sense my hesitation, he says, "Dacia, you cannot-"

"Will you just drop it? I don't want to fight with you." I lean my back against the wall with a sigh. "What happened at the restaurant before you saw me? Did your parents-"

He cuts me off with a scoff. "You have your things you don't want to talk about, and I have mine."

We've reached a stalemate. Neither of us forces the other to open up, and so the silence between us stretches on until I can no longer take it. I close and lock the door behind me when I reach my bedroom, as if I can lock out all the unsaid things between us. But I can't. I know this isn't over, but I'm not even sure what this is.

Another week passes, and reading is no longer enough to calm my restlessness. I finally break down and get a rental car and spend the lonely hours driving across town, getting myself acquainted with the San Antonio roads I'll never see again after August. When I pass the University, I wonder how many sleepless nights Marcus spends at the library. When I pass the public library downtown, I wonder how many weekends he spends reading, and which books he lost himself in. When I pass three different daycares, I wonder which one he works at. Another week passes, and I still can't quite place why I even care.

Okay, maybe that's not entirely true. I just don't want to care. It's the one road I refuse to go down.

When Friday finally rolls around, I ask Chastity if she has any plans with Jane.

"No, why?" She gives me a look of disbelief. "Don't tell me you actually want to go out for a change?"

"Maybe." I shrug. "It's been kind of boring being by myself. I finally got to finish a few books I've been dying to get to, and then I found myself missing going out like we have been lately. Is that crazy?"

"For you? Totally crazy." She shakes my shoulders excitedly. "But I love it! I'll call Jane and see if she has any plans. What do you think we should do? Another bar? Or maybe something more low key, like an all-night coffee shop?" We hash out the plans together and Jane texts that she and Marcus are free.

"Oh, they also want to invite that new friend of theirs." She adds with a scowl.

Her. Or an entirely different Sarah from Chicago. The one Marcus is pining over, complicating my paranoia even further. I answer with forced nonchalantness. "Whatever. Sarah's her name, right?" As if I could actually forget.

"That's the one." She groans. "Ugh, I'm not looking forward to this anymore."

"Are you kidding?" My brows furrow. "Going out is what you live for! Did something else happen with her that you're not telling me?" I hope I don't sound as desperate for information as I am.

"Just a comment she made. She probably didn't even mean anything by it, but-"

"What did she say?"

Chastity lets out another groan. "She visited the restaurant the other day and we ended up going to the mall afterwards. Well, we went up a flight of stairs and I got out of breath, because stairs, and I made a joke about being out of shape. And then she actually agreed with me."

"She what."

"It's been a long time since I felt insecure about my weight, but damn, that brought me back." Her tone tries to make light of it, but I know her better than to believe the false cheer. "I'm trying to repress her exact words, but they were along the lines of, 'maybe you should lay off the donuts'. She saw me eat a donut once."

"What the hell. That's so fucked up." My skin heats in anger on her behalf. Chastity is the most confident person I know. She doesn't even let hate comments get her down. This must have caught her off guard. The same alarm bells from last week ring in my head. "Want me to beat her up? 'Cuz you know I'll beat her up for you."

"Mm, I don't know. It might be bad for your career in the long run." She laughs. "Besides, you'd have to get in line behind Jane. She was livid."

"Good. You're way too nice, Chas. You need someone with a protective side." I tell her. "So what did Jane say when you told her?"

"She went straight into confrontation mode. You wouldn't think she'd be intimidating, she seemed so sweet and quiet when I first met her, but Jane's real scary when she's mad." Chastity says. "We both went to Sarah to talk about it, but..." Her face scrunches in thought, as if recalling the moment. "It didn't really go the way I thought it would."

"What do you mean?"

"Well, I can't really remember how, but she kinda turned it around on us and made it seem like we were targeting her. Sarah said if I had talked to her by myself she would've understood, but because Jane called her out while I was there it felt like we were attacking her over a comment that didn't even mean anything." She rolls her eyes, but her shoulders are slumped as she thinks it over again. "I guess she kinda had a point. She said she didn't mean to hurt my feelings. The whole thing just got blown out of proportion."

"Chas. I say this as your friend." I grip her shoulders like she so often grips mine when she's about to make me do something I don't want to do. "That's bullshit."

"But-"

"This girl is playing you." I say. "You know what you call someone who makes you feel bad for something they did in the first place?"

"You really think that's what she did?"

"I've seen it enough times to know." From the executives at work who refuse to take me seriously to the fake people I avoided in school. There's a reason people say high school follows us long after we graduate. Most people grow up, but some people just grow old. It all starts with how much responsibility you're willing to take for your actions. But there's a huge difference between refusing to take responsibility for your actions and manipulating others to take responsibility for you.

Sarah Bailey would know.

She was my best friend in high school, until our friendship turned toxic. I ignored all the warning signs, or I guess didn't know what to look out for back then. If I spent the day with my family, I was abandoning her. If I got an A on a test, it was because we studied together. If I thought she was wrong, I wasn't being a supportive friend. If I stood up for myself, I was attacking her. If I had something she wanted, I was selfish for not allowing her to have it.

The last straw came too late. The damage had already been done.

I'm not good at meeting people and making friends. I never have been, even before her. But it'd be naive of me to say she didn't affect every relationship I've ever had from then on. I'd rather someone want nothing to do with me than want something from me. It makes it easier on both of us.

"Listen," I say. "Try to keep your distance from her, okay? I've got your back tonight."

Her shoulders relax as she exhales. "What would I do without you, Dacia?"

CHAPTER 7

I've convinced myself so fully that I'm just being paranoid that I never take a second to consider what I'll do if I'm right.

When Chastity and I arrive at Snopioca, we spot Jesse and Jane sitting in a booth at the back. Jane tells us that Marcus and Sarah are running late, and we chat easily as we wait for them to arrive. Or rather, they chat easily while I sit silently and let them. Chastity kisses Jane on the cheek, and Jesse gags in good nature and exclaims how nauseatingly cute they are. I'm inclined to agree, though I'm always happy to see Chastity happy and in love.

"I can't believe it's been a month already." Chastity says. "Anyone else feel like the summer is flying by way too fast?"

"Me." Jesse raises her hand. "But that's because I'm not ready to go back to school yet. Remind me why I signed up for grad school?" Jane tells her as the bells of the front door chime, alerting us to newcomers. I watch as Marcus steps over the threshold, a short, dark-haired girl trailing behind him. I arch my back for a better look at her, but I don't see her face until it's too late.

"Hey, sorry we're late. They took forever to give us our bill at that Thai place." Marcus stands over our table. With her clutching at his arm, completely oblivious until her eyes fall on my face. I can't be here. But I'm already trapped. "Chastity and Jane you already know, but this is Jesse and Dacia. Guys, this is-"

"Sarah Bailey." I finish for him.

My eyes train on her like she's the only person in the room. She looks almost the same in seven years, and I can't help but mark how unfair it is. Same brunette curls falling past her shoulders, same fair skin untouched by the sun, same piercing blue eyes everyone fawns over, same doe-eyed expression when she's caught off guard, her pink lips forming a perfect O. There should be something - a witch's crooked nose and weathered skin, a blaring red warning sign slung over her torso, the words "Life Ruiner" scrawled across her forehead in sharpie, anything - on the outside to depict the evil within.

There's a ringing in my ears. Distantly, I can make out voices asking how we know each other. Neither one of us answers them, our eyes locked in a silent battle. Mine cold and hard, hers widened in surprise with a flicker of fear. I told her a long time ago what would happen if we ever met again. But seeing her now, in the flesh, is like the wind's been kicked out of me. I can't make good on my promise to make her life a living hell, like she made mine. I can't conjure that wild, menacing eighteen year old who refused to be intimidated by the likes of her ever again. I can't even get air to my lungs. For fuck's sake -

"Excuse me." The words are a weak rasp of breath. I burst from my seat, bumping into Marcus's shoulder and about five different chairs as I rush to escape the cafe. The night air is stiflingly warm on my heated skin, and it doesn't help me breath any easier. I pull at the collar of my plain T-shirt, the loose fabric somehow suffocating my lungs. That's what it feels like, at least. God, why can't I fucking breathe?

Once I cross the threshold, I realize I don't know where I'm going, only that I have to get out of here. I walk towards the torn, abandoned building next door that used to be a Sonic, all exposed metal and overgrown weeds. I come to a stop at the first pole, resting my head against the cool metal, trying and failing to get air to my lungs. Another panic attack. The first time I see Sarah Bailey in seven years, and I'm reduced to this.

"Dacia, talk to me." Chastity is at my shoulder, her hand light on my back. "What's happening? What do you need me to do?"

"Call me a car back to the apartment." I hear myself say. "I can't do this."

There are mumbled voices behind me, and I recognize the other as Jane's.

"I'll go with you." Chastity says. "You shouldn't be alone right now."

"No." I turn around, shaking my head. "I don't want to bring your night down anymore then I already have."

"Dacia, that's-"

"Besides," I cut her off. "I need to be alone right now. Please."

Chastity looks at me for so long I start to think she's going to force me to sit down and tell her everything that's going on right this second. It wouldn't be the first time. But maybe because Jane's standing behind her, Chastity's shoulders slump and she finally agrees. They wait with me outside until my Uber arrives.

When they return inside, some masochistic tendency makes me turn back and look into the giant cafe window. They're not sitting in the back booth anymore. Marcus, Jesse and Sarah have moved to a square table at the front of the cafe, a board game laid out in front of them and boba drinks in their hands, and I wonder how differently this night would've gone if Marcus had walked in with a different Sarah.

The uber driver gives my name, and I nod as I open the car door, but not before I catch Marcus staring straight at me. I keep my head down, pretending I don't notice him as I climb inside.

If I had the chance to redo any moment in my life from start to finish, I know exactly which one I'd pick. And that's not for a lack of worthy contenders. When my father died, the last words I ever said to him were, "Why couldn't we be a real family?". When Anthony didn't want to break up, I told him I liked the long distance part of our relationship more than the time we spent together. When Jorge refused to see what I saw in Sarah, we barely spoke for an entire year. I will never understand how people who don't believe in regrets can live with themselves. Or maybe I just have a lot more than most people.

But nothing could ever top the day I drove Sarah Bailey out of Chicago for good.

There's a soft knock at my door, and I know what's coming. I wipe the tears and snot from my face and call for Chastity to come in. She steps inside and plops herself across from me on the carpeted floor. Her expression is hesitant, as if not sure how she can comfort me. It's not surprising. I'm not a person who cries often. I didn't even cry at my father's funeral. I'd already wiped myself out of tears in the days leading up to it.

"I know you value honesty, so I'll just say it. You're scaring the crap out of me, Dacia." Her voice shakes as the words come out, and I notice her eyes are watery. I shut my eyes. I never intended to scare her. She let's out a long sigh before saying, "So. You know Sarah."

"Yup." I say tonelessly.

"How?"

"She's someone I went to high school with." I sniff. "She was actually my best friend before we met."

"Yikes. I take it things didn't end well?" She gives a nervous laugh, and when I don't return it she lets out another sigh. "What did she do to you, Dacia?"

"I can't..." I take a steadying breath, and then another. "Look, I'm sorry I kept this from you for so long. She's not someone I like thinking about. I just-" My eyes shut tight again. She can't do this to me again. But I know that's not true. After yesterday, she's more than proven that she can.

"Hey," Chastity sits down next to me, rubbing my back in circles. When I gather myself again, she asks, "Do you need your medication?"

"Probably." I say. "She's the reason I'm on it."

Her brows furrow. "What?"

"I got my diagnosis after I cut her out of my life." I tell her. "Situational depression, social anxiety and panic disorder. You think I'm at a low point now? You didn't know me back then." I let out a humorless laugh, the sound hollow to my ears. "I guess I can't blame everything on her. My mental health wasn't the steadiest even before I met her, but she certainly didn't help. In fact, a lot of therapists seem to think her manipulation tactics made it worse."

"Dacia..." She pulls me into her, wrapping her arms around me in a tight embrace. I let her, reveling in the support I always forget I need. "I officially hate this bitch. You don't have to tell me what she did. I mean, you can when you're ready, but you don't have to. I believe you."

"Thank you." The tears come again, falling over my cheeks in salty streams. I try and fail to sniff back the snot forming in my nostrils. "Can you pass me the box of tissues?" She does wordlessly, her mouth curling up slightly as I blow my nose. "I hate crying. There's much more snot involved than there needs to be."

"Now you know how I feel." Chastity says with a laugh, wiping away her own tears. While it takes a near apocalypse for me to cry, all it takes for Chastity is some light emotion. "What can I do to make you feel better?"

"You don't need to do anything more." I lean my head against her shoulder. "This is enough."

Chastity takes a week off from the restaurant to spend time with me, saying "Anything you want to do, I'm game." When I insist on staying in to read, she plucks a book from my shelf at random and reclines herself on the sofa next to me. My eyes widen in surprise at how seriously she's taking this before opening my copy of The Cruel Prince. I finish the trilogy in two days while Chastity dutifully reads the book she picked out right beside me. On the third day, when I come out of my bedroom to see her already on the couch with her book in hand, I'm flummoxed.

"You can't be having a good time." I say. "You hate reading!"

"But you love it, so I'm gonna do it. All week." She doesn't take her eyes off the page as she replies. "Unless you want to do something else today?"

"Do you want to do something else today?"

"This week isn't about me, Dacia." She reminds me.

"Okay." I take a seat next to her. "I want to go to the movies with you and Jane tomorrow night."

She puts the book down. "You do not."

"You don't know what I want." I shrug. "We can go see that new Marvel movie. They make them every month, don't they?"

"First off, you hate watching anything over two hours long because you can't sit still unless you're reading. Secondly, you hate Marvel! You said the last Avengers movie was the worst thing you'd ever seen since Dead Poet's Society."

"I fail to see why that movie had to be three hours long and kill off Iron Man. He was clearly the best one."

"Regardless, I know what you're doing." Her eyes narrow at me. If Amelia is my confidant, Chastity is my support system. A large part of our friendship has always been about building each other up when the world tries to tear us down. For her, it's haters on the internet and thoughtless comments from her brother. For me, it's the higher ups at Seidel and now, Sarah Bailey. I love her for that, which is why I need to return the favor now.

"Is it working?" I raise a brow.

"That depends on if we can change it to a movie night in. We can wear pajamas and buy junk food and wine and watch a 90's chick flick!" She gasps as if this is the best idea she's had in ages.

"We can even invite Jesse and Alex and make it a girl's night! But only if you want." She adds the last part after seeing my scowl.

"No, no, you're right. Up until you thought to invite Alex, that is."

"You really should be nicer to her, but this is your night so I'll give you veto rights."

"Okay, fine." I groan. "We can invite Alex."

Chastity squeals before taking out her phone to set the plan in motion, and I start to wonder if I've made a terrible mistake.

It's too quiet.

Aside from You've Got Mail playing on the flat screen, that is. Maybe it's my imagination, but there was a noticeable tension in the air when Jesse and Jane first arrived. Both girls avoided eye contact with me when we greeted each other at the door, but all night I catch them staring at me from the corner of my eye when they think I'm not looking. Now, as Meg Ryan tells Tom Hank off for being a jerk, I catch Jane's concerned expression pointed at me as I reach for the popcorn. She turns her head away quickly, her eyes trained hard on the screen as if she hasn't just given herself away.

I never thought I'd say this, but I'm glad Alex is here and completely oblivious, munching away on the store-bought chocolate-chip cookies without a care in the world. Why can't Jane be more like her?

The movie ends and I could almost cry out from relief, until Chastity asks what we all should do next.

"We could play a game." Alex suggests. "Do you have Monopoly? Or a deck of cards?"

When Chastity shakes her head, Jesse asks, "How 'bout truth or dare?" Jane nudges her with an elbow and a pensive look, leaning toward her to whisper something I don't catch. My skin heats from shame, but Chastity doesn't seem to notice.

"I'm game!" She claps her hands. "Is everyone down?"

I can't exactly say no, can I?

"But we gotta make this good." Alex says, downing her glass of wine. "We're not in middle school anymore. Give us something hard, and don't be afraid to ask us the real questions." I retract any nice statement I ever made about this girl.

"Who goes first?" Jane asks, studiously avoiding eye contact with me.

After Jane dares Jesse to tell off her ex in a text message and Alex asks Chastity what the hardest part of being on YouTube is, it's Jane's turn to ask someone -

"Truth or dare?" Her eyes train on me. "Dacia."

"Here we go." I grab my wine glass from the coffee table. A part of me wants to cut the bullshit and answer the question on everyone's mind. But a bigger part of me is sick of all the games. If I'm going to do this, I want to do it on my own terms. I look at her head-on. "How bout we make it interesting?"

"What do you suggest?" She asks.

"You want to know about Sarah Bailey." I say. Alex lets out a gasp from beside me. She knew her in high school, but she doesn't know the extent of my relationship with her. I'm not even really sure what she knows, actually. Jesse catches her up to speed, and Alex's jaw drops dramatically. I look at each of them in turn. To Jesse leaning forward eagerly, Jane rubbing her chin with a curious gaze, and Chastity biting her bottom lip in a nervous gesture. "You all do. I'm not willing to share the whole story, but I'm also not one to back down from a challenge. So here's how this is going to go. Ask me any question you want, and for any question I don't answer, give me the hardest, grossest, or most humiliating dare you can think of."

"Intriguing." Jane says. "How many questions do we get to ask you?"

"Three." I say. "So make them good."

"For the record, I don't think this is a good idea." Chastity says.

"Noted." I say dryly.

The four of them are silent for a beat. I take the time to finish off my glass, pouring myself a second as Jane and Jesse confer with each other.

Finally, Jane asks the first question. "Why did you react the way you did when you saw her?"

Chastity's mouth opens in shock. She turns back to me, concern burning in her eyes.

"Because she reminds me of past trauma." I answer. They wait a moment, as if expecting more. I open my mouth to explain myself, but think better of it. No one is owed that story.

"What past trauma? What did she do?" Jesse asks.

"That's two questions." I say. "You sure you want those to be the last ones you can ask?"

Jane gives her a stern look before turning back to me. "What did she do to cause you so much trauma?"

"Good combo." Jesse grins slyly at Jane, who just rolls her eyes.

I try to gather my thoughts into a coherent answer, but my mind can't stop replaying the memory. When I was at my lowest point, I was willing to give up a lot just to appease her. My belongings. My internship. The validity of my own emotions. It wasn't until she hurt someone I loved that I began to see her for who she really was. Who she really is.

"Our friendship was toxic." I explain. "She was a major part of my life for four years and she defined every one of them. She wasn't all bad, but that's how I was tricked. Otherwise we never would've been friends for as long as we were." She could make anyone feel special. Shower you with praise, raise you up on a pedestal just to knock you right off of it when your guard was down. I never saw it coming. Each and every time.

"I had a therapist once who said something that's always stuck with me. Emotional abusers are most effective when they get you alone. No one can dispute what they say to you if no one else is around to hear it. She was my best friend - my only friend, really - in high school. I think she liked it that way. She had more control of me like that, anyway."

I can't look any one of them in the face. This is the most exposed I've ever felt in years. But even though I know I don't owe them any kind of explanation for running out the other night, they should know what kind of person Sarah Bailey is. And I'm the only one who can tell them.

"Holy shit. I never knew she was that bad." Alex says. "She always seemed like a sweetheart in high school. I know you guys had a falling out, but I never would've guessed it was because she's toxic."

"She did make that comment to you about the donuts." Jane reminds Chastity. "And then we ended up apologizing to her."

Yes, I think. If Jane's starting to believe me, this will all be worth it.

"That doesn't necessarily mean anything, though." Jesse says. "I hate to be the only one who doesn't believe you, but you haven't exactly shown us that you want to be our friend."

"Jesse-"

"No, Jane. I need to say what you won't." Jesse turns back to me. "You haven't tried to get to know us all summer, and suddenly Sarah shows up and you want us to trust you? I don't buy it. I don't know what you're trying to gain from this."

"Whether or not you believe me is entirely up to you." I try for nonchalance, but every muscle in my body is tense. My jaw locks and I barely get the words out. "But if you can trust anything I have to say tonight, it's this. There will be serious consequences if Sarah Bailey sticks around. She might be a temporary presence in your lives, but the damage won't be."

"What did she do that was so terrible?" Jesse asks, eyes narrowed. "For you to say that, it has to be something more than emotional manipulation. What was it?"

I haven't thought of that day in years, but its just below the surface now. Jorge's face pressed into my shoulder, his tears staining the fabric of my shirt. My father shaking his head solemnly, like it's all he can do. Like it's already out of his hands. Amelia's face burning red in outrage. Fists clenched so tight my nails dig in to the tender flesh of my palms until I feel the satisfying sting of blood.

"Is it enough to say she hurt someone I loved?" I ask.

A beat passes. "No." Jesse says. "It's not enough."

"Fine." An intake of breath. Then another. "Then I choose Dare."

CHAPTER 8

I lean my forehead against the rim of the toilet. Sweat beads against my clammy skin as bile reaches up my throat for the third time tonight. Worth it, I think. There wasn't an ounce of regret in my body when Jesse mixed soy sauce, mayonnaise and a "mystery ingredient" into a shot glass and handed it to me with a flourish. Not even when I knocked it back to a chorus of high-pitched screams and discovered the mystery ingredient to be vodka.

Even now, my head resting on the cool tiled floor, there is no regret.

A knock at the door snaps me out of my thoughts, and when I yell for Chastity to come in I'm surprised when Christian is on the other side. I force myself to sit up, moving aside the sweaty strands of hair from my face.

"Here." He hands me a can of coke. "It'll wash out the taste."

"Thanks." I take a long swig from it. "Did I wake you?"

"No, I was already up. Chastity told me what happened when everyone left." He chuckles. "Who knew Dacia García was such a daredevil?"

I get out a groan as my stomach gurgles again. "I had my reasons. Believe me."

"I know." I look up at him in surprise. "Jorge told me about Sarah Bailey a few years ago. I can't believe she's here." He shakes his head, frowning. "What are you gonna do?"

There are so many questions spinning through my head. My brother told Christian about her? How did I not know this? But when I start to speak, all that comes out of my mouth is air.

"Look, I know it's not my place to tell you what to do, but they deserve to know the truth about Sarah." Christian continues when I don't reply. "I mean, this is so fucked up. Jane's got brother's his age when she-"

"I know." I shut my eyes. "And I tried, okay? But it's not that easy. I'm not even sure they believe me."

"They'd be stupid not to." He says, his hands clenched into white-knuckled fists. Then he lets out a sigh. "You should get some sleep. A clear head will do you some good, and maybe you can think of another solution."

He leaves without another word, and I gather myself off the floor and back to my bedroom. Maybe he's right. Maybe I should've swallowed my pride instead of that mystery shot. Then Jesse's words ring in my ears again. You haven't tried to get to know us all summer, and suddenly Sarah shows up and you want us to trust you? I don't buy it.

Or maybe what I have to say doesn't matter to them at all.

The next day, I'm completely done with being social. I pick up The City of Brass, easily the thickest book on my shelves, and plop myself down on the couch with a gigantic mug of coffee. Now this is my element. Who needs to hang out with strangers when you can read about their adventures instead? I'm only two chapters in when Chastity emerges from her room, dressed to go out.

"I'm going to brunch with Jane. Do you wanna join us?"

"I'm good." My eyes stay trained down on my book.

"Are you okay after last night?" There's a quaver in her voice that almost makes me look up. But the last thing I want to think about is last night, or anything to do with Sarah Bailey.

"Perfectly fine." I say, turning the page.

From the corner of my eye, I watch as she hovers by the front door. I can feel the concern coming off her in waves. But I'm afraid if I look up at her now, I'll completely break. Finally, she lets out a sigh and opens the door.

"Call or text if you need anything. I'll come straight back home."

I give a noncommittal nod and flip another page.

The day flies by chapter by chapter. When lunch rolls around, I bring my book to a French bakery at The Rim and eat the best grilled cheese I've ever had in my life. I stay until near closing and leave with a dozen macarons tucked away in my bag. I'm almost at the halfway point in my book when Chastity calls around dinner time.

"Hey, is it okay with you if Jane stays with us for a couple days?" She asks. "A pipe from her bathroom burst and her bedroom is completely flooded."

"Yeah, sure. Anything she needs." I reply automatically.

"You're the best!" She exclaims. "I'm helping her pack now, but we'll probably back in an hour. Do you have any plans for dinner?"

"I was thinking of ordering from a Vietnamese place that looks interesting. Do you want me to order something for you and Jane?" She agrees, texting five minutes later with their orders.

So much for being done with being social.

Jane and Chastity arrive back minutes after I do. Chastity has a duffel bag slung over her shoulder as Jane carts in a suitcase, two tote bags and a guitar case.

"Remind me how long you're staying for?"

"Not that long." Jane says. "This is everything we could save from the pipe burst."

"Yikes." My eyes widen at her meager belongings. "It must've been pretty bad."

"Only for me." She rolls her eyes. "Every other room in the house was untouched. Marcus was able to contain it, but not before wrecking every valuable thing I own." She rubs a hand over her face. "It took me three months to save enough for that amp, and now it's gone. And my camera-"

"I have tons of old ones. You don't have to worry about that." Chastity says. "In fact, you need to stop worrying in general. There's nothing we can do about it right now, so let's save that energy for tomorrow. I bet you're starving, we haven't eaten since brunch. Come on."

We settle in the living room to eat. Chastity puts a Netflix movie on the TV, and by the time we've finished eating Jane is visibly calmer. Chastity has her arm around her, and seeing them together brings a pang to my chest.

"God, I can't believe this took up my entire day." Jane says. "I bet I look like a hot mess, too."

"Nonsense." Chastity presses a kiss to her forehead. "You can never look bad."

"Like I can count on you to tell me how it is. You're supposed to say that." Jane rolls her eyes before turning to me. "Dacia, be honest. How do I look?"

I don't hesitate. "You've seen better days. In fact, you both have."

She lets out a loud cackle. Chastity wraps her arms around her and assures her I'm lying. Chastity plants another kiss on her forehead, and Jane leans into her. I have to look away, because I'm starting to feel less cynical and more...yearning. The last thing I need or want is a relationship right now, so why am I suddenly feeling like this?

"So, what are we watching next?" Jane pulls herself from Chastity's arms and reaches for the remote. For the next hour and a half, we watch a series Jane recommends. At some point in the night I fall asleep at an odd angle on the couch. When I wake up, the muscles in my back are killing me. I keep my eyes shut when I hear voices, the words steadily making sense as I fully wake.

"Come on, just let me post it. We look so cute!"

"I don't know Chas, you have so many followers. What if something happens?"

"They don't know you're my girlfriend. They'll just think I have beautiful friends."

"Wait, back up." Jane's voice grows. "When did we start using labels? I thought we were just dating."

"I know you think it's too soon, but it feels right, doesn't it?" A long pause, and then muttered words I can't make out. "...Know how I feel about you. I just don't see why we have to wait so long when we know."

"Because I've done this before, Chastity. Jumping so quickly into something new-"

"Look, let's just-" Chastity lowers her voice, and soon I feel their weight lift from the couch. Footsteps shuffle on the carpet before I hear a door shut.

I sit up from my awkward position with a stifled groan. This is exactly what I was worried about. Chastity has always gotten ahead of herself, and now Jane is pulling away from her. The last thing I want is to see her hurt over this, but I'm too exhausted to think what to do about it right now.

The next morning, I wake to the incessant chime of my phone. I let out a groan, flipping over and putting a pillow over my head to drown out the noise. When it doesn't stop, I bite the bullet and reach for it on my nightstand. Alex has sent four consecutive texts.

Hey there, friend! Thought I'd check in to see how you're doing.

I heard from Jesse that Chastity's planning a dinner party! Let me know if she needs any help.

I'm an excellent party planner.

;)

I let out a groan before typing a terse reply. Then I throw my phone on the bed with a grumble, wondering what part of town Alex staying. San Antonio is a big city, easy to avoid people you don't want to see. Or so you'd think, anyway. I've already run into two of them. I grab my phone and open Instagram to stalk Alex's page, which seems to be exclusively photos of food.

There's one of a mouth-watering ice cream cone from Kuma, a bowl of ramen from Suck It The Restaurant, and a plate of crispy tacos from the Barrera's restaurant (because of course there would be). There's no indication of what part of town she's staying. I'm about to close out of the app when Chastity's latest post catches my eye from the top of my timeline.

It's a photo of her and Jane from Jesse's birthday party. They're sitting on the couch, arms wrapped around each other. Jane is smiling into the camera while Chastity's eyes are glued on her. But it's the caption that throws me.

No, Chastity. This must be the picture Jane told her not to post. But Chastity does what she wants, and it looks like this time is no different. I stare at the picture for a few more seconds before a knock at the front door snaps me out of my thoughts. I must be the only one home, because the apartment doesn't stir. Another knock sounds, and I groan as I get up from the bed. Maybe someone forgot their key, but other than Alex no one has texted me.

I look down at my pajamas before answering the door. My shirt is vaguely see-through and oversized, falling over my shoulder and covering my pajama shorts. I don't care enough to change, though I hope it's not someone I'd be embarrassed to have see me like this at the door. But if my time in San Antonio has taught me anything, it's that luck is very clearly not on my side.

As if to prove my point, Marcus is standing on the other side of the door.

His tousled waves are pushed back from his face, with a few pieces sticking up out of place. He's wearing a white graphic tee tucked into worn out jeans that fit him a little too well. But its his eyes that have me pinned in place. Not quite hazel, but not quite brown, with long lashes framing them. Looking into them is like looking into pure sunlight, only not nearly as harsh. Just warmth.

How have I never noticed this quality in him before? How is this the first time his eyes have me completely hypnotized? They're trained on me now, brows furrowed in a look of question.

"Did you hear what I said?" He gives a light chuckle, and I snap out of my ridiculous thoughts.

"Sorry, no." I rub my eyes like I'm groggy from just waking up, as if my night shirt doesn't prove that already. Because that must be why I'm thinking of him like this. "It's been a slow morning for me. What's up?"

"I'm here for Jane. She said she needed a ride to work. On top of the burst pipe, she's also having car trouble now. Poor girl can't catch a break." He laughs. "Only, she wasn't in the parking lot like she said she'd be."

"I'll call Chastity and see where they are." I leave him in the doorway to fetch my phone from my room. When I return, I see him idling in the doorway like a lost puppy. I roll my eyes and motion for him to come in. Chastity's voicemail plays, and I hang up to text her instead. "She's not picking up."

"Jane isn't either." Marcus takes a seat on the couch. "Mind if I wait here for her?"

"Not at all. I'm sure they just got caught up with something." I tell him. "Do you want anything to drink?"

"Nah, I'm good."

I really wish he said yes so I could have something to do with my hands. The silence stretches, and my mind flashes back again to that night at the bar. You don't need to fill these silences. I wonder if he's learned to like me any better by now, and then I wonder when I started caring. Any good grace he's allowed me has probably been wiped clean after Sarah came into his life. If he asks me about her, I have no idea what I'll say.

But what if she's already beaten me to the punch? My stomach is starting to feel queazy just thinking about it. I start to ask, "How 'bout a-" when he says, "I hope you-", and we both laugh awkwardly.

"Sorry, what were you going to say?" I ask him.

"I was just gonna say I hope you're feeling better after the other night."

"Oh. That." I bite my lip, my heart pounding for no good reason. "Yeah, I'm...better." The words sound hollow and forced out of my mouth, but I can't give him an explanation. I could barely give one to the girls, and other than Chastity I'm not even sure they believe me.

"Whatever it is must be really bad." Marcus says. "Sarah wouldn't tell me anything, either."

Deep breaths, Dacia. At least I know she hasn't told him anything yet, but I probably can't count on her never telling him anything. A part of me wants to warn him about what kind of person she is, but I don't know what good that would do if I can't tell him the full story. I don't want another repeat of Truth or Dare night, and I highly doubt he trusts me enough to believe she's a bad person based on my word alone. Especially since Sarah is the girl he has feelings for. He might think I'm only saying it because I'm jealous of her, which would be mortifying. Soon I'll have to figure out what to do about her, because I have to do something.

But for now, I'm dying for a change of subject as much as I'm dying for a change of clothes. When I realize I'm not wearing a bra, I decide to kill two birds with one stone. "I'll be right back."

"Wait-" I turn back before I reach the door to my bedroom. "Jane just texted. She forgot to tell me Chastity wanted to give her a ride instead. Guess I wasted your time for nothing." He shoots me an apologetic smile.

"Don't worry about it." I see him the four paces to the front door, waving awkwardly as he leaves. I have no reason to be as disappointed as I feel, but I don't know what do about it either.

CHAPTER 9

I don't decide what to do about Sarah for another two days. When I do, I could kick myself for not thinking of it earlier. Chastity, Jane and Christian are gone for the day, leaving me free to make what's sure to be an hour long phone call uninterrupted.

Wilhelmina Seidel is my hero, and not just because she built Seidel Computers from the ground up in the 80's as a single mother of two. I see her as a woman unafraid to go the distance, no matter what she had to sacrifice. When she fell in love with my grandfather, a cotton-picker from a family of Mexican immigrants, it meant cutting ties with her family without apology. When he died ten years into their marriage, it meant picking herself back up and finding a passion to throw herself into. A passion that so happened to be a computer startup company.

But to everyone else, even Amelia, my grandmother is terrifying. A six foot tall German woman as silver haired as she is silver tongued, it's not hard to see why so many people find her intimidating. I've always admired her ability to speak her mind like she's never the felt the consequence of doing so.

"It's about time I heard back from you," Is how she answers the phone. There's no ire in her tone; it's simply matter-of-fact.

"I know. I won't give you an excuse, I know how much you hate that." I say. "I'm actually calling for a favor."

"You've been in Texas for two months without deigning to visit once, and now you have the audacity to ask for something?" She sounds amused, but that doesn't stop me from wincing. "What's this favor?"

"Are you still in contact with Ronald Weber?"

"I am." She says. "And say no more. I'll send you his information right away."

I breathe a sigh of relief that she doesn't ask any questions. "Thank you, Nana."

"Whatever you're doing, Dacia," She starts, and I hold my breath. "Promise me you'll be careful. I won't ask you what it is-"

"There's a first."

"You're a grown adult. I trust you know not to get yourself into any trouble. And besides, I'll have plausible deniability on my side if I don't ask."

I find myself smirking at that. "Thank you, Nana."

When I get off the phone, I pull up his email on my laptop. This isn't my first time contacting a private investigator, and I doubt it'll be my last. It was my father's idea to keep eyes on Sarah when Jorge went away for college. That was three years and a different PI ago. Back then she was in Arizona, and that was the last I'd heard of her. Even though I'm fairly sure her presence in Texas now is coincidental, I need to know for sure.

For the next two hours until I hear back from him, I pace the floor of my bedroom and attempt to start three different books, but none of them hold my attention. I'm too wired to focus on anything else. When my laptop dings with an email alert, I practically jump across the room to reach it. As I read the message, I find out Sarah's been living in Texas for almost a year after getting fired from her last job in Flagstaff. She moved to San Antonio four months ago. So this really was a coincidence. Sarah was already here when I got to the city.

I message Ronald to keep eyes on Sarah before shutting my laptop, still unsure what to do with the information I have. Seven years is a long time not to see or hear from someone, but with Sarah it was too soon. I don't know why I thought I'd be able to sleep tonight. When I shut the lights I toss and turn in bed, my mind reeling twenty different directions. Christian's words echo in my ears. I know it's not my place to tell you what to do, but they deserve to know. He's right. I know he's right. Then, another thought occurs to me. It's been almost a full week since we played Truth or Dare. Enough time for Sarah to have beaten me to the punch.

When my alarm goes off at five AM, I'm already wide awake. I swing my legs over the side of the bed and dress in my workout gear. The warm morning air heats my skin as I break out into a sprint. It feels like I'm running for my life.

Another week passes in a blur, a week in which Jane proves to be the perfect fourth roommate. The repairs to her bedroom at home are taking longer than she expected, so she takes it upon herself to make up for the inconvenience by showing her gratitude. Every morning, we wake to pancake breakfast and hazelnut coffee. (Or Chastity and Christian do, anyway. I arrive back from my morning run to it). She insists on cleaning around the apartment; every dish, every square surface, every nook and cranny we didn't realize needed cleaning in the first place.

Chastity has to force the Swiffer Duster out of her hand on most days, and I'm starting to feel guilty for everything Jane has been doing for us. She's our guest. We should be the ones making her breakfast and cleaning the apartment to make her feel more at home.

When Jane excuses herself to the bathroom after breakfast one morning, I clear the table and start loading the dishwasher before she gets the chance to.

"What do you think you're doing?" Jane asks, hands on her hips as she surveys me from the hallway. Hey eyes are narrowed, but her mouth is pulled up in the barest hint of a smile. "You know it's my job to do the cleaning up."

"We can't keep taking advantage of your kindness." I tell her. "Please. We're happy to have you for as long as you need, but the constant cooking and cleaning for us is unnecessary. You're our guest, not our maid."

"But I want to." She frowns. "It's my way of saying thank you."

"It's unnecessary." I assure her. "Truly. You've already done more than enough for us."

"Okay." But there's an uncertain tone in her voice. I puzzle it over when Jane leaves for work and Chastity and Christian leave for the restaurant. It isn't until hours later when Jane arrives back that it clicks. She walks straight to the kitchen, gathering pots and pans and necessary ingredients from the fridge to cook dinner. Before I can say anything, she gives me a pointed look from across the room. That's when I realize I hurt her pride.

"See, this is why I don't understand women." Christian says, and not for the first time in his life. Chastity and I are staring him down from across the kitchen bar. "You guys are making drama out of nothing. Why can't we let her cook and clean for us if she wants to?" Jane is at work, giving us free reign to talk about her while she's not here. I roll my eyes at Christian's statement.

"Spoken like a true midcentury man." Chastity scoffs. "It's not about that. I'm worried she doesn't feel comfortable here. There's been kind of a weird vibe between us ever since she started living here."

"I get it. She doesn't want to feel like a burden." I tell Chastity. "Her room will be fixed tomorrow, so things will go back to normal between you guys in no time."

"Maybe you're right." She crosses her arms over her chest, her expression no less worried. "Do you think I should talk to her about it anyway?"

"I don't really see the point." I tell her. "Just try to keep her away from the Swiffer in the meantime."

As the hours pass, the clouds outside turn grey with incoming rain. Christian leaves to get us dinner before the storm starts, and Jane arrives back soon after he leaves. I'm sitting on the couch when she walks through the door, hangs her purse on a hook and promptly falls to the floor face-first. I call for Chastity and run across the room to help Jane up. Her skin is hot and feverish, a sheen of sweat on her brow.

"Jane? Jane!" I give her shoulders a small shake, and her eyes flutter open. She mumbles something incoherent, and I yell Chastity's name louder.

"Calm down, I'm-" She freezes when she sees us on the floor, Jane's barely conscious form in my arms. "Oh my god! Jane!" Chastity pushes me out of the way to get to Jane, smoothing her hair back from her sweaty face. "Jane, can you hear me? What happened?"

"I'm fine." Jane lets out a groan. She pulls herself from Chastity's arms and attempts to stand up by herself. Chastity hovers over her with a worried expression. "I think I'm coming down with some sort of virus."

"What do you need?" Chastity asks. "I can go down to the drugstore and get you some medicine. Or do you think you need to go to the emergency room?"

"No." Jane bursts, and at Chastity's hurt expression she softens. "I don't get paid until next week, so I can't see a doctor. I think I just need to lie down for awhile, and I'll be alright."

"You just fainted. I don't think you can be the judge of that." Chastity pulls out her phone. "I'm calling your brother. Maybe he can pick up some medicine and soup."

"Please don't bother him, he's-"

"Marcus? Hey! Your sister just fainted in the living room..." Once she recounts the situation, she hangs up. "He'll be here in thirty minutes. Dacia, help me with her other side."

We carry Jane to Chastity's bedroom, setting her down on top of the covers. Chastity rummages through her dresser before slamming a drawer shut with a groan. "I don't have any pajamas that will fit you, Jane. Dacia-"

"Bottom drawer of my dresser." I tell her before facing Jane. "What else do you need?"

"Not-" Her voice comes out dry and scratchy. She clears her throat and tries again. "Nothing."

"And a glass of water." I tell Chastity, who nods before leaving the room. "You'd probably feel better in clean sheets. We can take care of that for you when you're in the shower."

"Is that your subtle way of saying I smell?" She smirks.

"Well, you did just come from working on cars outside all day." My brows crease in concern as I realize something. "Did the fever start today?"

"Last night, I think." She tells me.

"Going to work probably made it worse."

"I can't afford to miss a shift. They would've fired me if I hadn't shown up." I don't know what to say to that, mostly because I've never had to rely on a job where my presence was expendable. I'm well aware of my privilege, and how all my anxieties could never stack up to someone like Jane's. Even if I quit my job tomorrow, I'd be perfectly fine financially for the years to come.

"Do you go in tomorrow?" She shakes her head. "Good. You're not lifting a finger. Chastity and I will take care of you."

There's a soft knock at the open door. Marcus is standing in the doorway with a CVS bag in tow. I motion him in and he sits next to me at the foot of the bed.

"You really blacked out in the living room?" His brows are furrowed in a worried expression. Jane shrugs. "Jane! What happened to you?"

"Did you get a thermometer?" I snatch the plastic bag from his hand. When I find what I'm looking for, I tear through the packaging. "Feel her forehead. She's 102 at least."

Marcus does, and he heaves a sigh. "Pobrecita, Jane. What were you thinking going to work like this?"

"Open." I hold the thermometer above her mouth. "Lift your tongue." She does as I say and I insert the thermometer. Thirty seconds later, we have the result. "Told you. 102.7"

"Then it's a good thing I also bought these." He takes out a bottle of tylenol and a blue gatorade from the plastic bag. "To break the fever and keep your fluids up."

"You both are too much." Jane says with a laugh.

"And we don't even like each other." Marcus adds with a smirk. "Can you tell?"

I glance at him sideways. "When did I say I don't like you?"

"It was nothing you said, it's just your whole vibe." He motions a hand to me as if to indicate his point. I narrow my eyes at him. "See? That's what I'm talking about."

"Don't mind Marcus." Jane tells me. "He teases too much."

"So I've noticed." My eyes linger on him a second longer before I turn away.

We leave the room as Chastity enters with fresh pajamas, a bottle of water and a makeshift cold compress, and I have to smile at Chastity's efforts. I turn to Marcus when we reach the living room. "You can stay for awhile if you want. Just so you know she's okay."

"That'd be great." He tells me. "Thank you."

I amble to the kitchen, where Christian is sitting at a barstool with a plate of flautas. My stomach grumbles in response as I try to think of the last time I ate at the Barrera's restaurant. I steal a flauta off his plate when he's not looking, but he glances up from his phone when he hears the crunch as I take my first bite. His eyes narrow, but his lips curl in a sly grin.

"You're unbelievable." He says.

"That's what they tell me."

I spy two more bags of takeout and am about to offer Marcus a plate when Chastity emerges from her bedroom. "She's finally sleeping. Hopefully her fever will go down by the time she wakes up."

"Did she take any medicine?" Marcus asks.

"Two tylenol." Chastity nods. "Are you staying?"

"If you'll have me." He smiles sheepishly.

"Of course we will!" She clasps his shoulder. "We can watch a movie, or play a game-"

"Not truth or dare, I hope." I grumble.

"What?" Marcus's brows furrow, and I shake my head as if to say, don't ask.

"Actually, I think it's time Marcus and I had a talk." Christian gets up from the barstool. I look up at him in question. What the hell could Christian have to say to Marcus?

"We do?" Marcus turns his furrowed brows to Christian. "Oh, is this the 'if your sister hurts my sister, there'll be hell to pay' talk?"

"Come outside with me and you'll find out."

"You mean outside where it's raining?" I wave a hand toward the window, where rain slashes against the glass in torrents. "We already have one sick person living with us. We don't need two more."

"Fine." Christian rolls his eyes before indicating his bedroom. "Shall we?"

I watch as Christian snakes an arm around Marcus's shoulder and leads him away from the living room, the two of them talking in hushed tones. Here it comes. I should never have fought with Christian about the other man that day in the grocery store, because I was right. My words are about to come back and bite me in the ass. I need to do something, but I can't think with Chastity sitting beside me, drumming her long fingernails on the marbled kitchen counter.

"Your brother is transparent." I don't bother lowering my voice as I turn to Chastity. Out of the corner of my eye, I see Marcus turn his head. "What is it with men constantly needing to outdo each other?"

"I thought that's what women did." Christian answers from across the room.

"What your describing is society's need to pit women against each other." I sling an arm around Chastity. She leans her head against my shoulder. "We've always been above that. What I'm describing is the alpha-male tendency you two are displaying. What could they possibly be discussing that must not be overheard by the women of the room? Chas?"

"'If your sister hurts my sister, I'll hurt you.'" Chastity says, imitating her brother's voice perfectly.

"Nice guess, but your name never came up." Christian says. His face is blank, so I can't gauge if he's telling the truth. I narrow my eyes in disbelief.

"I don't trust you for a second. Marcus, is he lying?"

"Nope." He answers simply. He plops down on the couch facing me. "He mentioned nothing about Chastity."

"Which means they were talking about you." Chastity bumps my shoulder with hers, looking far more amused than I like. I roll my eyes, hoping my face isn't red.

"Oh, but of course." I lean into the sarcasm. "Two young and eligible gentleman vying for my attentions. What else is new?"

"My, my, but who will you pick?" I love when Chastity plays along. Marcus and Christian exchange glances, brows raised almost comically. "If you marry my brother, we could be sisters. But Marcus does have a certain charm about him."

"No, no, my dear. You need to think bigger." I say in an overly theatrical tone. "A lady must ensure she's made the most advantageous match. After all, what is an accomplished woman without an equally accomplished man on her arm?"

"And what constitutes an accomplished man?" Marcus asks, perfectly arched brow raised in amusement.

"Outrageously well-off, of course." I raise a finger. "Prestigious schooling. Fluent in more than three languages. Handsome. Passionate. Ambitious. Six figure salary. Physically fit. And oh, he must have his own private jet."

"And a well-stocked library." Chastity added.

"Yes, thank you." I agreed. "He simply must have a personal library. With all of the classics, none of that YA trash. God, could you imagine?"

Chastity and Christian laugh, probably thinking of the shelves in my bedroom in all of their Young Adult glory. They know I don't mean a single thing I say. But a laugh dies in my throat when I see Marcus's clenched fists in his lap. I'm about to assure him everything I said was only a joke, but he replies before I have the chance to.

"That's quite a list." His voice is light, and I think maybe I imagined his anger. "You must be completely faultless to demand such a suitor." His tone suggests he's playing into my joke, and my shoulders slump. Finally. Someone outside the Barrera's who gets my humor.

"Well, no one can be completely faultless. Even someone so far above others as I." I say, tone dripping sarcasm. In a more serious tone, I say, "I suppose if I had one flaw, it would be my penchant for grudge-holding. I never forgive and never apologize. If you cross me once, I'll never forget it."

"So you're unforgiving." Marcus says in an all-together different tone. I've shown too much of myself amidst the sarcasm. But how much of what I'm saying does he think I actually mean? "That explains a lot."

The game is gone in a flash. "What's that supposed to mean?"

"Nothing." He says, holding back his true thoughts, but I'm desperate to know what he meant. His tone reverts back to the theatrical one we've been using. "Just that you'll be doomed to a life of spinsterhood in a squalor mansion by the sea. All alone, with nothing but your books for company."

"You do realize you just described my dream, right?" I shut my eyes and let out a long sigh. "Ah, at last I've found it. Peace."

"Solitude."

"Quiet."

"Empty."

"Wondrous."

"Lonely. Forever."

When I open my eyes, Marcus's demeanor has changed. He's looking at me like I'm something inexplicable, and I feel small under his gaze. The tension in the room is palpable. I feel it mostly in my lungs.

Marcus looks down at his phone. "I should be going. Tell Jane I'll visit her again tomorrow." And then he pushes himself off the couch and out the door. Once again, the game has gotten away from me and spun into something I no longer recognize.

CHAPTER 10

Marcus picks up Jane the next day, not that I'm around to see it. I hear their voices from my bedroom, just short of pressing my ear to the door to eavesdrop on their muffled conversation. Ugh, I'm pathetic. When did I let myself become so invested in him?

For the rest of the day and the week following, I vow to put him out of my mind by starting the packing process. I set a few boxes aside and schedule the movers to come three days before the end of the month. Christian reminds us daily that we have less than a month left on the lease, but Chastity refuses to hear him. In fact, she refuses to hear any and all talk of moving out.

By the Friday of Chastity's dinner party her usual cheer rings false, with all the brittleness of a slowly cracking facade. She dances around me, setting up the table and double checking her to-do list.

"Wine and groceries are in the fridge. The apartment is pristine." She walks around me to the kitchen, looking down at her watch as she does so. I follow close behind, arms crossed over my chest. "Christian will be back with ice soon, and we can start prepping dinner in an hour. What else is left?"

"Talking about how you're in denial about leaving?" I'm far past subtlety by now.

"Music!" She strides across the room to her phone. "What are appropriate songs for a dinner party?"

"Farewell. Time of Your Life." I suggest. "Goodbye My Lover."

"I was thinking something instrumental for background noise. That seems classy." Her fingers fly across her phone screen. "Okay, it looks like we're all set."

"You did tell her our lease ends at the end of the month, didn't you?" My words finally seem to get through to Chastity. She looks up at me, expression hesitant. We both know who I mean when I say her.

"I was actually thinking of renewing when you and Christian leave." She tells me. "After the dinner party's over, I'm gonna talk to Jane about it. Do you think that's crazy?"

For a moment, I'm speechless. A lease is temporary, so it's hardly the worst choice Chastity could make for herself. But the problem is she's not doing this for herself. I remember the conversation I overheard between her and Jane when she was staying here. I know it's not fair to base my opinion of her relationship from one overheard conversation, but all I can think about is Jane pushing Chastity away for trying to push Jane into a more serious relationship than she's ready for. If Chastity stays in San Antonio, she's going to get her heart broken.

"Are you sure that's a good idea?" I ask.

"I can't help it. I'm in love with her." These are far from words I haven't heard from her before, but it's how they're said that gives me pause. Her voice is as serious as it is earnest. "And I know you think it's too soon, and lord knows Christian will freak out when I tell him, but this is something I really want to see through."

I've done this before, Chastity. Jumping so quickly into something so new-

"Is it what Jane wants, too?" I ask, already knowing the answer. At least, I'm fairly certain I do. "I thought she wanted to take things slow. She doesn't seem like the kind of person who'd let you make a big life decision like this for her."

"It's a six month lease, not a downpayment." She rolls her eyes.

"But your family and your job are in Dallas."

"I'm a YouTuber, I can work anywhere! And Dallas isn't too far a drive if my parents really need me."

"You don't know anyone in town apart from the people you've met through Jane-"

"Dacia, just tell me whether you support my decision or not." Her eyes are imploring, almost hopeful. "You know your opinion means everything to me. Am I making a mistake?"

I let out a sigh. "I just don't want you to get hurt."

"Is that a yes or a no?"

"Chas-"

"Dacia, please."

I want to tell her the truth, but I don't want to start a fight when our first guests will be arriving soon. "Can we please talk about this tomorrow?"

"Because you're going to tell me it's a mistake." The look on her face breaks my heart. I shut my eyes, because once again

she's spot on. Chastity is someone I admire for how different she is from me. Her resilience, her willingness to take risks, how she can wear her heart on her sleeve with complete abandon. But if I could stop her from making mistakes like this one, I would.

Chastity does what she wants. If she's already made up her mind, then nothing I say can stop her. But if there's any ounce of doubt, maybe I have a chance of being heard.

"Yes." I finally admit. "I think it's a mistake."

Chastity lets out a long breath. "Thank you for being honest with me. I need to-" She clears her throat as her eyes cloud. "I need to get some side dishes started. Can you help me chop some potatoes?"

For the next few hours, I help her prepare the scalloped potatoes and caesar salad. The air is awkward and tense around us as we skip around the truths we've laid out. We don't talk about Jane or what will happen when our lease is up, but it's right on the tip of my tongue until it's 6:30 and our first guests of the night begin to trickle in.

Chastity is avoiding me. We're an hour into the dinner party, and our apartment is already swarming with people. Chastity throws herself into hostess mode to ignore talking to not only me, but Jane as well. I've already caught Jane trying to pull her away from something keeping her busy three times, but Chastity is a master avoider when she wants to be. With my best friend occupying herself with anything and everything she can, that leaves me with Christian and Alex for most of the night. The former is nowhere to be seen (jerk) while the latter is following me into the kitchen (ugh).

I've never had a greater need for wine than right now.

"Oh, let me get that for you." Alex takes the glass from my hand before I can stop her. "Pick your poison. Red or white?"

"Whichever's stronger."

"That'd be the red." She refills my glass with a flourish and hands it back. I down half the glass in one long gulp. "Whoa there, girl. Rough night already?"

"Just killing time until it's over." I top off my glass and turn back into the living room, Alex close at my heels. Chastity walks by us on her way to the kitchen.

"You're already on your second glass? Dinner won't be ready for another half hour!"

"Actually, it's my third." I shrug, and she rolls her eyes before walking past me. Alex laughs for a full fifteen seconds as she follows me to the couch. Lord help me. From the corner of my eye, I spot Marcus across the room talking to Christian. Just from the look of it, the conversation seems heated. Christian is pointing his finger accusingly and Marcus is clenching his jaw in his telling sign of agitation. What the hell could those two be talking about? Alex says something to interrupt my snooping, but I only catch the tail end of it.

"...So glad we're finally getting the chance to catch up!" She says, and I snap back to attention. "And Dacia, I'm so sorry about what I said about your dad a couple weeks ago. I was kicking myself as soon as the words were out of my mouth. I wanted to apologize that night we watched You've Got Mail, but there never seemed to be a good time. I hope I didn't offend you, I just-"

Alex's stammering is the last thing I want to deal with right now. I watch over her shoulder as Marcus walks away from

Christian. I cut Alex off mid-sentence and make up an excuse to leave her, but not before catching her crestfallen expression. I'll feel guilty about it later. Christian is standing by the front door when I approach him, working a rough hand through his hair.

"Hey."

"Hey." His voice is soft, and I'm relieved to hear it. "I was just about to look for you."

"Well, here I am." I cross my arms over my chest. "Why were you talking to Marcus?"

"Because you barely let me get a word in with him last week." He says pointedly. "Though in hindsight, maybe that was a good thing. I doubt he believed a single word I said to him."

"Why? What were you guys talking about?" I feel my brows furrow.

"I tried to warn him about Sarah." My eyes widen. I'm not sure what I expected him to say, but it definitely wasn't that. "I thought it'd come better from me, man to man, but I think I just made things worse." He scrubs a hand over his face. "He said I have the whole story twisted, and he wasn't gonna let me slander Sarah's name like that. I don't know what she did, but she's got her claws in him deep."

I open my mouth to speak, but nothing comes out. He said I have the whole story twisted. I swallow back the bile threatening to rise at the back of my throat. "Did he say anything else?"

He hesitates before saying, "He thinks she's showing up tonight. He invited her."

My head snaps up. "He what."

He shakes his head. "I'm so sorry, Dacia. I tried."

"Don't apologize." I meet his eyes. "She wouldn't willingly step ten feet near me. She knows better."

I turn away from Christian, needing to be alone with my thoughts. The end of the month can't come fast enough. I want nothing more than to be rid of the Bailey's and the Henderson's and the Galindo's and this nowhere town once and for all. I'm halfway to the bathroom when I hear someone call my name, but I ignore it. The voice gets closer just as I reach the doorknob. Whoever they are is too late. I quickly lock myself inside and slide down against the door.

The first thing I do is email Ronald Weber, needing to know where Sarah Bailey is at this moment. If she comes anywhere close to this apartment, I'll lose it. I'll throw myself at her the same way I did seven years ago, only this time it'll be in a room full of people. It'll be worth the arrest warrant. While I wait for a reply, I stand up and push my hair behind my ears, smoothing the flyaways. When I look more manageable, I check my phone. One new notification.

My fingers are shaking as I pull up the email. It states briefly that she's been spotted at the airport, and that a full report of where she's headed will be following soon. I breath a sigh of relief, deflating against the door. She's gone. Maybe a whole state away, if I'm lucky.

I breathe easier as I step out of the bathroom, but that changes when I bump into Marcus. Literally.

"Ow." I slam against his hard chest, and he steadies me with a hand on my hip.

"Sorry." He says, but he doesn't particularly look it. His jaw is tense, and his expression eerily blank as he asks, "Can we talk?"

Stupid heart, stop racing so fast. I look out toward the living room, where everyone is ambling about waiting for dinner to start. No one will even notice we're gone.

"Sure." I lead him to my bedroom at the end of the hall, my legs shaking under me. I'm beginning to hate the effect he has on me. When did I allow this to happen? He walks in and I shut the door behind me, leaning my back against it. Marcus doesn't look at me. His eyes roam around my room; the perfectly made full bed pushed into the corner, the stack of boxes sitting beside it, to the two tall bookcases standing against the far wall. He walks over to them, scanning the titles.

"I thought you said you don't read YA." He says, picking up A Very Large Expanse of Sea off the shelves.

"It's called a joke." I roll my eyes at the back of his head. "Ever heard of one?"

He turns around to face me. "I'm never sure with you."

A lightbulb of realization must be hovering over my head. "That explains a lot."

"How much of what you say do you actually mean?" He puts the book down and returns to me. "Because I have to tell you, I've been trying to figure you out for weeks and I just...can't."

"And I guess that's a bad thing?" My breath hitches. His eyes are inscrutable. "Is this really what you wanted to talk to me about?"

"No." He says, looking away. "Well, maybe."

"Here's a thought: maybe I'm actually quite simple." I step forward. "Maybe you wouldn't be wracking your brain trying to 'figure me out' if you weren't so determined to hate me." I'm only teasing, but when his face reddens I realize I must've hit the mark remarkably well.

"I'm not-"

"Don't apologize. You'd be far from the first." I heave a long, dramatic sigh. "You're just one in a very long list of enemies. If you're lucky, you might be promoted to archenemy one day."

"So everything's a joke to you." Marcus rolls his eyes, but I can tell he's amused. "Thanks for clearing that up."

"Not everything." I say. "I wasn't lying about my biggest flaw. Unforgiving, remember? I tend to mix truth with sarcasm, so I understand why that would be confusing to some people. If I've ever hurt you, just know it was unintended."

"Really?" He asks. "Why do you do it?"

I shrug. "It's just my sense of humor. I know not everyone can appreciate it, but that's on them more than it is on me."

"Come on." He says unbelievingly. "I know there's more to it than that."

"There isn't." I step towards him. "I don't hide my true feelings behind masks of politeness. I use sarcasm instead. Call it a defense mechanism if you want, but when it comes down to it I'm not afraid to let you know where we stand. If I don't like you, I make sure you know it. If I like you, I don't make a big deal out of it. If I more than like you..." Our eyes meet and lock. "Well, that's when the line gets a little blurry."

I force myself to keep eye contact, hardly believing I actually said the words that just came out of my mouth. All that wine must be clouding my judgement. I've given myself away in this moment without ever really accepting that the feelings I have for Marcus are real. Even now, there's a part of me that still wants to push him away. Still a part of me that refuses to voice the truth. And the truth is...

He takes a step forward, and I no longer know what's happening. My heart is pounding so fast in my chest it's all I can hear. I take a step toward him without thinking, and we meet until our faces are mere inches apart. All he would have to do is bend his head down and all I would have to do is lean in for the tension to evaporate and a new kind of force to take control. We're staring at each other like we're under some kind of spell neither one of us has control over. His eyes fall to my lips and I'm leaning forward to meet him when the door opens with a loud crack and we jump apart.

"Dacia, I - oh." Christian is at the door, unable to hide the shock on his face as he looks between the two of us. When he turns back to me, his eyes are hard. I can't make myself look at him. My face feels hot from shame. "I didn't realize I was interrupting something. Sorry." The last word carries the weight of a loaded gun. Not sorry.

I clear my throat. "It's fine. What's up?"

"Dinner's ready." He says and immediately turns out of the room. Whatever spell previously over us has broken, and all I can think is what the hell was that? A momentary lapse in judgement or a quick descent into madness? I shake my head, clearing my muddled thoughts as Marcus and I make our way to the dining table. There are only two available chairs left, and they're right next to each other. I give a sigh before seating myself next to Christian as Marcus slides into the chair beside me.

"Oh, there you guys are." Chastity says. She gives me a puzzled look from the seat diagonal from me, probably wondering why Marcus and I were alone in my room. But if she has questions, she doesn't voice them. "Go ahead and help yourselves."

"What were you guys doing?" Luke asks his brother suggestively, wagging his brows. I feel a headache coming on and rub circles on my temples. Marcus doesn't say anything, but he shoves his napkin across the table at his brother.

The table is relatively quiet as we fill our plates, but soon the voices carry over into ten different conversations I can't make heads or tails of. I focus on eating and less on the people around me, but Christian isn't content to let me sit back and enjoy the meal I helped make for everyone.

"Are you okay?" He asks me.

"Why wouldn't I be?" I take a bite of chicken to avoid looking at his face.

"You just seem-"

I don't hear whatever he says, because Jane is raising her voice from across the table. "...Just don't see why you waited until now to tell me this."

"This can't honestly be a surprise to you." Chastity replies. "We talked about how I've been wanting to move away from my parents. I've grown to love this city, and I love-" She stops herself at Jane's expression. Her back is turned on me, but whatever look she gives Chastity must be bad. "Look, we can talk about this later."

"Chastity, I just don't want you to upend your entire life because of me." Jane says in a lower voice. "I wouldn't feel right about it. What if-"

"Your chicken is getting cold." Chastity says before taking a bite of hers, studiously avoiding Jane's eyes. I look away from them then.

"I need another drink." Christian grumbles as he leaves his seat. I couldn't agree more, but there's no way I'm following him anywhere right now. It's the grocery store argument all over again. I try to avoid looking at Marcus. I'm not sure what would've happened if Christian hadn't found us when he did. Or how much I found myself craving to find out.

When I finally do turn to face him, Marcus is staring down at his phone with a frown. I sneak a glance, but there are no notifications on his lock screen. But then, maybe that's the problem.

"She's not coming, you know." I tell him. His head snaps up to me. "Sarah. That's who you're waiting to hear back from, right?"

His jaw clenches. "What did you do?"

"Nothing." I say evenly. There's that inexplicable look in his eyes again. He doesn't believe me. "I'm not lying to you. I know her much better than you should ever hope to, so you can trust me when I say that you don't want to know her. She's more harm than good."

"Funny. She told me almost the same thing about you."

I look up at him in surprise. "Whatever she said-"

"Let me guess, isn't true?" He asks, shaking his head. "You don't even know what she told me and you're ready to jump to conclusions. How do you know she didn't tell me the truth?" I think of what Christian told me earlier. He said I have the whole story twisted.

"Because you wouldn't be so clearly on her side if she did." I say through gritted teeth.

"I'm not on anyone's side here-"

"Now you're the one lying." I cut him off in a voice louder than I intend. I'm about to go on when his brothers' heads to turn to look at us, and I keep my mouth clamped shut.

"Look, I'm just trying to hear you out." Marcus leans in and whispers once everyone has turned away from us. "I thought the least I could do was give you that chance." But I don't believe him. She beat me with whatever twisted tale she spun for him. He doesn't know the damage she's done to my family, and I can't tell him. Not when a large chunk of it isn't even my story to tell, and not when I don't have half a chance of being believed.

"Oh, I get it. You think you're being gracious. You've not only taken her side, but now you're trying to 'figure me out' to see if I'm redeemable in your eyes. After all, if Jane and Chastity make it you know you'll be stuck with me, and it'd be awfully inconvenient for you if you still hated me in ten years."

"Dacia, come on-"

"What did she tell you?" I ask.

"Why can't you just tell me your side?" We sound like children the way we're going round and round like this. Tell me yours and I'll tell you mine. But this has never been a game to me, even when I was playing Truth or Dare with Jesse and Jane. If they didn't believe me, there's no chance Marcus will.

"Because it's not my place." I tell him. "Just like Sarah knew it wasn't hers to be here tonight. You do know that's why she stood you up, right? Because she wouldn't dare face me after what she did."

"You don't know that." But he's not looking at me.

"Oh, yeah? What excuse did she give you for not coming? Did she even give you one?" He's silent for too long. "Sarah Bailey knows better than to step foot anywhere near me."

"Because she's terrified of you." He meets my eyes, and I see the venom there. As if his anger could make me back down from the fight.

"She should be." I can barely hear over the blood pounding in my ears. I've had enough of this shit for one night. I excuse myself to the balcony for some air, but when I get outside the heat is stifling.

Seven years have passed and Sarah Bailey still isn't done fucking up my life. I plop myself down at the edge of the railing and reach a hand under the wooden plats. My hand closes around the box taped there when the door cracks open and I turn my head, already dreading who could be behind it. But of course it's Marcus.

"Haven't had enough yet?" I don't even look up at him as I light a cigarette.

"You really shouldn't smoke those."

I roll my eyes. "Why don't you tell me something I don't know?"

He lets out a long sigh before looking down at me, wearing an expression like he's bracing himself. "Look. I'm sorry, okay? I'm sorry I got in the middle of whatever happened between you and Sarah. I shouldn't have brought it up. Can we go back inside and forget this ever happened?"

I touch the lit cigarette to my closed lips. Three months clean. This argument isn't worth throwing all that progress away. I stub it out on the railing before standing up to face him. There's a reason I never apologize unless I know for certain I've fucked up, and it's not because I'm the shitty person most people think I am. I have an uncanny way of seeing through insincerity. You don't grow up surrounded by business people without learning how to see through the masks. Sarah eluded me for so long because I saw what I wanted to see in her.

I'm through with that. Once and for all.

"Why are you here?"

"I just said-"

"But you don't mean anything you said." I tell him. His eyes widen in shock, and I can't help but laugh. "I was the one who brought her up, remember? Tell me why you're really out here."

"Alright, fine. You're right. I'm not sorry." He throws out his arms. "Christian saw you walk out and thought I needed to apologize for whatever we were fighting about. Is that what you want to hear?"

"It's the truth, so that's exactly what I want to hear." I cross my arms over my chest. "Apologies mean nothing if you don't actually mean them. Let's be more direct, shall we? You're being manipulated by a woman who can't be bothered to give a reason for bailing on you. Do you realize that?"

His brows crease. "What the hell are you talking about?"

"Okay, so you don't." I step forward. "Either that, or I just realized what your greatest flaw is."

"And what would that be?" He scoffs.

"Fatally stubborn." I tell him. "Once your mind has been made up, it can't be changed by anything or anyone. Not even the truth."

He opens his mouth to speak, but nothing comes out.

"The signs are all there, but your eyes are closed to them." I continue. "This isn't the first time she's bailed on you. Hell, I'd bet this wasn't even the second. I'm sure Jane told you what she said to Chastity. And let's not forget how she acts around your much younger brothers - Chastity was quick to let me in on that mess. None of this is new to me. I know who she is, but that was never a question." I take a step forward. "The real question is, do you?"

"I do." His voice is rough, his eyes burning through me. "I know exactly what kind of person she is. The same can't be said for you."

"Fine. Think whatever you want about me." I shrug. "That I'm too unforgiving, that I'm dooming my life to an eternal spinsterhood, but know this: I'd much rather end up alone than be as narrow-minded as you." I look up at him. "Ah, there's that clenched jaw. Right on schedule."

"I'm 'narrow minded'?" He seethes. "How can I be narrow minded when I asked for your side of the story?"

"You don't care about my side. You've made that abundantly clear." I tell him. "Don't think yourself so high and mighty because you pretended to be concerned for me. I thought you wanted to be an actual nice guy. Not a fake one."

"You want honesty? Fine. I don't really want to be a nice guy right now." His eyes flash as he takes a step toward me. "You're right. Nothing you say would make me believe you, because what you did to Sarah is too despicable. You ran her out of town not once, but twice. You ruined her reputation beyond repair that even her parents will never look at her the same way again.

You attacked her in public, and she was the one who took the blame for it. You made her spend a night in jail for a crime she didn't commit. You made her cry herself to sleep every night for an entire year. You spread lies that she-"

"Stop." My eyes snap shut. I feel my heart beating in my throat. Breathe. Just fucking breathe. My vision swims as I'm transported back in time, to Sarah trying to convince me that everything I saw was wrong. What kind of person do you take me for? You're supposed to be my best friend, Dacia. How could you possibly think that I'd ever-

"I thought you wanted me to be honest, Dacia." He gives a dark, humorless laugh. "Make up your mind. What exactly do you want?"

I'm done. If Sarah wants to fuck up his life the same way she did mine, he can go right ahead and let her. Maybe I'm a terrible person for thinking that, but I tried to warn him. I can't help someone who doesn't want to be helped.

"I want you to leave."

"Yeah, I think we're finally on the same page about something." He walks past me to the door, never giving me a second glance as he leaves.

CHAPTER 11

When morning comes, I don't feel any better than I did last night. I want nothing more than to return to my life in Chicago and forget all about the drama this stupid, nowhere town caused us. But more than that, I need to put Marcus out of my head for good. Out of sight, out of mind, right? Plus, there's no grander statement than leaving town without saying a single goodbye to anyone. Sarah's not the only one who knows that. And if last night showed me anything, I'm not the only one ready to leave San Antonio behind me. After everyone went home, Chastity came to my room in tears and told me she had a huge fight with Jane. I just wish I hadn't seen it coming.

"You were right. She thinks we're moving too fast. I'm pretty sure it's over." She couldn't give me any details apart from that, because she burst into sobs. I held on to her until they passed. I never wanted to see Chastity so hurt, and a part of me can't help but feel responsible for not warning her in time. Not that I really believe it would've done any good. Chastity does what she wants, and nothing I said could've stopped her.

Now, I find Chastity furiously packing up her room. I suppose she's making up for lost time since she's neglected packing up a single thing until now. Her Spotify playlist blasts from a speaker as she takes her clothes off their hangers and shoves them into a large suitcase open on her bed. I lean against the doorway, arms crossed over my chest as I watch her. When I knock on the doorway, she turns around and lowers the volume.

"Are you sure this is what you want to do?" I ask her.

"Isn't it what you and Christian want?"

I bite my tongue. She's not wrong, but the guilt of it still stings. "This isn't about what we want. You have to know that we never wanted to see you get hurt. That's what we were trying to avoid."

"I put my heart out there, Dacia. I always have, and I'll never apologize for that." She shakes her head, but she doesn't look at me. "There were so many moments when I thought Jane and I were on the same page about what we wanted from each other. But then she'd back down, like she was afraid of wanting something more with me. I thought if I could show her that I'd never hurt her, that I was actually serious about her and she had no reason to be afraid..." Her eyes cloud with unshed tears. "But in the end, it just made things worse. I know I pushed her too far, and that's my own fault. That's why I lost her."

"No, Chastity." I shake my head. "If she can't see how great you are, then she's crazy. I saw how much you cared about her, Chas. It broke my heart to see she couldn't feel the same for you."

"Is that what you really think?" Tears fall from Chastity's eyes. "You don't think she cares for me the same way I do?"

"Fuck." I mumble under my breath. "Chastity-"

"You've always told me the truth, Dacia." She says, eyes cloud-ing over again. "Don't stop now because you're afraid of hurting me. I can take it. Just tell me."

"Okay, you're right." I take a deep breath. "It just seemed to me like you were putting more into the relationship than she was. And everything you told me now about her just confirms to me that you were."

She sniffs, wiping the tears from her cheeks. "Maybe you're right. I'm just so tired, Dacia." She takes a seat at the edge of the bed, and I sit down next to her. "What should I do?"

"Well," I say. "We still have a week until our lease on this place ends, but that doesn't mean we have to stay here."

"What do you mean?" Her brows furrow.

"I mean your parents don't need your help at the restaurant anymore. Christian has perfectly capable hands, and he does owe us each a favor for being a giant dick to us this summer. He can finish packing up the place for us." I tell her. "Let's skip out early."

"Oh yeah?" She asks unbelievingly. "And go where?"

"Well, you know how much I've been missing Chicago, and I know how much you love their pizza." I say conspiratorially, slinging an arm around her shoulders. "How much convincing do I need to do to get you on a plane with me tomorrow morn-ing?"

"For you?" Chastity gives a small smile. "Not much at all."

"Yes." I fist bump the air.

"Maybe you're right." She says. "I need to get all this drama out of my head once and for all. If it's over, there's nothing I can do about it but show Jane what she'll be missing."

"There you go." I smirk.

Chastity and I pack up a majority of our rooms in half a day, and by the time the sun has gone down we've bought two plane tickets for Chicago. I email Mr. Banks to schedule a meeting with him on Monday, but that leaves Chastity and I almost an entire week to get San Antonio off our minds for good.

Christian takes longer to convince, but I plead with him on his sister's behalf until he's forced to relent. "Fine." The word is more of a reluctant sigh as it comes out of him, but I take the victory for what it is. "You think you're ready to go back to work?"

"Definitely." I nod. "I'm fairly sure this trip was the definition of too much vacation. But I am gonna miss you and Chastity."

"We're gonna miss you, too." He pulls me in for a hug. "And you can always come to Dallas if you have another mental break-down."

I shove him away from me, but I find I'm smiling as I do so.

Our flight leaves in hour and I'm dead on my feet, but I flinch awake when Chastity nudges my shoulder. The action spills half my coffee on the knee of my jeans and the carpeted floor.

"Shit, sorry. I forget how useless you are in the mornings." She grabs some napkins to soak up the spill. "Do you think this is a good idea?"

"You waited until now to ask that question?" I raise a brow.

"I know, I'm sorry. I almost texted her, you know." That catches my attention. "I must've typed out at least twenty different messages, but none of them seemed...right, I guess. Is there a right way to say 'goodbye forever' through text message?"

"That's a joke, right?" I deadpan. She flashes a small smile. "Goodbyes suck, but goodbye texts are criminal."

"You're right." Chastity sighs. "She probably doesn't want to hear from me anyway. I guess it's time to hit the reset button. Go back to normal."

"I think that's the best thing you can do."

She holds out her phone to take a selfie of us, and I put my sunglasses over my eyes to shield my zombie eyes. Then I look over her shoulder at the picture. Chastity is bright-eyed and fresh while I look like a hot mess. She types "Onto the next thing..." above our heads and hovers over the location icon. I don't say a word, but I watch as she quickly taps San Antonio International Airport before sending it to her story.

We get up from our seats when our flight is called, gather our luggage, and shuffle in line behind other passengers. It isn't long before we're boarded on the plane. Once we reach our seats, Chastity turns and asks me, "You ready to get out of here?"

"Fuck yes." I sigh.

I put in my earbuds and open a book on my kindle. Five minutes into the flight, I can't concentrate on a single word. I take out an earbud and nudge Chastity with an elbow.

"Any regrets yet?"

"I'm not sure." She admits. "You?"

I will never see Marcus again, but as long as Sarah Bailey is out of his family's life for good, I'm okay. Even if we did end our friendship (a generous term, but what other word is there to describe what we were?) on horrendously bad terms. Maybe it's easier for everyone this way. He can think whatever he wants about me. I don't mind. I won't be around to care.

"No." I tell her, but I'm not sure I entirely believe myself. "Onto the next thing."

I lose myself in my kindle book until our plane lands, and I'm finally home.

For the first time in three months, I can finally wear a power suit again. This morning's outfit of choice is a white lace blouse with a high neckline tucked into black slacks and chunky heels. My hair is pulled up into a high chignon, and my makeup look is a coat of mascara and under-eye concealer. I can't be bothered with anything more than that. But the look isn't complete until I pull my favorite black blazer over my shoulders. Simple, understated, yet just elegant enough to give me the confidence I need to return to the office. Today, I'll show Mr. Banks that time off work was just the trick to clear my head and that I'm ready to tackle anything he can throw at me.

There's a reason I was eager to invite Chastity back with me. Ever since my dad died, home doesn't exactly feel like home. I moved back in with him when he was first diagnosed, and in the eight months since he passed I still haven't moved out. When I was working, I didn't have to think about how empty these walls were. I didn't have to think about how my remaining family is scattered across the country and how I'm the only one left in this city. You'd think I'd be more relieved to be back home after the shit-show that was my time in Texas, but I'm surprised to find that I'm not. Not if it means staying in this house again. I'll have to ask Chastity about helping me find a new apartment. I don't know if I have the heart to sell this place, but I can't stay here by myself for one more night. Otherwise, I'm sure another mental health plummet will soon be coming.

But in the meantime, I have a train to catch.

Normally I'd take my Tesla, but I used to think there was something cinematic about riding the train. When I was in college, I'd commute home this way every other weekend, reading the distance away while red-colored leaves breezed by through the window. In truth, there's nothing magical about public transportation; just people going where they need to go and underusing hand sanitizer along the way.

Fall hasn't quite hit the city yet in late August. The trees passing are dried and browning, letting the rest of the world know the dying season is coming. When the train arrives in the city, I can't conjure the love I used to have for it. It lies in nostalgia, but that only reminds me of everything I've lost. There's only me, now.

A balmy breeze blows in my face as I arrive at the tall, imposing building that is Seidel Headquarters. I bypass it to the Starbucks half a block over. Chastity told me to wake her up before I left so she could wish me luck, but I didn't. If I need Chastity to wish me luck, then that means this meeting is a bigger deal than it is. Which it isn't. It'll be an hour tops with Mr. Banks, and then I can go home and finish the book I started on the plane.

At ten till seven, I leave the coffeeshop with my iced coffee before heading back to the building. Mr. Banks's office is at the top floor next to my father's old office, which has remained empty since his death. Mine is at the second to the top, and I stop there first to center myself. The glass desk is arranged just the way I left it, overlooking the view of the Chicago skyline. Pictures of Jorge, Amelia, Chastity, and Christian are taped to the bottom of the monitor. A picture frame is sitting facedown on a stack of files pushed to the corner of the desk. I walk over and pick it up for the first time in months. My father's image stares up at me, flashing his hundred-watt smile. I haven't had the courage to look at it since he died.

Jose García, later called Joseph Seidel, was far from a perfect man. But that didn't make him any less my father, and that doesn't mean I could ever love him any less. I'll always miss him, and I can't imagine a time when his memory won't make me sad, but right now it's also strangely comforting. Give me the courage you had, I think.

I take a seat behind my desk, boot up the PC, and pull up my work email. Before I face Mr. Banks, I have to face up to the biggest mistake I've ever made in my career. I find what I'm looking for at the top of the drafts folder. My resignation letter. I started it the day my father died and have been updating it for the past few months, every time I'm overwhelmed by the urge to give up. Even though I never had any intention of sending it out, part of me thought it would be cathartic to get these feelings out. In a few ways it was. But if I've realized anything about myself lately, it's that writing this draft was nothing but an act of fear. I've been so afraid to hold my father's seat, to want this position as badly as I do, to put in everything I possibly can into this company and have it still not be enough. I've let that fear hold me back for far too long, but not anymore.

Clicking delete doesn't erase the very real anxieties I'm still harboring, but I like to think of it as a stepping stone.

Mr. Banks is sitting behind his desk when I knock at his door and step inside his office. He's a broad-shouldered man in his early fifties, the sides of his hair greying and thinning, which makes the hair piece sitting at the top of his head stand out in an obvious way. I've had to train myself to maintain eye contact with him, otherwise I'd never be able to peel my eyes away from that thing.

"Ah, Miss García." He minimizes the browser on his screen and turns his desk chair forward to face me. "Punctual as always."

"At least I can do one thing right."

"Let's not begin with that attitude again." He gives me a stern look and I shrink. Damn my self-deprecating humor. "Your father was a strong believer that a change of scenery can do a person a load of good. With you, I'm inclined to believe that logic."

"You are?" I raise an eyebrow.

"Very much so." He tells me. "I just got off the phone with Mrs. Henderson. Her daughter told her you looked incredibly well in San Antonio."

"She did?" Alex's mom is head of the Austin office. Its how our parents have been friends for years; my dad hired her for an internship over twenty years ago.

"I've been doing a lot of thinking while you were away." He tells me seriously. "You were so overwhelmed when your father died and your responsibilities at work increased. I can't even imagine what it must be like to be a fresh-faced twenty-five year old just out of grad school, having to watch her father die while grappling with a new and intimidating job position. I believe your father pushed you far past your limits."

Fuck. He's not letting me go, is he? No, he can't. It goes against all the contracts we signed. Tears fill my eyes, and I furiously blink them away. "What exactly are you saying, Mr. Banks?"

"I owe you an apology." He says. I look up at him with surprise. "The entire board does if you ask me, though most members are inclined to disagree. Especially James," He scoffs, surprising me again. "I believe we did wrong by you, and that we need to take some responsibility for your, ah-"

"Panic attack?" I offer.

"Yes." He nods, but he won't meet my eyes. His shoulders are stiff like he's uncomfortable. "I'm so sorry, Dacia. We should've taken your well-being more into account and offered you time off to grieve immediately following your father's death."

"But you did." I remind him. "I had a week off to arrange the funeral."

"I think we can both agree you needed longer than a week." He says. "You know, I've been thinking a lot about the forty-three years your father spent with this company and the ways his mother set him up to replace her. Wilhelmina wasn't prepping him for her inevitable death. She was showing him what this company meant to the different people who work for Seidel Computers. He shadowed computer engineers and programmers working in our labs. He visited our offices across the country to learn how our computers are advertised and study the ways our offices were efficiently managed. He bonded with a great number of employees from different backgrounds and understood the heartbeat of Seidel before he ever sat in that office." He points to the dark, empty room across the hall. My father's office. "I've talked it over with the board. We all believe that you'd benefit from a similar path your father took before he succeeded Wilhelmina as CEO."

"Okay." I nod. "Yes, that sounds perfect. I'm up for the job. Where would you like me to start?"

"Wilhelmina had a visit with the head technician at the San Marcos lab. We think you'll get firsthand knowledge of how our products are developed by shadowing the engineers there."

"San Marcos." A sinking dread pours over me. "You want me to go back to Texas."

"I think you'll be most comfortable starting out there." He tells me. "Your grandmother will be staying for the Fall, and I hear Mrs. Henderson's daughter just started school at Texas State, so you'll be far from lonely."

"Sounds perfect." I grit my teeth. "When will I be going back?"

"We're set for the Monday two weeks from now." He tells me. "This should give you sufficient time to pack and find proper living accommodations. Perhaps Alex can help you find an apartment." And with that annoying note, we end the meeting and he wishes me a good journey. I get from my seat, but I turn back around when I reach the threshold.

"I'm not changing my name, by the way."

Mr. Banks looks up at me. Then, the edge of his mouth slides up in a tired smile. "No one should've ever asked you to."

Words can't express what this sort of satisfaction feels like. On the Metra, I check my missed messages and find five from Chastity. I send her a quick text that I'm on my way back with news. When she asks if its good or bad, I send her an upside down smiley face emoji.

Chastity is sitting on the couch watching a Netflix show when I arrive back. She pauses it when I plop down next to her and immediately inquires on my news. I fill her in on the highlights.

"San Marcos. Wow." She blinks. "To think we were just an hour away from there."

"The universe has an incredible sense of humor." I roll my eyes. "I'll just have to grin and bear it. See if I can keep my interactions with Alex to a minimum. Though, it will be nice to visit Nana again."

"I don't see how. That woman scares me." Chastity shudders.

I chuckle. "She scares everyone. That's why I love her."

For the next week, Chastity helps me find a suitable apartment and offers encouraging words when I start to doubt myself. We also spend a night barhopping until I vomit in an alleyway, our usual cue to head home. I see Chastity to the airport on Sunday morning. When we arrive at the gate, she wraps her arms around me in a bone-crushing hug.

"These three months went by way too fast." Her voice is muffled against my shoulder. "Way too fast."

"I know." I tell her, tears stinging my eyes. Of all the people to come and go from my life, temporarily or otherwise, Chastity is always the hardest to say goodbye to. "Take care of yourself in Dallas."

"I'll try to kidnap Christian for a road trip to you soon." She says with a laugh. "And don't be nervous. You know you've got this."

Texas, again. Hopefully this time I won't completely lose my mind.

Chapter 12

Alex is more than willing to help me move in to my new apartment. I feel bad for taking advantage of her kindness since I've been less than nice to her lately, but I promise myself to make it up to her later, no matter how much I'm already dreading it.

I managed to find a three-month lease on a townhouse in the middle of San Marcos, ideal only in that I won't be staying in it for very long. A fine layer of dust covers the countertops. The bedroom carpet still carries the faint smell of smoke (by mid-afternoon I'm running to the drugstore for nicotine patches). Alex has already tripped twice over the loose floorboard in the living room. But it was the only listing with a three month lease and washer and dryer inside the unit, so I took what I could get.

When we finish up, Alex asks, "Do you have any plans for tonight? Jesse and I are going to get dinner."

My first instinct is to decline, but I did just promise myself to be nicer to her. Seeing Jesse might be awkward, though. I'll have to focus on Alex the entire dinner. How fun for me.

"Sure." I say, and her face lights up. "I don't have anything to eat here yet. I probably would've ordered a pizza."

"Great!" She exclaims. "We're going to have such a fun time, I promise you won't regret it." Alex must know me better than I give her credit for because I was just thinking I might, in fact, regret this. "So how 'bout I pick you up at seven? You haven't had the chance to rent a car yet, right?"

"I'm picking it up Monday morning." I tell her. "Seven sounds fine."

When the time arrives, I'm dressed in leggings and an oversized T-Shirt because that's what I napped in immediately after Alex left my apartment. I wake up five minutes before she texts that she's here, and promptly throw my feet into flip flops, sling my purse over my arm and walk out the door without checking a mirror. What was once a bun tied at the top of my head now flops uselessly against my back as I climb down the stairs. If the restaurant we're going to is fancy, I'll be severely underdressed.

"Hey, girl!" Alex says once I'm situated in the passenger seat of her small Audi. She's wearing jeans and a red polo, so I think I'm good with my lack-of-trying outfit. "Hope you're ready for Indian food!"

My stomach gurgles. I'm starving and Indian food sounds like a dream come true. "Like you wouldn't believe."

"Awesome! Jesse's meeting us there since she's coming from an interview." Alex tells me. "I forgot to tell her I invited you, but it should be fine. She likes you, right?"

Since mysteriously leaving town with Chastity without saying a single goodbye to anyone? Doubtful. "I hope so."

"Ha! I always forget how funny you are." Alex shakes her head with a grin. "Your humor is so dry. It's like you don't care about anything."

Is that really the impression I give people? "Uh, thanks? Maybe?"

"You're welcome." She shoots me a sly smile, like we've come to some kind of understanding I missed. "Here we are!"

Inside the restaurant, Jesse is sitting on a scratchy sofa in front of a Please Wait To Be Seated sign. Her face immediately falls when she spots me, which is all the sign I need to know where we stand.

"How many?" A waitress shuffles forward to show us to a table.

"Four." Jesse tells her.

"Four?" I ask Alex with a raised brow.

"Oh, cool! So he's coming after all?" Alex asks Jesse, who nods before giving me a weird look.

He? A sinking feeling starts low in my belly, like a stone dropped to the pit of my stomach. My skin heats as I imagine I already know who they're talking about.

I avoid eye contact as we're seated at a table in the far corner. It's not long before I discover who this mysterious fourth dinner guest is. I barely have time to look down at a menu before a figure emerges from behind me.

"Hey, guys! Sorry I'm-" Marcus's eyes find and lock on mine. Shit. "Dacia. What are you doing here?" His face falls much like Jesse's did when she saw me. Now I'm really starting to regret coming.

"Oh, I invited her!" Alex beams, oblivious to the noticeable tension. "She's new to the town, so I figured she'd benefit from spending the evening with some friends." Funny how I only have one friend at this table and I don't even like her. Is this the universe's way of paying me back for all the times I went out of my way to ghost Alex Henderson?

I rub my forehead with a hand, sensing a stress-induced headache coming on. Just stick it out for the chicken tikka masala, Dacia. You've attended more awkward dinners than this.

Marcus reluctantly takes the remaining seat next to me. "Cool."

Why did it have to be him? And why is he even here?

I train my eyes on the menu in front of me, my pulse racing. The waitress interrupts our awkward bubble to take our drink orders and ask if we need more time to decide on our entrees. We all mumble in agreement, but Alex is still deciding between the butter chicken or the shrimp curry and asks the waitress which she prefers.

"You and Chastity left town pretty quickly, huh?" I startle when I realize Marcus is talking to me. He tries to take an easy tone, but his voice wavers like he's nervous.

"Yup." I keep my eyes trained on the menu. "I felt like she needed a quick getaway."

"Interesting." That one little word says more than a full sentence could. When I chance a glance at him, his expression is eerily blank. "I thought Chastity cared about my sister more than that." And I thought Jane couldn't care less about what happens to Chastity, I think to myself. Not that I'd dare say that in public with two of our "friends" right beside us. That's another fight waiting to happen.

"They broke up. What does it matter how they ended things?"

He's about to reply, but seems to think better of it and shakes his head. Alex finishes asking the waitress's opinion and orders the shrimp curry. We all put in our orders as well and once she leaves, the table descends into another awkward silence. Jesse's brows crease in concern as she looks at Marcus, and her mouth shifts into a scowl when she flicks her eyes to me.

I wonder if it's too late to shadow a lab in a different city.

"Is something wrong?" No one bothers answering Alex. I roll my eyes. We've reverted from awkward small talk to tense small talk, which is somehow so much worse. "Seriously guys, something feels weird. What am I missing?"

"It's me." I say. "They don't like me."

"That's not-"

"Jesse, you don't have to do that." I tell her. She's no longer wearing a scowl - her face is more stricken now. "I'm not being spiteful, I'm just being honest. It's okay that you don't like me. Not a lot of people do."

"It's not that I don't like you." She says. "I just don't really know you outside of what I've heard from other people, which is never a good way to decide if you like someone. But I'll admit it is hard to get other's people's opinions of you out of my head. I didn't mean to give off a bad vibe, so I'm sorry if I did." Her words sound sincere, but there's something like hesitation in her expression. When her eyes shift back to Marcus, I can sense what it is. A protectiveness over her best friend. I understand that more than she can know.

"Okay." I shrug. "We're good."

"Good!" Alex claps her hands. "So we're all good, then."

"Most of us, at least." I feel Marcus tense up beside me as I take a sip from my water. Jesse smirks into her hand despite herself. Before Alex can ask what I mean, our food arrives. I tear into a piece of naan and dip it into the sauce on my plate, nearly moaning in delight when I take my first bite. Finally, I can ignore the people around me and enjoy what I really came out for. Now that the air has semi-cleared, conversation comes easier.

"So, how are you and Jesse getting along in the dorm?" Marcus asks Alex.

"So good! Thanks for asking." Alex claps her hands again. "I know Jesse's your best friend, but I think you have some competition with me around."

I meet Jesse's eye across the table. She gives a subtle shake of her head when her roommate isn't looking, and I know she likes Alex about as much as I do. Marcus teases Jesse about being offended, putting a hand over his heart in a dramatic gesture. All seems well again, until Alex asks what I was hoping she wouldn't earlier.

"What did you mean when you said 'most of us, at least'?" She faces me before turning to Marcus with a faux gasp. "Do you not like Dacia?"

"Let's not get into that right now." I say. "The restaurant closes in three hours and we don't have nearly enough time."

Jesse snorts into her rice and Alex's jaw drops in shock. Marcus just rests his head in a raised hand, avoiding eye contact three ways. He doesn't say a single word, even when the check arrives and we get ready to leave. Once outside, we say our goodbyes and head different directions. Marcus lingers outside the restaurant like he wants to say something more, but I'm not sure that there's anything left to say. He tries to meet my eyes, but I look down at my shoes to avoid his gaze.

I assume he's just visiting Jesse for the weekend, and that he'll be heading back to San Antonio in the morning. Whatever's left to hash out between us doesn't matter. Chastity and Jane are done, and after tonight we'll have no reason to see each other again.

He must be thinking along the same, because he finally drifts off to his car and I'm left with Alex. She chatters on like nothing's wrong for the entire drive back to my apartment and I let her, answering in monotone syllables and halfhearted mhmm's. It crosses my mind more than once to ask her why Marcus is here, just to confirm what I think I already know, but I chicken out each time.

She reaches an arm out to hug me goodbye when we reach my building, and I'm surprised that I let her. I've been dodging all forms of physical contact from her for years. Alex says she'll text me soon to make plans to see each other again, and I'm so disoriented that I actually say I'm looking forward to it. Her face lights up at my words, and I scramble out of the car as fast as I can before I have the chance to say something else I'll regret.

Tomorrow will be different. I'll be back at work, with other matters to focus my mind on. There will be no more surprises to throw me off my game and I'll fall back into my old routine like this summer never happened. I'll forget all about Marcus and finally move on from what should've been a stress-free summer.

I should know better by now than to actually believe that.

CHAPTER 13

Nana meets me for breakfast on Monday morning before work. She's dressed elegantly in a pale blue pantsuit, her neck and wrists adorned with pearls. When I arrive at the table, she stands up to envelop me in a hug, squeezing my shoulders with Chastity's bone-crushing strength.

"My Dacia! It's been far too long, darling."

"I know. You should visit Chicago more often."

"Oh, we both know how I feel about that city." Her mouth sets in a frown, hardly any lines at the edges of her lips. The botox must be working, I think distantly. We take our seats across from each other. She's already ordered for me: a plate of pancakes and a cold brew coffee with two pumps of classic sweetener, no milk. She knows me well, even though she cringes every time I drink black coffee in front of her. "You know I was ready to get you back down here the first chance I got. It doesn't take much for me to convince Arthur Banks of anything these days."

"I don't doubt it for a second." I take a sip from my coffee and Nana shudders. "But I'm thinking you both were right. Its embarrassing how little I know about the computer side of

Seidel Computers." Finance was a specialty of mine, and I can dabble in marketing in a pinch. But advanced technology has always gone over my head. I'm far overdue for a crash course.

"And you will." Nana says. "The engineer you'll be shadowing just transferred a few months ago from California. I think you'll be quite happy to be working with her."

"Sounds great." I say. "Is there another reason you invited me out to a whole meal before work?"

"What ulterior motives must you think I have up my sleeve?" She laughs. "Well, since you brought it up, I may as well let you know about some ideas I have for the company's future."

"What kind of ideas?" My eyes narrow in suspicion. Even though she retired over a decade ago, my grandmother has never strayed far from Seidel. I suppose retirement means little to nothing when you're the founder of a corporate legacy.

"A decision was made years ago for the benefit of the company, and while I felt I was backed into a corner making it, it's a decision I still stand by. That being said, now that I've established myself as a fixture of Seidel, the company has grown and it's time for you to step forward, I think it's high time this decision was corrected."

"The suspense is killing me." I say drily, though I have to admit I am curious.

"I hope you won't be too angry with me for starting this process behind your back." She says. "Nothing has been set in stone yet. That will ultimately be up to you to decide, and I'm hoping you'll make the right choice."

"Okay, seriously. What are you talking about?"

"Moving headquarters back home." She says. Silence follows her words, mostly because I'm stunned silent. "I started this company out of my two-door garage in Austin. Seidel was born and bred in Texas. Seidel belongs here. It always has. And so do you. I know you've dealt with a lot of changes this past year and this will be one of the biggest, but I think this is exactly what you need after everything you've been through."

"No." It's the only word I can think of to stop the ringing in my ears. No. This can't be happening. Not when I've finally been given a fresh start to prove that I'm ready to take on this role.

"Dacia, hear me out. You owe me this much." Her voice is gentle, but it does nothing to soothe the thoughts raging in my head. I've blown it. I've blown my chance at CEO, and now it's being taken from me.

"What is this really about? Are you trying to take Seidel back?" Panic ices in my veins. I'm all but hyperventilating just at the thought of Nana pulling me out. "I knew it. I knew Mr. Banks didn't want me to be CEO, but I really thought you wanted this for me."

"Dacia, honey, I want this for you more than anything." She assures me, her eyes softening as she reaches across the table for my hands. "You have no idea what it means to me to see another woman in charge of my legacy, someone of my own flesh and blood. But you have to understand something about the seat you're stepping into. Aside from Mr. Banks and myself, no one wants to see you take over Seidel. The board is just waiting for you to fail or quit on your own so they can fill your seat with someone they can control."

"You don't think I know that? How will moving HQ to Texas make that any better? If anything, they'll only hate me even more."

"Hate is irrelevant as long as they're listening to you." Nana says. "They liked your father, but what good did that do him? They made him into nothing more than a pawn. Once Seidel got bigger, the more it weighed on him to do what his shareholders wanted to make more money. Then that was all it became to them. A way to fill their pockets, no matter who got hurt in the end. Our computers were made and manufactured here before the pressure to produce faster led your father to open factories in South Asia. Thousands of good, hard working people lost their jobs and we exploited a third world country to make Seidel a multi-million dollar company."

This isn't anything I haven't already heard before. "I know he sold out, and I'm threw making changes to appease them. None of this tells me why you're suddenly so hellbent to move HQ back to Texas."

"Because Seidel has lost sight of it's roots." She explains. "The truth is I always wanted to base headquarters in Austin, but that decision wasn't entirely mine to make." She looks down, as if ashamed. "I didn't step down as CEO simply because I missed my home. The truth is, I couldn't stand what I had let my own company become. Just another money-hungry, corporate machine." She scoffs.

I'm quiet for a long moment, letting her words sink in. Finally, I ask, "Why did you never tell me that?"

But I already know why. I can see it in the defeat in her slumped shoulders, the shame flushing her cheeks. How she looks down at her wrung hands instead of at me.

Pride must be a family trait.

She doesn't answer me. Instead, she says, "I played the long game to see my vision become a reality, and though the stars have finally aligned for it, I'm afraid it's at your expense." She finally looks up, meeting my eyes with her steady gaze. "Your father, my only son, is dead. Your brother is in New York. Amelia hasn't lived in Illinois for years. There is nobody left in Chicago for you. It isn't just time for Seidel to come home, Dacia. It's time for you to come home, too."

Tears sting my eyes, but I'm too stubborn to let them fall. She's right. I hate how she's always right. I clear my throat and square my shoulders to regain some dignity.

"You can think on it." She finally says. "I wouldn't expect you to come to a decision like this one right away."

"Do you really think this is this something the board will agree to?" I ask. "You said yourself they only want me to fail. They'll never agree to move HQ."

"Don't worry about them right now." She says. "Arthur is on my side, and he owes me a favor or two from over the years. First, you need to make a decision about whether this is something you want."

"This isn't about your legacy at all, is it? You're just trying to do what you think is best for me." I realize. On my way back to Chicago - all throughout summer, if I'm being really honest with myself - I was pushing back a feeling of dread for all the reasons my grandmother laid out as easily as breathing. In Chicago, I'm all alone.

I haven't felt alone in months.

Taking Chastity with me was an attempt to delay that inevitable feeling. While I can't deny that this summer was a disaster, it was also the happiest I felt in a really long time. I wasn't ready to lose that. I'm still not.

"Seidel has had many a facelift over the years. This will just be the newest." Nana says, snapping me out of my thoughts. "And you need to surround yourself with the family you have left. I know the time you spent up there after your dad died were killing you. There's no weakness in asking for help or needing to be with people who love and support you. The board will see that. A happy CEO makes for a happy company. Put yourself first."

"Okay." I let out a long sigh. "Fine. I promise I'll think about it."

"Good. Now off to work with you." She smiles slyly. "I think you'll understand where I'm coming from more by the end of the day."

Oh, that woman is sneaky. I find out how sneaky when I reach the office of the lead engineer I'll be shadowing.

"Amelia?" My cousin looks up from a pile of paperwork. She brightens when I enter her office, getting up from her chair to run and hug me. I haven't seen her since the beginning of the year, but she hasn't changed since. Her hair is a shade between blonde and brunette, and it falls past her shoulders in loose waves. She's wearing a white button-up tucked into a grey pencil skirt, a pair of glasses sitting at the crown of her head.

"Dacia! I can't believe you're finally here!" She says when she pulls away, but she's still gripping my shoulders, her brown eyes inspecting my face for any changes. "And it looks like you've finally been getting some sleep. That break did you some good after all."

"You didn't tell me you transferred!" I swat her shoulder. The last time I saw her was at my father's funeral, but we didn't get much time to talk. She was busy with a secret work project and had to fly out the same day.

Now, I'm wondering if that "secret project" involved moving across the country.

"Nana swore me to secrecy. She wanted it to be a surprise." She smiles conspiratorially. "Did she tell you her plan, yet?"

"So, you're a part of her shameless ploy to force me back to Texas." I shake my head, but my lips pull up in a grin despite myself. "How'd she convince you to leave California?"

"A ridiculous pay raise, of course."

I follow her down the hall to a lab with disassembled computer parts, where Amelia shows me a blueprint for the model tablet she'll be working on. I ask her a few questions and she answers them in a way I'm able to understand. She tells me about the process behind the technology, and I write down some notes in a notebook. The day goes by as I shadow her through a regular day's routine.

"What are you doing for dinner?" Amelia asks me once we've clocked out for the day.

"I have no idea. I'll have to go to the grocery store and figure something out."

"I'll go with you. Alex invited me out with her roommate, but I already hung out with them last week. I like to keep my time with Alex to a minimum." She says with a laugh. We both have that in common.

"You met Jesse?" I ask, wondering if she also met...

"Yeah, and her friend Marcus. He is so cute." She gushes, and my heart picks up pace. "And he's apparently staying in town for awhile. Wait, I think Alex mentioned you know him, too. Longish dark hair, light brown eyes."

"Oh, I remember." I sigh. He's staying in town for awhile? How long is awhile? I thought he was just visiting when he showed up for dinner on Saturday. Amelia's brows crease as she senses more than I'm telling her. "Wait, what do you mean he's staying in town? I thought he was still in school."

"Oh, it was something about his financial aid not going through for his student-teaching semester. I can't believe he wants to teach first grade, bless his soul." Amelia shakes her head. "Anyway, Alex set him up to nanny for her little niece and nephew while her aunt's out of town for work. She thought it'd be a fast way for him to save some tuition money. You know her family tips big. I'm pretty sure she pushed him into it without letting him say no, in true Alex fashion."

"Oh. That's..." I trail off, wracking my brain for the right word for how I feel about this, but I don't know how I feel about it at all. Terrified? Excited? I take a deep breath, giving my heartbeat time to regulate. "Did he say how long he's staying?"

"Only another week, but they may hire him full time if they like him." She says. "I'd hope they do if I were him. Can you imagine getting to live in that place for free? You know I still have dreams about their in-home sauna." She lets out a dreamy sigh. Now I can't stop thinking about Marcus in that sauna, his brown skin glistening with sweat, nothing but a lush, white towel wrapped around his -

"Hello? Earth to Dacia!" I snap out of my decidedly not-safe-for-work daydream and turn to my cousin. My face feels like it's on fire.

"Sorry. I'm just hungrier than I thought." Wrong choice of words, Dacia. I shake my head to clear it. "Let's go get groceries."

I walk past her to the parking lot, practically running to my Tesla rental. Amelia calls for me to wait up, but I don't until I reach the car. We make plans to meet at my apartment and then ride to HEB in one car. At the store, Amelia helps me stock up on everything I need for the next two weeks, and we gather ingredients for a recipe she found online.

When we get back to my apartment, Amelia takes over the kitchen. Cooking has always been a hobby of hers, and whenever we're together I'm always well fed. She almost lived out her culinary dreams until she discovered her mother's love for computer engineering, but the world's loss is my gain. I practically moan when I take my first bite of roast chicken. "That good?" She asks.

"So good." I sigh. "And you made enough to feed an army. How are we supposed to finish all this?" I indicate my countertops, where the leftovers surround us. In addition to the roast chicken, she also made creamy mashed potatoes, baked zucchini and dinner rolls. There's no way I'll be able to finish it all by myself.

"I actually thought I'd divide it between you and Marcus." She says, and suddenly my mood has plummeted. "The poor guy's been surviving off fish-sticks since he's gotten here. I promised him a home-cooked meal when he found out I was this close to becoming a chef."

"Oh. I didn't realize you guys were so close already." I wonder if my cousin is developing feelings for him, and why the thought bothers me so much. Amelia's a great person, and she deserves someone great. And Marcus is...

"Hardly. We've only met twice." She rolls her eyes, and I'm more relieved than I have a right to be. "Let me catch you up on some recent events. The very first day we met, my front left tire burst while I was driving on the highway. Everyone was in the car with me; Marcus, Alex and Jesse. Alex started screaming, because of course she would, and then I started sobbing at the wheel because I didn't know what to do at that point. We skidded into the next lane and cars were honking at us like they couldn't clearly see I had no control over what was happening. And Marcus calmed us all down immediately; he assured Alex that everything was going to be fine, he guided me to the curb and then got out of the car to replace the popped tire with the spare donut in the back. He even offered to go with me to get a new tire and make sure they give me a good deal. He's the reason we're not all dead right now. That boy is a saint and I will cook for him every day of my life, even if he marries someone who isn't me. Hell, I'll even cook for his wife and kids, too."

"Wow." I say, because it's all I can.

"I am indebted to him forever." She says solemnly. "Wanna come with? I'm sure it'll be fun for you guys to catch up."

"'Fun' might not be the right word for it." I tell her. "I'm pretty sure he hates me."

"What?" She does a double take from packing up the leftovers in tupperware containers. "I can't imagine him hating anyone, least of all you."

"I guess I just don't really know how he feels about me." I shrug. "Especially since he met Sarah Bailey."

Amelia Siegfried is the only soul I've told the truth to, because it's the kind of truth I couldn't bare telling a second time. She was with me the day I found out what Sarah did, the day I bought a plane ticket and signed a check I had no reason signing. The day I thought I'd seen Sarah for the last time. When I couldn't face my father to tell him what she did to Jorge, Amelia told him for me. Amelia calmed me down through my first panic attack and came with me to every doctor's appointment when I struggled to get a handle on my mental health in the weeks following. There aren't many people I can say that I truly trust, but I trust Amelia with my life and the lives of everyone I care about.

"What the fuck? She was there? Why didn't you call me? What happened-" I explain everything to her then. Not just about Sarah, but about my entire time in San Antonio. About Chastity and Jane's whirlwind romance, about meeting Marcus and the slight comment made in bitterness that got us off on the wrong foot, down to our tense standoff the last time we saw each other and the disillusionment of Chastity and Jane's relationship. By the end of the story, all Amelia can say is, "Wow."

"Yep." I say. "So I don't really know where we stand now."

"I think you're right. She had to have manipulated him against you. I remember how good she was at that." She says. Then she scoffs. "Sarah fucking Bailey. What are the odds?"

"I think the universe has more than proved to be against me by now."

"Now that we're finally back together, I think your luck's about to change." She winks. "And don't worry about Marcus. We'll change his mind." She gives me a sly grin I don't like the look of whatsoever.

"I don't know if I want to do that."

"Sure you do." She says, poking my cheek. "It sounds to me like someone has a little-"

"If you say the word 'crush', so help me god I will-"

"You'll what?" She counters, way too amused for my liking. "You know you love me too much to threaten to kill me. Chastity might be your best friend, but I am your person." I can't say anything to that. She's not wrong. "Now come on. We have a Postmates order to fill."

CHAPTER 14

The last time I was at Alex's aunt and uncle's house in San Marcos, I was twelve years old. It was the dead of summer, we had just come back from the Prime Outlet Mall and I was sulking about the millions of freckles covering my body. Our parents made a big of deal of taking a picture of me and Alex side-by-side in all our freckled glory. I'm pictured with a scowl because I refused to smile, much to their chagrin, but Alex was grinning ear to ear.

The house is on the outskirts of town in a gated community, a massive red brick two-story with rose brush on either side of the front gate. Amelia parks in the driveway and picks up her phone to call him. Marcus's name pops up on the bluetooth screen, and when he answers his voice fills the car from all sides.

"We're here with food." Amelia tells him.

"Oh, cool!" He says. "Wait, who's 'we'?"

Amelia mouths for me to say something, and my eyes widen. I shake my head so hard my skull rattles. She insists, nodding vigorously and motioning with her hands as if the action will convince me more. I continue to shake my head, and Marcus's "Uhhh" sounds from the speakers.

"Amelia, you there? Should I just come outside?"

"No!" Amelia bursts. "We'll come to the front door! Okay, bye!" She hangs up, turns off the ignition, and slaps my arm repeatedly. "Why didn't you say anything?"

"Ow!" I rub my arm where she slapped me. "You put me on the spot! You know better than anyone how much I hate that."

"Come on, we'll try that again." She gives me a pointed look before getting out of the car, and I reluctantly follow. Marcus is waiting for us at the front door. When he sees me, he can't hide the look of surprise on his face. It would be laughable if I wasn't having such a hard time breathing.

"Hey! Here is your home cooked meal as promised, sir." Amelia hands him the large tupperware of chicken and his face brightens.

"Thank you so much! You can't imagine how much I appreciate this. If I have to so much as look at another fish-stick, it'll be too soon." He says, smiling until his eyes find mine again. "I didn't know you knew Dacia."

"She's my cousin." She links her arm with mine, and the small action is enough to give me my confidence back. "Actually, she's practically my sister. We're very close."

"Closer than Chastity?" He asks me, his expression guarded, but I can tell he's close to thawing.

"Amelia beats her by the barest percentage." I tell him. "Just don't tell Chastity that."

"No danger." He says, and I sense a hint of bitterness behind it. "Come on in."

I make it two steps inside before we're cut off by a three-foot screaming menace. Marcus and Amelia manage to step aside just in time, but I fall flat on my ass to the tiled floor with Alex's nephew gripping my leg.

"Whoa! You see Tyler, this is why I had to cut you off at three juice boxes." Marcus grips the kid by his shoulders and pulls him off me in one smooth motion. "Apologize to Dacia right now."

"I'm sorry," Tyler stumbles over my name, as expected. I repeat my name back to him, but he doesn't even try to say it. I think of James Felding and have to bite back the wave of irritation that washes over me. But Tyler's only a kid. He can't know any better."

"Hey, it's okay. Just repeat after me." Marcus kneels to meet Tyler at eye-level. "Dah - see - ah."

"Dah - see - ah." Tyler repeats slowly.

"Good. Now put it all together." Marcus guides Tyler with a gentle hand until he's facing me again. "Now, let's try that apology out again."

"I'm sorry, Dacia." Tyler says to me, pronouncing my name perfectly. I'm impressed, and if it shows on my expression I can't help it. I dumbly assure him it's no problem, and Marcus sends the kid upstairs and helps me off the floor with a hand.

"That's only half of what I've had to deal with today." Marcus says. "Dacia, I'm so sorry about that." But he's smiling like he's amused.

"Don't worry about it." I say, dusting off my slacks. There seem to be very clear signs that the odds are against me, but I just keep barreling through them anyway. Amelia and I follow him into the kitchen, where Marcus transfers the food to a dinner plate before sticking it in the microwave.

"I hope y'all's day wasn't as exhausting as mine."

"I sat in a corner and watched Amelia work all day, so probably not." My cousin turns away from us and slaps a hand to her forehead, no doubt cringing at my blunt remark. Marcus just crosses his arms over his chest.

"Well, I played with a lego space shuttle for four hours, so who's the real winner here?" He shoots me a smirk. I shake my head, but I find I'm smiling back.

"Fair enough."

"So other than playing with legos and wrangling kids all day, how goes the nannying?" Amelia asks. "Do you know if you'll get to stay longer yet?"

"It's been good. And actually, I do." Marcus says. "They want me to stay on full-time for as long as I'm up for it."

"That's awesome!" Amelia exclaims. "I'm sure Jesse will be thrilled to hear you'll be staying for awhile longer."

"Yeah, it just feels a little weird." He says. "The last time I was away from my family this long didn't go so well for me."

"Oh?" I find myself asking.

"I was at UT my first two years of college." He says. I feel as my brows raise in surprise. "God, those were the worst years of my life. Please don't ask me why, I'm not ready to share the trauma." His tone is lighthearted, but I notice his smile doesn't quite reach his eyes.

"I bet you missed your family a lot." Amelia notes. Marcus doesn't say anything, but he nods. His expression turns unreadable, hiding a part of himself I'm suddenly curious to know.

"Excuse me, I need to use the bathroom. I haven't been here in awhile, but I think I remember where it is." She leaves, and I heave a sigh. I highly doubt she actually needs to use the bathroom, but just wanted an excuse to leave us alone together.

"How is your family, by the way?" I ask to change the subject.

"They're good." He says, but his jaw clenches, giving him away. "Actually, Jane's up in Dallas now visiting our aunt. I know she wanted to get in contact with Chastity, but she hasn't heard back. You wouldn't know anything about that, would you?"

My eyes widen. If Jane is trying to get in touch with Chastity, it's news to me. "I haven't heard a thing. Chastity and I are terrible at keeping in contact when we're in different cities."

"Well, maybe you could ask her about it." He says. "Jane was pretty heartbroken over the way they left things."

"So was Chastity." Which is why I'm not sure getting them together again would help. Not that I say as much. "I'll ask her what's been going on."

"Thanks. I appreciate it." On a different note, he asks, "So, what are the chances your work would bring you back to Texas?"

"Oh, you know, it was just a regular day of the fates conspiring against me." I tell him. "And by 'fates', I mean my grandmother. Not that I can argue with her when she built Seidel from the ground up."

"That's impressive." He tells me. "Especially that you'll get to run it at such a young age. That must be incredible."

"Yeah, I suppose. I didn't have much of a choice, though. Nana is hellbent on keeping the company in the family, so that never left me with much room to decide what I want for myself." I tell him. "When I was in middle school, I actually really wanted to be a doctor. I fought with my parents about it for a full year."

"Really?" He asks. "What happened?"

"My brother accidentally cut his hand open with a kitchen knife. I fainted from the sight of gushing blood." He lets out a surprised laugh. The way his face lights up is intoxicating, and I'm more happy than I should be that it was my doing. "Safe to say I let go of that dream without any hard feelings. But it was all for the best. I started interning at Seidel when I was sixteen and haven't looked back since."

"Nice." He says. "I can't imagine following in either of my parents' footsteps. My mom is a dental hygienist and my dad does social work. Neither calling has ever appealed to me."

"But screaming children do?" I counter. "What is it about teaching elementary that calls to you?"

"I've always liked working with kids." He shrugs. "I just love how innocent they are, you know? They haven't been shattered by the world yet. But I also think that can change so easily depending on what kind of teacher you have, especially at that young of an age. English isn't my first language, so I had it rough the first couple years of schooling. None of my teachers really gave a shit about me until I got to fifth grade. Mrs. Rodriguez was the first teacher who really took the time to help develop my English, and a lot of that was through books. She not only taught me how to be a better English speaker, but she gave me my love of reading."

"That's amazing." I say, leaning forward in interest.

"Yeah. My parents always spoke Spanish at home, but once they learned how badly I was doing in school they switched over.

The crazy thing now is my three youngest brothers can only speak English. Luke's actually failing his Spanish II class." He laughs.

"Damn. That sounds like me and my brother. We never learned Spanish, even though our mom really wanted us to." I tell him. "I can understand it when spoken to me, but Jorge only knows the bad words. Our mom didn't like speaking English even though she could, and I'd always get embarrassed when she spoke Spanish in public. It's something I really regret now, especially after she died. I feel like I let her down." I'm not sure why I'm admitting all this to Marcus when I hate admitting it even to myself. "Everything was just so focused on Seidel. I saw the way my dad's coworkers looked at her, you know? Like she clearly didn't belong in their world. She was so proud of her culture while my dad hid every Mexican part of himself when he went out into the world. Clearly I followed in his footsteps, but that's what I thought you had to do to succeed."

"I definitely get that." Marcus says. "It was embarrassing being the only one in my class struggling to speak the language. The other Latinx kids weren't struggling, and a lot of them didn't speak Spanish to begin with. It felt unfair that I was the only one who couldn't keep up. I took a lot of that frustration out on my parents, so I understand exactly how you feel. Growing up, we put more value in the country that doesn't want us and ignore the one we come from. That's got to fuck us up in some monumental way."

I look up at him in surprise. His eyes dart away from me, and then back. "What?" His brows are furrowed in question.

"You just said 'fuck'." My lips pull up of their own accord, forming what I'm sure is an amused smile. I try not to think about what this is going to do to my fantasies now that I know what that word sounds like out of his mouth, but I fail spectacularly. My arms cross over my chest as I lean toward him. "Say it again."

He rolls his eyes before shaking his head. "I was doing so good for weeks. Do you know how hard it is to give up cussing?"

"Sorry to make you fall back into dirty habits." But I can't wipe the grin from my lips.

He narrows his eyes at me. "You don't look sorry."

"I'm not." I shrug, and then we're quiet as I really think over his response before I got distracted. "My father made the choice to leave behind his last name and half his heritage when he became CEO. And because I've spent my entire life following in his footsteps, I'm expected to do the same." I shake my head. "But I can't be like him. I won't."

"Good." He nods. "We shouldn't have to choose between success and holding onto where we come from. No one ever says outwardly that we can't have it both ways, but it's too ingrained. It effects everything we do, whether we know it or not."

"Yeah." I sigh. "I remember that from living here. But it gets much worse when you leave Texas."

"What do you mean?" He asks.

"Half the board members are racist, sexist fucks. I don't know how my father could stomach working with them. Once, I overheard one of them ask my dad why he thought it'd be a good idea to marry his housekeeper. My mom was a nurse." I roll my eyes, but I'm getting heated by the comment all over again.

"That's insane." Marcus says, his jaw clenched. "What did your dad do?"

"Nothing." I shake my head. "He couldn't afford to burn any bridges. Those are the kind of people I'll be returning to. And I'll have to keep kissing their asses if I want to keep Seidel funded."

"Jesus. No wonder you needed three months off from that place."

"But I didn't want them." I say. "You want to know the real reason I took time off? The pressure got to me. I embarrassed myself in front of all of them by yelling at the only person on my side. The looks on all their faces..." My eyes cloud. "I couldn't take how they were all staring at me, so I ran eight stories down to the lobby and out into the street during rush hour. My eyes didn't register a single car. I needed out of the building that badly."

"You had a panic attack." His eyes are sympathetic. I'm surprised by how quickly he realizes it.

"I had a meeting with Mr. Banks, the acting CEO now, the next morning and he suggested I take some time off." I say. "It took me awhile to see it, but I really did need a break."

"Wow. God, I don't even know what to say to that."

"You don't have to say anything." I tell him. "I'm incredibly privileged. My punishment for yelling at my boss and subsequent mental breakdown was three months off with pay." He doesn't say anything more, and I can't place the emotion crossing his eyes. Does he pity me? Is ashamed of me as much as I'm ashamed of myself?

I shrug it off and decide to change course, mostly because I don't want to focus on how much I've admitted to Marcus and how much I may regret it later. "So, you want to be the teacher you needed when you were younger."

"Yeah." He blinks. "I never really looked at it that way before, but definitely."

"For the record, I think that's far more impressive than what I'm doing." I tell him. "And I am sorry, by the way."

"For what?" His brows crease.

"What I said about you the first time we met." I say. "It takes a lot of courage to follow your dream, especially if its an unconventional one. I shouldn't have judged you for that."

"Thank you." Surprise colors his tone. "You know, I thought you were a jerk for not giving me a real apology, but now I think I get why you didn't."

"I've always valued honesty over politeness. It might be the reason I only have a handful of friends, but they're the only ones I've ever needed." I say, hesitating before adding. "And listen, I know we weren't exactly friends in San Antonio, but I do hope that can change. As long as you're willing, that is."

His eyes are inscrutable, and I wonder if he's still trying to figure me out like he said all those weeks ago. Finally, he nods. "I'd like that."

"Good." I give a small smile. "Now, where is Amelia? Did she fall in the toilet? I swear to god-"

"I'm coming!" Amelia's voice conveniently (too conveniently, if you ask me) sounds from above the stairs, and I follow it to the living room, Marcus trailing behind me. She reaches the landing and meets me downstairs. While Marcus is still two feet away, she whispers, "I was eavesdropping the entire time. You did so good!" I roll my eyes and push her away with a light shove.

"We should probably get going. I know you're exhausted from playing with legos all day." I say, and he gives a light chuckle.

"Maybe we can all meet for lunch tomorrow!" Amelia says. "You must be so bored while the kids are at school. It'll be fun."

"That sounds good." He says. "Just text me a time and place and I'll be there."

Once we're safely tucked away in the car, I let out a groan. "I can't believe you made me do that."

"You'll get over it. I gave you the push you needed." She laughs.

"So you really didn't go to the bathroom?" I ask her. "You just made up an excuse to leave me alone with him?

"It wasn't an excuse. I really did have to pee." She says. "When I came out, you guys were sharing your aspirations and talking about being friends, and it was just so cute to listen to you having a civil conversation with someone who wasn't me or Chastity for a change." I scowl, and she laughs at my expression. "I think he might like you back, by the way."

"Yeah, right." I roll my eyes again.

"Once he realizes what a great friend you are, he's going to see what a catch you are." She tells me. "Let me help! Chastity was too busy focusing on her own love life to help you with yours, but since mine is totally nonexistent I'm free to help you out."

"Then maybe we should focus on you." I tease. She rolls her eyes before giving me a pointed look. "Why are you so fixated on this. I'm not even sure I like Marcus."

"That's a straight up lie, and you know how I can tell?" She asks, and I shrug. "You can't even say his name without blushing." I roll my eyes when she isn't looking. I'm really going to need some Advil after this ride. "Plus, I haven't seen you this happy since your dad died. Even before then."

I take in a deep breath. "You think I look happy?"

"I really do." She says. "I know I never told you this, but I never thought Anthony was the one for you." I turn my head around to look her, surprised. "He was always the safe choice, but 'safe' doesn't always mean 'right'. You never had to go too far out of your comfort zone with him."

"Amelia, we were together for four years. Why did you never say anything to me?"

"Because what kind of supportive cousin would I be if I had?" She shakes her head. "Besides, it was something you needed to figure out for yourself. And you did."

She drops me off at my apartment, and we say goodbye. I toss and turn that night trying to sleep, but I can't help wondering if Amelia is right. Do I have feelings for Marcus? Is he the kind of man I should be pursuing? When I wake, I don't have the answers but I do have a lunch date with Marcus to find them.

CHAPTER 15

The next day, we meet Marcus at an Italian restaurant close to work. Things have been slow at the lab, so we can afford to take an hour-long lunch break. Whenever Marcus isn't paying attention, Amelia glances back at me with a knowing look that makes me roll my eyes. We're not twelve year olds, for Christ's sake. Once seated, we share stories about our day and what are jobs are like. Though I'm loathe to admit it, I was a ball of nerves at the start of lunch but by the end of it I can hardly remember what I was so nervous about.

The next few weeks pass like this. Sometimes Alex or Jesse will join the three of us for lunch, and we pass the time laughing at nothing. There are days when it's just me and Marcus, and though we never quite reach an easy back-and-forth with each other, it's still nice hanging out with him alone. It's during one of these lunches that he decides to ask about Chastity again.

"I heard from her last night, actually." I answer, though I don't want to. The awkwardness that surrounds us whenever we talk about Chastity and Jane's relationship puts me on edge, but I know it could be much worse. I'm counting myself lucky he's gone this long without bringing up Sarah. "She says she's doing great in Dallas. Her parents have her designing the layout for their next expansion in Corpus Christi."

"Good for her." He says, twirling the spaghetti on this plate with a fork. He's dressed in a cream-colored button-down with the sleeves rolled up to his elbows. I can't say what it is exactly, but the sight of his forearms have me breathing more shallowly than I'd prefer. I find myself wanting to trace my fingers along the veins bulging from the inside of his wrist-

"Has she mentioned anything about Jane?"

"What?" I shake my head to shake me out of the daze. Stupid. "Oh, no, she hasn't." I answer when he repeats the question. "This is her MO - she avoids talking about negative feelings like they'll go away on their own. If she's heard from Jane, it's best to let her tell me on her own."

"You can't ask? I just know it'd mean a lot to my sister if they could-"

"Okay, look. I'm sure it will surprise no one to say that I'm not good at dealing with other people's feelings. Or even my own, for that matter." I say. "Chastity and I are close, but we really never talk about this kinda stuff."

"What do you mean by 'this kinda stuff'?" He asks, brows furrowed.

"Breakups." I say. "Or other heartbreak-related feelings. We never have."

He opens his mouth as if to speak, and then closes it. Finally, he says, "That doesn't make any sense."

"Why? Because we're girls?" I give him a sardonic smile. "You surprise me, Marcus. I didn't take you for a midcentury man."

"You're seriously telling me you and Chastity never talk through your feelings?" He sits back in his chair, surprise etched in his features.

"Sure." I nod. "We vent when we're angry, we share our excitement over good news, but we don't cry in front of each other. Neither of us is really the wallowing type, unless we're wallowing by ourselves." I shake my head. I think back to the morning after I saw Sarah for the first time in years, sobbing on the bedroom floor. Chastity's soft knock on my door. You're scaring the crap out of me, Dacia.

I should've told her the truth, right then and there. There are so many things I've held back from her and I can't even really say why. I've excused it as not my story to tell, but if I can't even trust my best friend, then who can I?

"We support each other in different ways." I explain. "Back in college, she'd drag me out to every social event there was in an attempt to get me out there. Our habits don't change, because she did the same at her cousin's wedding. But that changes when one of us is sad. When my anxiety got so bad that I couldn't make myself leave our dorm, she'd push our beds together and we'd watch Netflix together for entire weekends. When negative internet comments used to get to her, I'd plan a road trip somewhere we wouldn't get cell service."

I think of Chastity reading a book beside me on the couch when I couldn't bring myself to talk about Sarah. My heart feels full knowing she's always stood by me without a single word exchanged.

"I get it." Marcus says, but there's hesitation in his expression.

"But?" I offer when he doesn't add anything more.

"But at what point does that become avoidance?" He asks. "I'm not saying everything needs to be talked to death, but what about something serious? Not everything can be solved with a spontaneous road trip."

"Chastity has other friends for that." I shrug. "And I have Amelia."

"Huh." He rests his chin in his hand. "Does that mean Amelia's the friend you cry to? If you cry at all, that is?"

I cock my head at him. "Is that your subtle way of asking if I'm really a robot in disguise?"

"Maybe." He smiles wide, flashing teeth. There's something sly about his grin, even if he doesn't mean it to be. Like he's letting me in on a secret no one else knows. Every time he smiles like that, I'm reminded of the first time. In his car, driving me home from Jesse's birthday party. How he'd turn to face me every so often, between stoplights and stop signs. Back then I thought we were becoming friends, and maybe we were. Now it feels like we're finally getting that back.

If I can quiet my incredibly inappropriate thoughts about him, that is.

"Robot? Nah. Sentient AI with the means to take control over the humans who created me? Perhaps." He lets out a light chuckle. "By the way, yes. Amelia is the only friend I cry to. But don't go trying to make her spill my secrets. Her vault's locked up tight, and for good reason."

"Sounds intriguing." He smirks. "But we'll all have to go out drinking soon so I can properly put that theory to the test. You know, for science." He flashes his teeth again and my skin heats. There's something dangerous about that smile...

It's killing my brain cells, one shiny canine at a time.

I wasn't lying when I said Chastity and I are terrible at keeping in contact when we're in different cities. We have to make three different Skype call dates before one finally sticks. It isn't until the weekend after Halloween that we're both finally free. It's an unseasonably sunny Saturday morning, and before I shut the curtains I can see joggers getting their exercise in (since work started again, my daily runs have turned more into suggestions) and tenants walking their dogs through the window. Too idyllically summer for the start of November, if you ask me.

I have an iced coffee prepared on the coffee table when Chastity's call comes in. Her face appears on the screen in full makeup, her hair styled in loose curls that fall over her shoulders. How she can look this good at nine AM on a weekend is beyond me. She's in the bedroom of her Dallas apartment, from the baby blue painted walls behind her.

"Dacia!" She shouts my name, and it echoes off the bare walls of my living room. "Oh my god, it's been way too long already. How did we let two whole months pass without a single video chat?"

"Time flies when you're having fun." I take a sip from my drink.

"So you're actually having fun down in San Marcos?"

"Oh, no, not at all." I correct her with rolled eyes. Only now that the words are out of my mouth, I realize they're not true.

"Is it really that bad?" Chastity asks, brows creased in concern.

"Surprisingly, no." I confess. "I wouldn't say it's been fun, but it's actually been kind of...nice."

"Wow." Chastity says, eyes widened. "Does that mean you're thinking of becoming a full-time Texan again? Because you know I've been dying for us to be roommates again."

"You just hate living alone." She pouts, but she knows I'm right. "And as for becoming a full-time Texan again..." I tell her about Nana's proposal to move HQ, and she squeals before I'm even finished speaking.

"You have to do it, Dacia!" She moves closer until her face fills the screen. "We can finally see each other for longer than a handful of days in the year!"

"I'm still thinking it over." I say. "There's a lot to consider-"

"Like what?" She counters. "Being close to your friends and family and getting some space from your asshole board members isn't enough? Sounds like a no brainer to me, but I do know how stubborn you can be." She sits back, a knowing look on her face.

"It can't just be for me." I tell her, but I think back on my grandmother's words. How Seidel became something unrecognizable to her, and how much it broke her heart. "Anyway, for now I'm just trying to focus on getting back into the groove of work. If I'd known taking three months off to visit you was just going to propel me into more drama, I would've swung for a trip to England instead."

"I hear you, girl. I probably would've gone with you." Chastity laughs. Then she hesitates before adding, "I haven't told you or Christian this, but Jane's still texting me."

I try to look surprised. "Have you messaged back?"

"I did a few times, just to tell her how I've been." She tells me. "Then she started asking to meet up. Apparently she's in town staying with an aunt or something. Part of me really wants to see her again, but I don't know." She lets out a sigh. "She said she wants closure, Dacia. I can't give her that because if I see her, I'm afraid I'm going to break down and ask her to take me back."

"Oh, Chastity." I sigh.

"I know I messed things up with us." She continues. "It was all too much too soon for her and I get that, but I couldn't help it. I can't remember the last time I felt that strongly for someone. Those feelings don't just go away overnight. If I give her closure, then it means that we're done for good and that's the last thing I want. But if I don't see her at all, then we're already done." She takes in a deep breath. "I just don't know what to do, Dacia."

"I'm sorry you're still going through this, Chas." I say. "If you think meeting her will help you move on in the long run, then do it. Because either way, it looks like that's where this is headed."

"You're probably right." She tells me. "You know, I keep thinking about what would've happened if we hadn't left San Antonio a week early. Would we have made up and gotten back together? Would I still be living in San Antonio right now?"

"There's no use asking 'what if'." I tell her, even though I'm wondering those what if's too. Did I ruin any chance of happiness she had with Jane by bringing her to Chicago? Guilt builds in the pit of my stomach. I make a mental note to talk this over with Amelia later. If I can count on anyone to tell me the truth, it's her. "You just have to decide what you want to do from here."

"What would you do?"

If this were the start of summer, I'd tell her to cut Jane out of her life completely. I'd tell her that no one is worth that much hurt. But I can't decide for her who's worth hurting over. Not when I'm fairly certain that Jane is her first real love.

"I don't know." I say. "I can't tell you what to do. Just trust yourself."

She heaves a sigh. "Thanks for being no help at all." She shoots me a smile to show she's teasing.

"You're quite welcome."

The work week passes by in a blur. I'd forgotten how fast time flies when you fall into a routine. Summer in San Antonio seemed to drag on forever, but the months here have sped by with me hardly noticing. I shudder to think what I'll do with a week off for Thanksgiving, and how I'll even be spending it.

On Friday after work, Amelia asks me if I have any plans for the night. "Ha! Just kidding. I know you don't." She slings an arm around my shoulders affectionately when I glower at her. "But we should change that. Marcus invited us to Shade tonight."

"And by 'us', do you mean 'you'?" I ask, already knowing the answer.

"Nope, and I'm not even lying for your benefit! Here, look," She holds out the evidence in the form of Marcus's last text message to her. She clears her throat. "And I quote, 'you should tell Dacia to come'. Booyah."

"Like that means anything. He's just being nice." I say. "And what is Shade, by the way?"

"It's apparently a really cool patio bar." She says. "It'll be fun! Jesse and Alex will be there. Oh-" Her phone pings with an incoming message just as I feel mine vibrate in my pant's pocket. "It looks like he started the group chat."

I scan the message detailing the plans for the night. "Wait a minute, he says we're bar hopping. Ugh, I'm definitely going to puke tonight."

"Don't worry." She flashes a grin. "I'll hold your hair back."

CHAPTER 16

"Of course you didn't do anything wrong."

The words are a welcome relief to my conscious, but a small part of me can't help but consider Amelia's bias. She's always been able to see my side of the story, but I've never stopped to wonder if she can see it from an outside perspective as well.

"I don't know." I'm applying a second coat of mascara in front of a mirror, trying to fix the clumps the first coat made. Amelia is getting dressed behind me. I find it easier to say exactly what's on my mind when we're not facing each other. "You didn't see Chastity this summer. She fell hard for this girl. I know she falls in love quick, but I've never seen anything like this."

"But from everything you've told me, it doesn't sound like this other girl was that into her." I hear the springs sag as she takes a seat on the edge of my bed. "Chastity deserves better than that, doesn't she? You were right to get her out of there when you did."

"Maybe." I'm still not convinced, but we don't have enough time for the amount of convincing I need. I stare at myself in the full length mirror, moving left and right to inspect myself from all angles. I'm wearing black skinny jeans and a teal top with thin straps. Autumn is a joke in this part of Texas, so I don't even need a jacket. I push my hair behind my ears and off my shoulders, watching as it falls down my back in a sleek waterfall. Chastity would be proud, if not for my meddling in her love life, than for my appearance now. I learned everything I know from her.

"Ready for this?" Amelia asks.

"Not in the slightest." But I shoot her a grin to show I'm joking.

"Let's just focus on having fun tonight, okay?" She grabs her purse and hands me mine as we leave my apartment. "You know I got your back tonight, girl. And if at any point in the night you want me to leave you alone with a certain somebody-"

"Don't even go there."

"Maybe we could come up with a code word! Just say the word 'buttercup' and I'll distract Jesse and Alex in a heartbeat." She says. "Come to think of it, I'll probably do that anyway."

"You're ridiculous."

We take an uber to The Square, where restaurants and bars are all lit up with string lights. I roll my shoulders back to shake out the nerves, but I'm not sure it helps. There's no reason to be nervous. None whatsoever. We walk across the cobbled walkway to Shade, where Marcus is waiting for us on a bench outside. He gets up from his seat when he sees us and waves.

"Hey!" He greets us both with side hugs. I'm not expecting it, and the spice of his cologne fogs my senses. I hope he doesn't hear me breathe him in. "Alex and Jesse are running late, so I say we start the party without them."

We follow Marcus up a narrow staircase to the bar. It has a rustic feel, with wooden benches and plants everywhere. It's around ten at night, so the bar isn't as crowded as I feared. Marcus asks for our drink orders and as he heads to the bar to place them, Amelia and I find a table.

"Rum and coke." Marcus hands me my drink. "Raspberry mojito." He slides the drink to Amelia, and she barely stops it from spilling on her sweater in time.

"Sorry." He smiles sheepishly before taking a seat next to me. "Have you guys ever been here before? This is a nice place."

Amelia and I shake our heads. We're stopped from saying anything more when Jesse and Alex arrive. Alex squeals as she goes around hugging each of us, as if she hasn't seen us in years and not three days ago at lunch. "Aw, you already started drinking without us!" Alex exclaims before taking a seat across from me.

"You better catch up quick. I'm ready for round two." I drained half when my glass when I spotted them as they walked in, truth be told. Force of habit takes over when Alex walks into the same room as me. I get up from my seat and head to the bar.

"I'll go with you." Marcus says, following after me quickly. Weird. He couldn't have finished his beer that fast. I shrug off the thought when we reach the bar, where the bartender is busy making drinks for a couple with their arms wrapped around each other. That stupid yearning feeling fills my chest as I glance back at Marcus. We take seats at the barstools as we wait.

"You drained your glass pretty fast back there." Marcus says with a laugh. "You've really known Alex since high school and she still has no idea you don't like her?"

"Not a clue." I tell him, marveling again at how much he seems to notice. "Our families are incredibly close, so my parents used to get after me to be nicer to her. I really tried, but my attempts never really stuck for long. When I dislike someone, I can't hide it. But alas, Alex either remains oblivious or chooses to ignore the fact that I can't stand her."

"Wow." He says. "So of all the people we know, including me, how many of us do you hate?" His expression is amused, telling me the question isn't asked in malice. I'm not sure why I decide to play along, but I count them all in my head and hold up three fingers. "That's it?"

"Did you expect more?" I give him a knowing look. Like I don't already know the answer.

"Kinda, yeah." He flashes a sly grin. "Okay, come on. 'Fess up."

The bartender interrupts to ask for our drink orders. Once we have our drinks, I take a sip and shake my head. "Guess."

"Okay." He taps a finger on his chin in thought. "Me."

"No." I shake my head.

"Really? I passed your test?" He almost looks pleased. I just roll my eyes. "Okay, okay. Luke."

"You got one."

"I knew it. You seemed pissed at that dinner." He tells me.

"Because he was being a brat. But if it makes you feel better, all teenagers are brats, therefore I hate all teenagers by default."

"Fair enough." He chuckles. "Okay, oh. An obvious one. Alex, duh."

"Ding ding ding."

"Last one, who could it be?" He takes a swig of his beer. I watch as he bites his lip, almost hesitating to say, "Jane."

My brows furrow. It's not the name I expected to hear. "Of course not. Why would you think that?"

"Just had to check." He confesses. "She actually kinda hates you."

"Well, that's less surprising." I sigh. "I'm not an easy person to like, remember? That list would be a lot longer than this one. Go ahead, count how many people hate me off the top of your head." I mostly say this to avoid him from guessing the third person correctly. Sarah Bailey. It's such an obvious answer, I have to wonder why he didn't say it. Maybe because we've been so good at not fighting since meeting up again. I don't want to lose that.

"Okay, I'll bite." Marcus says, then rests his chin between his thumb and forefinger in thought. It doesn't take him very long. "Yeah, you're right. I'm already up to eight."

"Told you." I take a sip from my drink. "In fact, once upon a time you used to hate me, too. Or did you count yourself in that list?"

I chance a glance at him to find him already staring at me. His eyes are cloudy, locked on mine. I'm caught in his gaze, the people surrounding us long forgotten. The music and noise fade to a dull register, and the air shifts between us, creating a tension entirely new to us. Or maybe it's exactly the same. When his eyes flick down to my lips, something primal and wanting awakens in me. In the very back of my mind, I think maybe he actually doesn't hate me at all. He confirms my suspicion when he finally answers.

"I don't hate you, but I'm not sure how I feel about you." He confesses, his voice rough. "Please tell me you're just as confused as I am."

"Probably more." I tell him. Our faces inch closer, until we're at a standoff. This feels an awful lot like the last time we saw each other in San Antonio, back in my bedroom. What would've happened had Christian not interrupted? I think I'm about to find out. I'm aching to. "Much, much more."

"Doubtful." He's off the barstool, our noses almost touching. "Whatever this is has been messing with my head since...I don't even know when. I can't pinpoint the moment."

"Neither can I." It's like he's taken the words right out of my mouth. I can't make heads or tails of my muddied thoughts. Everything is hyper-focused on this moment, on this inevitability I hadn't realized until now that I've been waiting for. "This is a bad idea, isn't it?"

"It's definitely not a good one." He says. We're breathing the same air. Every thought in my head is evaporating. "Dacia-"

I cut him off, finally out of patience. My hand snakes up his chest to the collar of his shirt, curling into a fistful of fabric as I pull him down to meet me in an earth-shattering kiss.

This. This is what I've been waiting six months for. The warmth of his mouth against mine, the scruff of his cheeks against my skin, his lips parting just enough for our tongues to meet. Admitting it feels more freeing than I thought and less embarrassing than I predicted, but that's because I'm not focusing on the repercussions. Just him. It's been two years since I've kissed anyone. I thought I would've forgotten the mechanics of it by now, but if anything the opposite is true. My lips capture his, dominating him in a way I've wanted to for far too long. My hands move up to cup his jaw, keeping him where I want him.

I have no idea who I am in this moment. Not once in my life have I been the one to make the first move. Even the mere thought of it has always been too nerve-wracking. But Marcus is more than eager to comply, one hand wrapped around my waist and another lost in my hair. His lips are so soft, and I wonder how we could've gone for so long without doing this. When his tongue slips into my mouth, I let out a groan and pull him closer. I'm practically straddling him at this angle, him standing between my legs. It's only once his hand reaches my thigh that I realize we're still very much in a public space and pull away, breathing hard.

"Sorry, I forgot myself there for second." He says, his forehead resting against mine.

"Me too." I hardly recognize my own voice. "We should prob-ably-"

"Yeah. You're right, we should..." He trails off, and neither one of us moves an inch. It isn't until a throat clears that we turn away from each other. Alex is standing right in front of us, arms crossed over her chest as she surveys the mess we must look like.

"So this is where you two snuck off to." Good lord, of all the people to catch us. "We're ready to head to the next bar, but if you guys want to...explore whatever this is-"

"No!" I jump off the barstool and move a good foot away from Marcus. "We're ready. Let's go." I can't quite meet his eyes, but he follows Alex and I to our earlier table.

"Heeeey, you guys." Amelia drawls, obviously drunk. She pulls me away from the others, swinging her arms out to reach me. Her elbow knocks into a beer glass, spilling the contents across the table in an acrid puddle. "Whoops." She hiccups before bursting into laughter.

"Amelia, this thing was full." I lift the glass bottle with two fingers, careful not get any liquid on me. "You just wasted a full five dollars."

"You mean Marcus wasted a full five dollars." She corrects, raising her index finger like she's informing me of something important. "He left it here to follow you to the bar."

"He..." He had no reason to follow me to the bar. Marcus, who's saving every penny he can for tuition money, left a five dollar beer behind to be closer to me? My heart practically leaps out of my chest.

Amelia wraps an arm around my shoulders. "I may be a li-" I cringe when she hiccups in my ear. When I try to untangle myself from her arm, she pulls me right back with ease. "I may be little drunker than I planned," She whispers faux-conspiratorially. "But you can still count on me as your wing-woman. I got your back tonight!"

"That's not at all necessary." I tell her. "How many drinks have you had?"

"Just two," She waves my concern off.

"Try five." Jesse says. "Alex and I didn't want our second round of shots, so she drank them."

"Jesus, Amelia."

She's already moved on from me to Jesse and Marcus. "I'm so glad I met you guys!" She gushes. "You guys make Texas fun. We should do this every weekend!"

"Maybe we should just call it a night." I say. "If she has one more drink, I'll be holding her hair back when she vomits onto the street."

"But it's barely midnight!" Alex exclaims. "The night is young!"

"You guys can go on without us." I try to pull Amelia's hand, but she's having none of it.

"Nooooo!" She says, fighting me. "I'm not ready to quit the night!"

I heave a sigh as we head out to the next bar. Alex and Jesse walk with me while Amelia and Marcus trail behind us. I don't like the idea of leaving them alone while Amelia is this drunk (I shudder to imagine what embarrassing story she's telling him now), but I don't want to make a big deal of it.

The next bar has a divey feel to it. A couple of patrons play pool at the table in the corner, others are sitting around chatting casually. Jesse and Alex head to an open pool table and I order Amelia a water and myself another rum and coke. When Amelia and Marcus trail in, I already have the drinks and a table. I wave her towards me, and she drunkenly ambles to my table.

"Drink this." I hand her the water, which she slides away. "No, no, Amelia-"

"Its too early in the night to be cut off!" She tells me. "Tell her, Marcus."

When I catch his glance, it's deja vu. I'm transported back to summer in San Antonio, right to the beginning of all of this. The Brass Monkey, where I caught him glaring at me for seemingly no reason. Back then, I blinked and it was gone but now when I blink, his eyes remain narrowed on me. Then he looks away like he's disgusted with me, and when he meets my gaze again its with forced politeness.

"I can't do this." He tells us. "I'm gonna head out."

"Whaaat, no!" Amelia pulls on his shirt sleeve, but he works his way out of her grasp. "You can't go yet!"

"It's been a long night, and I have to take the kids to a soccer game in the morning." He says. "Really, it's been fun. I'm glad we did this."

"I can walk you out." I tell him, because I need to know that we're good and if we're not, I need to fix whatever I somehow broke.

"Don't." His voice is hard, and it freezes me in place. I don't know what's happened to suddenly change his mind, but I need to change it back. "Just...don't." His voice is softer, but his eyes are still cold. Then he walks out. I force down the urge to run after him and make him tell me what the hell just happened. He obviously doesn't want that, and I don't want to be where I'm not wanted.

Only, just a moment ago I thought he did want me.

"I think I'm gonna be sick." Amelia puts a hand to her mouth and makes a run for the restroom. It's a sentiment I can relate to.

Chapter 17

I can't sleep. All night I toss and turn, wondering what the hell happened with Marcus. How could he go from leaving behind a five dollar beverage just to follow me to the bar to completely icing me out at the end of the night? By the time morning comes, I still don't have any answers. When did he change his mind? Did Amelia say something between the five paces we walked from one bar to the next? She was determined to talk me up, so I doubt she would've said anything bad. Embarrassing, yes. But something to make him hate me all over again? No chance.

But a small part of me can't help but wonder, would something romantic between us really kill him so much? Our relationship has been rocky, but there's obviously something between us that isn't going away. I swallow my fear and send him a text asking to talk. Then I finally get out of bed to start a pot of coffee. An hour passes and he doesn't text me back. I've been dreading this, but I think I have no choice. I find Amelia's number and call her.

She answers with a loud groan. "You should know better by now than to call before eleven AM after a night like last night."

"I'm freaking out." I tell her, hating how shaky my voice sounds. "Can you come over?"

I hear the ruffle of sheets as she gets up. "You better have the coffee ready by the time I get there."

"Already done."

Seven minutes later, Amelia is at my door wearing sunglasses, her blonde hair piled at the top of her head in a bun that's barely a bun. I hand her a mug and lead her to the couch. "Okay. What's wrong?"

"How much of last night do you remember?" I ask her.

Her eyes squint. "It'll all come screaming back to me in a minute." She puts a hand to her head and winces. "After some Advil."

I take the bottle from the coffee table and rattle it at her. "Here. Maybe this will speed up the process."

"I don't say this very often because it's usually not true, but you are an angel."

"Yeah, yeah. Hurry up and take it." I open the bottle and put two pills in her open hand. "I'm gonna need your full attention when I tell you what I have to tell you."

"Mm." She washes the medicine down with a sip of coffee. "Okay, go. I'm ready."

"I kissed Marcus last night."

"You WHAT."

"And then he completely blew me off." I tell her. "He's not texting me back and I have no idea what I did to cause this. You're an expert in my social blunders. I'll give you the play-by-play and you can tell me where I went wrong."

I give her the details, the conversation before the kiss to the actual kiss itself to Alex catching us in the act. I even tell her about the beer bottle she spilled, because it has to mean something. Then I tell her about his cold behavior just before leaving Cats Billiards as soon as we'd gotten there. By time I'm done, Amelia is just as confused as I am.

"Dude, that makes no sense."

"Oh, good. It's not just me." I breathe a sigh of relief. "Do you think he just regretted it happening and that's why he walked out?"

"No, this sounds like something more than that." Amelia shakes her head. "I'm just not sure what - hold on." She pauses as her phone chimes. "It's Marcus." She looks up, brows furrowed.

"Great. He texts you before bothering to text me back." I grumble.

"He's asking if we can talk about what I said last night..." She trails off, brows furrowing. "What did I say last night?"

"You were walking with him on our way to the next bar." I remind her. "I was just going to ask if you remember him acting weird."

"I remember telling him to cut you some slack." She says. "I was talking you up. I was-" Her face scrunches in thought. She takes a sip of coffee, and I can feel my patience thinning.

"What? What did you tell him?"

"What's his sister's name again?" She asks cautiously.

"Jane." I say. "What does that have to do with-"

"And what's the name of the girl Chastity was seeing over summer?"

"Jane." I say, more slowly this time.

Amelia starts and stops herself from speaking. Finally, she whispers, "Are they the same person?" When I nod, she gives a nervous laugh and says, "I think I may know what the problem is."

An hour later, I track him down at the elementary school's soccer field. The sky is grey with a coming storm, but that doesn't seem to the stop the game. He's sitting on the bleachers with Alex's aunt and uncle. Mrs. Henderson spots me first, frantically waving me over with an excited smile. When Marcus's head turns and his eyes lock on mine, his expression nearly makes me turn right back around. But Alex's aunt is shouting my name, so it's too late for that now.

"Dacia! How are you?" Mrs. Henderson wraps her arms around my shoulders in a tight hug. "Gosh, we haven't seen you in years, have we John?" She asks her husband.

"Almost ten, if I'm remembering correctly." Mr. Henderson says. "What brings you down here?"

"I actually came to see if I can steal Marcus for a moment." I tell them.

"Oh, I didn't realize you two knew each other." Mrs. Henderson says. "Go ahead and take him off our hands! He's been a wonderful help to us today already."

"Are you sure? You already paid me for the whole day-"

"Nonsense, you work hard." Mr. Henderson claps a hand on his shoulder. "Enjoy the day off. We're actually headed to Austin after the game," Alex's uncle turns to address me now. "So you kids are free to hang out at the house without being bothered. It was nice seeing you again, Dacia."

Marcus looks far from happy to be free of his employers, but he follows me out to the parking lot anyway. It's starting to drizzle, so Marcus suggests we talk in his car. Once we're inside, the rain comes down harder. Figures. I can't help but think how awkward it will be if this ends up being a short conversation and we're stuck in here waiting out the rain.

I turn on my side to face him. "I know you don't want to talk to me, but I think we have to."

"It's not that I don't want to. There are a lot of things I want to say to you right now, believe me." He looks straight ahead out the windshield, his jaw clenched. Not a good sign that he won't look at me. "But a calm mind makes the best decisions, so I don't think this is a conversation we should be having right now. Especially after what Amelia-"

"What exactly did she say to you?" I ask him.

"Answer me honestly." He finally turns to look at me. "Did you breakup Chastity and my sister?"

"No." I shake my head. I'm still not sure how Amelia told the story exactly, but I don't want him to think that's what I meant to happen.

"Are you sure about that?" He asks, eyes narrowed. "Are you sure you didn't talk Chastity into that Chicago trip to get her away from Jane?"

"That was-" I stammer, trying to think of the best way to explain. When he puts it that way, it doesn't look good. I have to backtrack, start from the beginning - "After the party, Chastity said she got into a huge fight with Jane and that they broke up. She was heartbroken-"

"And two days later, she was on a plane." Marcus interrupts. "Was that her idea?"

Fucking shit. This is going downhill fast. "No." I admit. "I wanted to get her mind off of everything that happened with Jane. I thought she needed that."

"Yeah." Marcus scoffs. "And what about what Jane needed? That wasn't a breakup to her. She never got the chance to apologize for everything that went down between them."

"What use is it arguing about what happened six months ago?" I ask him. "I can't change the outcome."

"So you don't care." He realizes. Then he lets out a humorless laugh. "Of course you wouldn't. I don't even know why I thought you would."

"What do you want me to say?" I ask him. "Do you want me to apologize? Would that honestly change how you view me as a person?" He doesn't say a word. "I'm so tired of the emotional whiplash from you. We hate each other, we're friends, we hate each other again, we're kissing, and now we're right back to hating each other."

"Maybe its because right when I think I'm starting to like you, I find out you're no different from who I thought you were in the first place." He seethes. "Sarah was right. You could care less about anyone not in your little circle. You don't care who gets hurt, as long as you get what you want. And god forbid you actually admit when you're wrong and apologize."

I blink once, twice, three times, but all I see is red. "Of course. Because it all comes down to her, doesn't it?" I laugh, and once I start I can't stop. Nothing about what's happening is remotely funny, but that doesn't stop me. The sound is humorless and cold and doesn't sound a thing like me. "You've been holding a torch for her all this time, haven't you? Even now, hundreds of miles away, she's still under your skin."

"This isn't about her!" He bursts, a vein in his forehead bulging. "If you want to know the truth, I could care less about where she is. It was clear she didn't like me the way I liked her, and she made me look like an idiot multiple times. But putting all that aside, there's still something she said about you that rings true to me."

"Why are you so determined to hate me? Because everyone else does or because you can't stand being wrong?" I ask him. He looks away then, jaw clenched and fists white. "I already told you once. Apologies don't mean anything if you're not actually sorry. I did nothing wrong when I invited Chastity to Chicago after the breakup, or whatever it was. There's only so much you can know about a relationship you're not in, but everything I saw suggested that Chastity was giving and giving and getting nothing in return from your sister. I had-"

"Because she was scared." Marcus interrupts. "She didn't know if Chastity was for real or not. How do you think it looked to Jane after she left without a word? She had to find out on Chastity's Instagram story-"

"I had enough of seeing her hurt," I continue as if he didn't say a word. "So I asked if she wanted to leave early. She said yes." He shakes his head, but he's not looking at me. "I won't apologize for doing what I thought was right at the time for my best friend. So maybe Sarah's right in this instance. Outside of the people I truly care for, I couldn't care less about who gets hurt along the way." He still won't look at me. I'm not sure what possesses me to spill my heart out, but the urge to make him listen is too strong for me to ignore. "And you're in that circle, too. I care about you."

He pauses, uncertainty in his eyes. Now that I have his attention, I can't stop myself from putting everything out there. "I tried to fight it for months, but it's there. The more we get to know each other, the more I find myself falling for you. I can't name what, but there's just something about you I can't shake, no matter how hard I try. Maybe it's just that I'm a masochist for wanting what I can't have. You've given no clear indication that you feel the same about me, and I'm sick and tired of the constant push and pull between us. For once and for all, Marcus, give me the clarity I desperately need." I make myself keep eye contact despite the alarm bells ringing in my head, urging me to run while I still can. "Do you feel the same way I do? Am I alone in this?"

His mouth opens and closes, eyes wide as saucers, starting and stopping himself from answering. What thoughts must be raging through his head right now? I thought I was finally onto a hint of his feelings last night, but now, waiting for an answer after making myself the most vulnerable I've ever been, I'm terrified that I've been completely off base the entire time we've known each other.

"I can't." He finally says, shaking his head. I swear I can feel as the organ inside my chest splinters and breaks. "I can't even let myself start with you. There are too many unanswered questions-"

"Like what?" I ask, pushing his words to the back of my mind to deal with later. I can't even let myself start with you. If I think about that now, I'll completely lose it.

"What you did to Sarah." He tries to keep a neutral expression, but the fists balled in his lap are clenched so hard they're white. "She said you attacked her, but she was the one who spent a night in jail. Not to mention those rumors." His voice isn't accusatory, but tears sting my eyes at how matter-of-factly the words come out. "I don't know what to believe anymore, Dacia. It doesn't make sense for the person I know you to be to have done everything she said you did. Maybe at first, but now-" He shakes his head, turning in his seat to better face me and hope builds in my chest. "What's the truth, Dacia? Help me understand."

Those light-colored eyes train on me, brows furrowed in question. My thoughts rage and war, a distant feeling in the back of my mind wondering if this is some sort of trick. For the first time since I can remember, anxiety and pride are in full agreement. Don't tell him. But another part of me wants to, a part I'm too frightened to name. I want him to trust me, and more than anything I want to trust him. If that means telling him the truth...

"They're not rumors." I find myself saying, voice shaky. "I've only told one person the truth, and that was Amelia. Everything else-"

He shakes his head, looking away from me. When his jaw clenches, I know made the wrong choice. It took me barely opening my mouth for anxiety and pride to win in one fell swoop. "Come on, Dacia. I thought you valued the truth too much to lie."

The truth, because that's what it is no matter what he or anyone thinks, at the tip of my tongue chokes and dies in the back of my throat. Shock washes over me before anger quickly takes its place. "Excuse me?"

"Christian knew." His eyes narrow. "He was spreading that story at Chastity's dinner party. He even tried to warn me about her." He scoffs and shakes his head. "How do you explain that?"

My skin heats at the accusation. I'm through. I'm sick and tired of being the only one on trial for Sarah's crimes. Once and for all.

"My brother told him!" The words tear through my throat in a scream. "Because it is entirely possible for someone to know what you don't explicitly tell them yourself, Marcus. Just like I know exactly what 'rumors' Sarah said I spread about her. She twisted the truth, just like she twisted the truth to me for four fucking years before I finally saw through her act." The urge to scream again is right there, but I don't want to give him the satisfaction of watching me come undone. "Is it gonna take you as long as it took me? Because I don't have that kind of time to waste anymore."

He stops in his tracks, mouth open in shock, eyes widening slightly. Neither of us says another word after my outburst. It's only now that I notice how loud the rain slashing against the windshield is. A roll of thunder sounds above our heads and I flinch, not expecting it. I didn't expect any of this. The fight has drained out of me. I lean back against my seat, not looking at him anymore. He's quiet for so long, but I hardly care what his reply will be now that I've finally admitted the truth to someone else, even as small a fraction of the truth as this. I try to look out the window, but I can't see a thing through the blur of water. It isn't until he finally speaks that I realize what I'm looking for.

"How do I know what you're saying is true?" I roll my eyes, because it's all I can do at this point. I'm too exhausted to keep arguing when it's going nowhere. It always does when it comes to Sarah Bailey. With my brother. With my father. Now, with Marcus. "How do you know that she really..." He trails off, not able to say it.

"You know what?" My car. That's what I'm searching for through the rain. The getaway I deserve. From the confessions I've laid out to a man who doesn't believe me or doesn't care or both. When I've laid my heart bare for the first time in my life just to have it go this badly. "I don't care what you believe anymore."

I open the passenger door and run, barely remembering to slam the door behind me. If Marcus calls me back, I don't hear him over the storm above my head. My feet pound against the wet pavement all the way to my car, and once inside I lock the doors and scream into my steering wheel.

CHAPTER 18

The rain stops an hour later, but the afternoon sky is still darkened by rain clouds. I change into a hoodie and joggers before leaving my apartment. It's been hard to schedule my morning runs once work started again, but right now it's all I can think about. I put in my Airpods and blast the volume to it's highest setting before breaking out into a sprint.

I can't even let myself start with you.

His words pierce through me all over again, and it's only now that I realize it wasn't an answer. Not a clear yes or no, but a full stop. I must be so starved of human affection for that realization to bring me hope. To wonder how he'd truly feel, if he'd only allow himself to feel it. But no. I can't let myself hope at what he's actively stopped himself from feeling. Even if I know why he's doing it, and maybe even how to fix it.

Except that I don't. Not really. My head is a mess of rebuttals and half-hearted apologies. But I'm not sorry for anything I've done, just the way it affected our...whatever our relationship is. Whatever it almost was. Maybe if we'd both been calmer, like he said, we wouldn't be in this mess now. I don't believe in closure.

The world is far too cruel to ever allow us that, so we have to find and make it for ourselves. I've done more harm then good, and my time in San Marcos is coming to a close soon. In time, Marcus and I will forget we ever met each other and move on with our lives. Until then, there are things I never told him that need to be said. But they don't necessarily need to be heard...

When I circle back to my apartment, I know exactly what I have to do. I quickly shower off and change into pajamas before rushing back into the kitchen to make a pot of coffee. There's no outward need for urgency, but I still feel it within myself. I need to get this out - once and for all. Once I've brewed myself a cup, I compose a text message I'll never, ever send.

I had a therapist once who suggested journaling to let out my anxious feelings. This is a lot like journaling, only the stakes are higher. It feels more real to me, but I'm ultimately in control of the final outcome - hitting send or backspacing every word. When I drafted my resignation email, I knew I'd never actually go through with sending it. But there were low points where I considered pulling the trigger - when I hovered over the send button with my cursor for whole minutes before finally clicking away from the screen.

I've even written a number of letters to Sarah over the years, to the address in Flagstaff I found in her original PI file. They currently live divided among three shoe boxes in a storage unit located in downtown Chicago. I've thought about burning them or dumping them in the Chicago River, but there's something about letting them rot in a cold, forgotten storage unit that has a sense of poetic justice to it.

The words spill out of me, unedited and unfiltered. I didn't hold back then and I don't hold back now, even with the secrets that aren't entirely mine to tell. Even with the emotions I'm ashamed to have ever felt. An entire hour passes and I hardly feel it.

Once I finish typing, I down the remainder of my coffee and walk to the sink. I scroll through the message, rereading it all over before I start backspacing. I only wish I had his email or physical address, because I'm cut off at the end and there's so much more I could say. This doesn't feel over, but I can't help but wonder if even with a fully thought out, complete message, this thing between Marcus and I ever will.

I'm not ready to hit backspace, so instead I lock the screen and put my phone on the coffee table. Now that the words have drained out of me, my energy has done the same. I don't remember closing my eyes or when I fell asleep, but I wake up later to find myself sprawled out on the couch, my limbs aching from whatever odd position I slept in.

What time is it? I lift myself off the couch with a yawn, stretching my arms above my head before reaching for my phone. But the first thing I see when I unlock my phone is the drafted message to Marcus. I read over the message again, though my brain is still groggy from sleep. Coffee. I make my way into the kitchen to see if I left the pot on when the hem of my pajama pants snag on a loose floorboard, pulling me backward before I make it to the kitchen. I'm falling to the floor before I can untangle myself, twisting my body around to save my phone, but to no avail. It falls out of my hand and hits the floor facedown beside my head.

"Fucking shit-" I sit up and rub the back of my head, grimacing at the pain. I hold my breath as I turn my phone over, letting out a sigh of relief when it comes up without any scratches. Then I do a double take when I catch a flash of blue on the screen. "No." I gasp. No no no no -

Somehow in the chaos of my fall, my message to Marcus sent.

Oh god. Oh god oh god oh god oh -

It's five AM, and I'm driving at a dangerous speed on the empty highway. I'm afraid to admit how many times I've called Marcus. Of course he won't answer - its fucking five in the morning. It's only once I'm parked in the Henderson's driveway that I begin to wonder if I'm overreacting. Maybe I should've gone to bed and waited to deal with the aftermath in the morning. But I promised my brother to never betray his confidences. We had such a hard time rebuilding the trust broken between us when I told Amelia everything that happened. I remember his face when he asked me to promise not to tell anyone, just as clearly as I remember his face when he discovered I broke it.

I turn off the engine, but then I just stare up at the house. The Henderson's aren't home, but this feels like crossing a line. I'm still wondering how much the text message is worth when the front door opens and Marcus emerges. He's wearing a white T-shirt and gym shorts, and his hair is all kinds of disheveled. My heart picks up pace. What thoughts must be going through that bedraggled head of his? He walks over to my car, and I let out a sigh before rolling down the window.

"What the hell are you doing here?" He asks, not with accusation but sleepy confusion. "Did something happen? Are Amelia and Alex okay?"

"They're fine." I say, and realize what a mistake this is. He thinks there's been some sort of emergency. That would actually warrant a five AM visit. "Did you read any of your messages?" I ask him.

"I was about to until I saw your car parked outside." He said. "What's going on, Dacia?"

"Don't read them." I tell him. "I sent you a long, rambly message that I never meant to send. I was trying to clear my head after our fight, and I-"

"You came all this way over a text?" He asks, brows creased. His tone threatens to diminish my resolve, but I've come too far to let that happen.

"It's not over the text, it's what I said in the text-"

"What did you say?" He asks before pulling out his phone. "Jesus, you sent a lot more messages after that."

"Because I betrayed someone's confidence. That's all I can tell you." Panic bleeds into my voice, making me sound more high pitched than I like. "Please, Marcus, don't-"

"'I'm beginning to think you were right to-'" I burst out of the car as he starts to read my message aloud, tackling him for the phone in his hand. We land in a heap on the grass, a tangle of limbs as we fight each other for the phone.

"Marcus, please just erase the message!" I scream as he pins my wrists over my head. "I know you think this is stupid and it probably is, but it's important to me. Please."

His face hovers over me, mere inches from mine. We're both breathing hard, and I desperately try to shove away the memory of our bar kiss. Pinned underneath him, feeling the warmth of his skin through my thin shirt, it's all I can think about.

But I can't afford to get distracted, even though I'm liking this precarious position more than I'm willing to admit.

"I'll make you a deal." He tells me. "I won't read the message on one condition."

"Deal."

He chuckles, and I feel the vibration of it on my chest. "Don't you want to hear what the condition is first?"

"Fine." I roll my eyes. "What is it?"

"You have to read the message to me."

I pause, looking up at him. "But I told you-"

"I know, you betrayed someone's confidence." He says. "I want to trust you, Dacia. I really do. But that means you have to trust me, too."

I take in a long breath. If there's anyone I want so badly to trust, it's him. "Okay. I'll give it a shot."

He lifts himself off of me and offers his hand to help me up. His palm is warm on my skin despite the chill in the air. He leads me inside the house to the guest bedroom where he's staying, never letting go of my hand. There's no fear of waking up the Henderson's since they're out of town, and if I'm grateful for anything it's that my madness has impeccable timing. I should feel nervous, but something about Marcus's touch calms me down enough that I'm breathing easier.

"I need to see you erase the message before I do this." I tell him.

"Okay." He shows me his screen as he pulls up his messages and erases the long one. "Done."

I nod, placated. "I want to tell you about my brother first."

"Okay?" His brows crease.

"His name is Jorge, and he's nothing like me." I tell him. "He's the kindest person I know. He inherited our father's hundred-watt smile - it could even rival Chastity's. He's not nearly as outgoing as she is, but unlike me I think he wishes he were and that kind of kills me. He makes the best buttered croissants, and he just uses the Pillsbury ones you put in the oven. I don't know, he just does it better than anyone else I know." Marcus chuckles at this. "You'd like him if you ever met him. Everyone does."

I let out a breath. "Okay. Now, the text. And please try not to interrupt me, or I won't be able to get through it."

Once he nods, I begin.

"I'm beginning to think you were right to want to wait to talk to me. I like what you said about calm minds making the best decisions, even if it does sound like it was ripped off an Influencer's Twitter bio." He opens his mouth as if to respond, but I cut him off before he can. "No interrupting, remember?" He grumbles to himself before giving a begrudging nod, and I continue.

"Neither of us were in any fit state to talk calmly about the things between us, and now that I've had some time to reflect, there are many things I regret saying to you." My voice shakes, and I hate how weak I sound. I look down at my phone so I don't have to look at Marcus, pretending I'm just reading aloud to myself. It makes it easier to get through this.

"Here's the first: I said I'm not sorry for doing what I thought was right for Chastity at the time. While I still stand by that, what I do regret is the effect it had on you and your sister. If Jane truly felt more for Chastity than what I saw, I'm sorry for any hurt I caused her in putting my best friend first. I know how close you two are, and that you must have also felt any hurt that she did.

"Here's the second: Sarah Bailey. As much as I hate to admit it, what I said about you holding a torch for her was said out of jealousy and a need to hurt you the way you hurt me by blindly taking her side. If you only knew half the truth of what she's done to my family, you'd understand why I felt that way. Believe it or not, I used to call her my best friend. Obviously things fell apart between us, and I've had trouble trusting people ever since. Even Chastity doesn't know the full extent of the story.

"When Sarah and I were eighteen, my brother had just turned fourteen. She used to tutor him in Math after school, and one day I-" My voice breaks, reliving the memory. I clear my throat. "One day I stumbled across them in the dining room, heads bent together, her hand on his thigh. The four year age gap between them may seem like nothing now, but at the time she was a senior in high school and he was an eighth grader. She knew him when he was ten and she was fourteen. But even beyond that, Sarah has always known how to get what she wants from those around her.

"When I confronted her, she tried to convince me that what I saw with my own two eyes wasn't the truth, and she almost succeeded. That's how convincing she is. It was Jorge that gave away their relationship in the end. When I caught him rifling through our father's things weeks later (weeks I'm still ashamed to this day of letting pass), I knew. He begged me not to say anything to her, that his love for her was being tested. I'm not sure you can imagine how I felt. Even now, remembering is too painful.

"I asked him what she wanted. I had to ask multiple times before he answered: a check for a quarter of a million dollars. My brother was going to forge our father's name. So instead, I did. But not before pulling a few punches, first. I still have scars on the back of my neck from where her nails dug into my skin.

"I gave her the check along with a plane ticket to Flagstaff, with specific instructions not to cash the check until she reached Arizona. She didn't listen, which is exactly what I was banking on. I told my father she was the one who stole his checkbook and forged his sig..." I take a deep breath and look up at him. "That's when I ran out of room. Do you...have any questions?"

I stumble over my words from the expression on his face. He has both hands clamped over his mouth, and his eyes are wide as saucers. "Uh, yes. I have so many questions. But first, I have to-" He let's out a groan, shaking his head. "An apology doesn't even begin to cover what I need to do. Groveling at your feet might be a good start, because how the fuck did you put up with me? After what I said to you on the balcony-"

"Marcus-"

"And then again yesterday." His eyes shut tight, his mouth pressed into a fine line. "Dacia."

"You didn't know." I cross the room towards him. "Marcus, look at me."

His eyes open, creased with regret. I push the curls out of his eyes, running my fingers through the thick strands. He catches my wrist, pinning it in place.

"You didn't know, Marcus." I repeat. I'm not sure how I thought I'd feel after telling him the truth, but I never expected to feel relieved. Like a weight seven years old has finally been lifted off my back. My eyes shut as I let out a sigh, leaning into the warmth of his body. "There was no way you could have."

"I don't deserve your forgiveness." He wraps an around my shoulders, pulling me into his chest. "God, I was an even bigger idiot than I thought."

"Ignorance tends to do that." His muscles tense around me. I give myself enough space to look up at him without leaving his arms. "I don't mean that in a bad way. I should've told you a lot sooner, but I couldn't get over my own trust issues. And...I don't want you to beat yourself up about this. I forgive you, okay?"

He shakes his head, but he pulls me back into his arms.

"I just can't believe I fell for her." He says. Now I'm the one tensing up. What exactly does he mean by that? He can't believe he fell for her act? Or he can't believe his own feelings for her? "I've thought a lot about that night, when you told me she was manipulating me. I didn't believe it. I didn't want to believe it. But you were right." He meets my eyes again. "She had an uncanny way of using my own words against me, and anytime I tried to question her was like an attack on her character. And if she was too harsh, she'd apologize by saying her relationship with you really did a number on her." He shakes his head, his jaw clenched. "I knew there was something that wasn't adding up, but I ignored it. I wanted to be angry with you, and I wanted to show her I would always be on her side. That obviously backfired on me."

I don't respond right away. It's like I'm hearing myself, all those years ago when I first discovered the truth. Finally, I look up at him and say, "She's good at that. I didn't want to believe she was capable of all this, either. For years, I was so caught up with proving myself worthy of her. So much so that I never asked myself whether she was worthy of me."

He laughs humorlessly. "She could never be." His hands stroke my hair back from my face, and I melt into the warmth of him all over again. "You said you would answer some questions..."

I nod. "Go for it."

"What happened when she tried to cash the check?"

"She was arrested." I shrug. "That's what her night in jail was for, not our fight like she said. My father didn't want word to get out to the press and Jorge blabbed that I was the one who really signed the check. I guess in that regard she was right, and her night in jail was my fault. She left for Arizona soon after that, and to my father that was enough punishment." I can't keep the bitterness out of my tone. "There's a stigma surrounding victims of rape and sexual assault, and in some ways its much harsher for male victims. Especially when there's emotional abuse involved. For a long time, Jorge didn't believe that what Sarah did was wrong. Since the damage wasn't written on him in any obvious way, my father told us to let it go. We were never to speak of it again."

"I'm so sorry." Marcus says. "I know it's useless to say, but-"

"No." I shake my head. "It's not useless. I don't think I realized how much I needed to clear the air between us. I always would've wondered..." I clear my throat, looking away. "Anyway. Do you have any more questions?"

"Yeah." He says. "How is your brother now, after all of this?"

I let out a long breath. "I've never really known, if I'm being honest. We can't talk about her without it turning into a screaming match, so we just...don't. We're still close, and he gives every indication that he's a fine and well-adjusted person, but I just don't know." Admitting this is more painful than I can even begin to explain. I blink back the tears gathering in my eyes. "But he's apparently talked to Christian about her, which I'm taking as a good sign."

"Christian, huh?" His mouth quirks in what's meant to be a smile, but it doesn't reach his eyes. His eyes narrow in thought, and I'm about to ask him what he's thinking when he shakes his head and asks, "What about you? How are you, after all this? I know I didn't make it any easier on you."

"I'm good." I say, and I mean it. "I was so scared you wouldn't believe me. That's why I never planned on sending that message, because I wouldn't be able to bear it. Now that it's all out in the open, I'm just relieved. Maybe it's a good thing I tripped on that stupid loose floorboard after all."

He laughs lightly, pulling me to him again. My face hits his chest and he rests his chin on top of my head. "I'm glad you trusted me."

Through the window, the sun casts a golden glow on the walls around us and I suddenly realize I have no idea what time it is. But we've stayed up together past sunrise. The light makes his eyes glow, so clear they're almost transparent. Ironic, since I'm the one without a single secret left.

He walks me out to my car, idling as I step into the driver's seat. We stare at each other for a long time before we finally say an awkward goodbye. The pressure builds in my chest as I watch him walk back into the house. Then, I put the car in drive and head off into the morning glow. Even though we've finally said all that we needed to say, I can't help but feel like there's still something between us left unsaid.

CHAPTER 19

The week before Thanksgiving brings a rare cool front, dropping the temperature to the forties overnight. I arrive at the office Monday morning bundled in my thickest sweater under a wool blazer, wishing I'd at least packed one scarf. I'm running late to a meeting with my grandmother. She's waiting on an answer from me, and I have no idea what I'm going to tell her.

If I'd known a few months ago that I would have to make a decision to move HQ back to Austin, it would've been an easy choice to turn down. There are many reasons I hate Texas. The constant heat. Country music. Football. Barbecue. Republicans. Southern accents. The lack of decent public transportation. But when you stack them against the very real reasons I'd be staying, they don't even compare. If I stay in Texas, I'll be closer to almost all of the people I care about most in the world. Chastity, Christian, Amelia, Nana Wilhelmina. Even Alex, who I'm turning out to hate less than I thought. And...

I lied before. I know exactly what I'm going to tell her.

My grandmother is waiting for me outside an empty office, thermos of coffee in hand. She holds the door open for me and follows me inside. Wilhelmina is a smart woman, so when she takes one look at my face I can tell she already knows what my decision will be. She wears a small smirk, but she doesn't give away what she already knows. Instead, she asks, "Have you thought about what we spoke of a few weeks ago?"

"I have." I tell her.

"Well, don't keep me in suspense."

I shake my head, but I find I'm smiling. I'm actually smiling about moving back to Texas full time. "My vote is yes. Of course my vote is yes."

"I'm glad to have influenced you." She crosses her legs and rests her hands on a raised knee. "I'm also glad to see you doing remarkably well, considering all you've been through."

"It's funny, everyone seems to think that." I shake my head. "I'm not sure what they're seeing."

"Strength." She answers. "Determination. Resilience. Never sell yourself short."

"Right." I nod, avoiding her eyes. I never could take compliments well.

"Now, all that's left is for the board to come to a vote, but before we do that we're going to have play our cards right. Your next placement will be at the Austin office, which will become HQ if all goes according to plan. What Mrs. Henderson is going to have you do is write up a full report of how each department is managed compared to the Chicago office. In the meantime, you'll still be visiting all our other locations and learning how our offices are managed. It could be a year until the board meets to vote on the move."

"An entire year?"

"We're playing the long game, remember Dacia? They have to see that this is the best possible decision for Seidel, and if they put it to a vote now it'll be split too many ways." I nod. She's right again, of course. "In the meantime, you should get used to the idea that one day soon you'll be calling Texas home again. Have you talked to Jorge about anything that's been happening?"

I shake my head. "It's been awhile since we've talked. I doubt he'll be happy about the decision."

"Call him soon." She tells me. "The holidays are coming up. Maybe he'll change his mind after spending a Christmas in Austin, hm?"

We leave soon after, and all I can think about is that in two weeks I'll be leaving for Austin, and that there's a chance that move will be permanent. It feels like the right decision, but it's not my decision alone to make. The new year is going to have me traveling more than I like. I'm already dreading having to move into a third apartment this year, and who knows how many more I'll be moving into next year? But Nana was right about one thing. We have to play the long game in the hopes that I'll finally be at peace with where I belong.

Texas, again. No one's more surprised than me.

My brother has only lived in New York for two and a half years, but with the way he talks about it you'd think it's been longer. He's a full convert. When we moved out of Texas, he was still in elementary school and claims not to remember a single second of living there. I can only imagine what he'll have to say about HQ moving to Austin.

"What's up, sis?" Jorge smiles at me from his dorm bed. I can make out the Spiderman sheets from the angle he has his computer placed. His hair has grown out from the last time I saw him, a Skype call on his birthday back in April. It now grazes the tips of his shoulders, making him look like a lanky caveman. He's wearing an NYU sweatshirt with a clearly identifiable Hot Cheeto stain at the collar. "How's work life treating you?"

"Good, for the most part." I tell him. "I'm shadowing the Austin office for the next three months, so there's that to look forward to."

"Austin?" His brows crease. "Is this one of Nana's schemes to get you to move back? I know we love her, but you know how she can be."

"If only you knew" I shake my head. "Anyway, we can chat more when we have the time to. I know you're probably busy studying and not partying or slacking off whatsoever-"

"Of course not." He moves the bottle of Vodka sitting on his nightstand out of view.

"But I just wanted to check in, see what your plans for Thanksgiving are. I'll still be in San Marcos with Nana and Amelia. If you don't have anything going on I can fly you down here."

"I was actually meaning to talk to you about that." He says. "My roommate invited me to spend it with his family. I hope that's okay."

"Of course." I say, but my chest aches anyway. We've never spent a major holiday apart. I clear my throat and work past the grief threatening to spill over in the form of tears. Our first

Thanksgiving without dad, and we won't even be spending it together. "But you're definitely coming back for Christmas."

"Definitely." He nods. "I'm sure you'll be glad to be back in Chicago, too. All this Texas can't possibly be good for you."

I wasn't planning to talk to him about everything now, but since he's brought it up...

"Actually, I'm not sure I'll be going back up there after all." I say. "All this moving around has been exhausting, so I just don't have it in me to fly up there. I'll have enough on my plate arranging a new place in Austin as it is"

"Wait a minute, where will we be spending Christmas this year?"

"Austin." I tell him. "It might be better this way. We'll get to be with Nana and Amelia-"

"But they always fly up to us. Why can't we just-"

"Jorge, it's just easier this way." I let out a sigh. "Look, I know this is another big change on top of all the big changes we've had to deal with this year. But maybe this could be the start of a new tradition, you know?"

"Can't I just stay in New York for Christmas?" He asks, the hesitation in his voice clear. I'm sure he already knows the answer to that question.

"Do you want me to pay your tuition for next semester?" I counter, raising a brow.

"Fair enough." He sighs, but he looks far from happy.

A few hours after we hang up, Amelia texts me about Thanksgiving plans next week. We text back and forth for awhile until the topic of my next placement comes up.

Amelia: Don't let them take you away from me!!!

Me: Take it up with Nana.

Amelia: It feels like I just got you back and you're already leaving.

Amelia: :(

Me: Stop being so dramatic. Austin's only a half hour away.

I'm waiting on her reply when my phone vibrates with an incoming call. Marcus's name flashes across the screen. I pick it up immediately.

"Hey." He says. "Are you busy?"

"No, but I do have news." It's only occurred to me now that I've yet to tell him about moving to Austin, or that HQ might be moving there soon.

"Me too." He says and surprises me. "Do you want to get a coffee?"

"Sure." He gives me the address to an indie coffeeshop and we agree to meet in thirty minutes.

I'm already on the road to meet him when I realize this might be one of the last times we ever see each other.

He's sitting at a table in the corner when I arrive. His hair is pushed back from his face and he's wearing dark jeans and a white long sleeve henley. I almost consider turning back before he sees me, but then I remember Chastity's words from a few weeks ago. If I don't see her at all, then we're already done for good. Not seeing him now won't change the fact that whatever we have is about to end before it even begins.

"Hey." He looks up when I reach his table.

"Hey yourself." I sit down at the seat across from him. "So what's this big news you have?"

"I'm leaving tomorrow." He says, surprising me once again. "I think I've overstayed my time at this nannying gig. Plus, I miss my family and Jane's coming back home for the holidays, so."

"Right. That makes sense." I nod. "What will you do now? Go back to school?"

"Probably not for Spring semester, but hopefully next Fall." He says. "I'm still trying to scrounge together the tuition money, and while I made more than I expected to at this job, I'm still not quite there yet. I'll probably go back to my old daycare job in the meantime." He tells me. "But enough about me. What about you, hotshot CEO? What's your news?" He's smiling, but it's a sad smile.

"I'm moving soon too, actually." I tell him. "I'll be in Austin for the next three months, and then after that probably a site in California."

"Oh, wow." His eyes crease, and there's something distant in his voice. "I didn't know your job required so much traveling."

"It usually doesn't, but the board's preparing me to step in as CEO by shadowing all of our offices and labs. That's what I'll be doing for the next year." I tell him.

"And then back to Chicago?" He asks, his expression unreadable.

"Hopefully not." I say. "The board votes in a year to decide if HQ will be moved to Austin."

He blinks once. "Wait, what? You could be moving here permanently?"

"Possibly, yeah." I nod, and I find I'm smiling. "But I won't know for sure until next year, which sucks. I'm trying not to get my hopes up."

"Wow. I didn't know that's what you wanted." He says. "They'll say yes if it's good for the company, won't they?"

"That's what I'll be spending the next year trying to prove: that it will be good for the company." I say. "It'll be good for me too, I think. My remaining family is here, aside from my brother. But I'm making him stay with me in Austin for the holidays, much to his annoyance. He hates Texas." Marcus chuckles at this. "I'm actually from Austin originally. I'm not sure if I ever told you that."

"You did not."

"My father wasn't CEO yet, but he was head of the office there until I was in middle school. Then my grandmother decided it was time for her to step down, and we moved to Chicago." I tell him. "And now, it's like I'm returning to my roots. I grew up in my father's office. He worked most weekends and he always brought me with him so he could show me the ropes early on. I was the oldest which meant I should inherit the company, but really I think Nana just wanted a woman running the company again."

"Down with the patriarchy." Marcus says with a solemn nod. "I like it."

"I do, too." I say. "And I've grown to like Texas a lot more than I thought I would."

"We converted you, huh?" He asks. I just laugh. "Well, I hope this isn't goodbye for us. Austin isn't too far. A year from now we could be bar hopping through Sixth Street with Amelia and everyone again."

I heave a sigh, my heart suddenly feeling like deadweight in my chest. I want to believe him, but I don't. It's the kind of thing you say to someone you're not sure you'll ever see again. Something you're supposed to say instead of goodbye, because goodbye is too...messy. But after everything we've been through together, I want more than that. More than what I should realistically hope for. Even without accounting for the drama and other outside forces against us, my job ensures that after tonight we won't be in the same city again for an entire year.

If my relationship with Anthony proves anything, it's that long distance relationships don't work. Even before we were long distance, we were in a committed relationship of two years. What are Marcus and I, at this very moment? Even if we decided tonight that we want to be together, we couldn't be. Not really. Not the way we deserve to be.

If that's what he even wants. Because that's at the crux of it all, isn't it? I've made my feelings for him perfectly clear, and he still hasn't.

"Let's not kid ourselves, Marcus." I finally respond, shaking my head. "It's so easy to say that we'll see each other again soon or that we'll keep in touch without making any kind of definitive plan, but we won't do any of those things. Let's just call this what it really is. Goodbye."

His expression stiffens in shock. I watch as his chest rises and falls as he takes in a deep breath. Then, he flashes a wry smile. It doesn't reach his eyes; as it is, it barely lifts the edges of his mouth. "There's that honesty."

"Maybe it's better that we end it now while we've cleared the air." I tell him. "I'd hate for us to try to stay in contact and have it fall apart because we're too busy in our everyday lives to keep up with each other." Like how my relationship with Anthony ended. Because it ended long before the day we called it off in his apartment. That was just a formality.

"I guess you do have a point." Marcus rubs the back of his neck. "Even if I don't like it."

My heart races at his admission. Maybe he feels more for me than I'm giving him credit for. But ever since I foolishly told him I was falling for him, I can't help but feel like I'm hanging at the edge of a cliff with no ocean to catch me. There's one loose end left between us. I may not believe in closure, but I don't have to to still crave it.

"I don't like it either." I tell him. Then I let out a sigh. "I wish there wasn't so much stuff getting in our way, you know? We could've gotten to know each other like normal people."

"And how do normal people get to know each other?" He asks over his mug.

"Well, like this." I gesture between us. "Coffee and conversation. For instance, I didn't know you liked so much foam. Is there even any coffee under there?"

He lifts a hand to his mouth, choking down an ill-timed laugh. "And black is so much better?" He asks once he's recovered himself. "Let me guess - bitter coffee, bitter soul?"

"Please. I'll have you know there are five pumps of sweetener in here." I raise my mug. "No better way to fuel up, my friend."

"I can't think of anything more terrifying, actually." He laughs. Then, with caution and an unmistakable note of hope, he asks, "You wanna get out of here?"

My mouth quirks up of it's own accord. "I thought you'd never ask."

Marcus Galindo is in my apartment.

He's inspecting the lone bookcase standing in the corner of the living room. I didn't bring as many books here as I did to San Antonio, but even with work I've still managed to get through a decent stack of them. He peruses each shelf slowly, and I can imagine him reading each title in his head as his eyes pass them.

"Is it weird that this is the first thing I do when I visit someone's apartment for the first time?" He asks, crouching down to inspect the bottom shelves. "Jesse made fun of me racing to Alex's small bookcase when I went to their dorm."

"It's not weird." I tell him. "I'd do the same to you if I'm ever invited to your place. Bookshelves are like windows into a person's soul."

"How romantic of you." He rises, shooting me a sly grin. "I didn't think you were capable of such a whimsical notion. I'm learning so much about you already."

"Of course I'm a romantic." I assure him. "I'm also deeply cynical, so the latter often overshadows the former." I step forward to meet him. "So, tell me what you learned about me based on the books I own."

"You have varied tastes, so that tells me you have an open mind." He says. "Not a lot of nonfiction, though."

"If I were interested in true events, I'd actually have a life." I explain. He just shakes his head and laughs at me. "Anything else?"

"I counted about fifty-three books, so that tells me you're a hoarder. These are all your unread books?"

"Well, not all of them. I have more packed up in my Chicago apartment." I say. He looks aghast. "What? I like having options on hand."

"That would give me so much anxiety, owning so many books I haven't read yet." He says. "I read the books I own before buying new ones, otherwise I'd never be able to keep track of them."

"Oh, you're that kind of reader." I roll my eyes. I turn my back on him and head to the kitchen. "Do you want anything to drink? More coffee?"

"Only if you have milk, you monster."

Once a pot is brewed, we sit across from each other at the kitchen bar. I watch as he blows at the steam billowing from his mug before taking a tentative sip. It makes him look more adorable than he has a right to be.

"Can I ask what will probably be an uncomfortable question?" He looks up, brows furrowed. "About Sarah..."

"Oh." He straightens, meeting my eyes. "Of course. Whatever you want to know."

"Did anything ever..." There's no decent way to ask this question. "You know, happen between you guys? Were you guys dating, or-"

"No." He shakes his head. Then he takes a deep breath. "No, nothing ever happened. We never even kissed." He gives a scoff. "I won't lie, we did come close a couple of times. But something held me back from taking it that far. Well, a couple of things, actually."

"Oh?" I ask, intrigued.

"My sister, for one." He says. "Jane was wary of her after what she said about Chastity. I tried giving Sarah the benefit of the doubt, but Jane's worries did stick with me. Then, there were the mixed signals..."

"What do you mean?" I ask.

"As you clearly noted months ago, she always stood me up." He explains. "Those two times you saw weren't even the half of it. I don't know, that just never sat well with me, you know? I hated feeling like I wasn't worth her time, not even worth a text to say she couldn't make it. But the feeling had a habit of going away when I was with her. That's why I always tried to hold onto it, keep it in the back of my mind, because-" He's silent for so long I think that's the last of it. "I'm not sure you want to hear this."

"I do." I tell him. "God knows its hard to hear, but I want to know."

"Okay." He nods, releasing a breath. "She was...charming, I guess? She always knew exactly what to say, and I guess that should've been a red flag right there. But I fell for every word. When I was around her, I just got so caught up in her. Nothing else seemed to matter. Not what anyone else thought, and not even what I thought. She'd change my mind, anyway. She was good at that."

I force myself to take in a breath and let it go. "You really did like her."

"Not anymore." He reaches out a hand to my wrist. "And not in a way that was healthy. I know that now."

"I'm glad." I shoot him a small smile. "Okay, enough Sarah talk. Once and for all."

"Agreed." He nods. "Otherwise we might need something stronger than coffee to get through it."

"Good call. And I think I've had more than enough alcohol for one year. I always say the wrong thing when I'm drunk." I finish off my coffee in one long gulp. "Hey, speaking of. Remember when you called me out for telling Chastity that you failed to live up to my dating standards?"

"Uh huh," He nods warily, no doubt wondering where I'm going with this.

"I loved that." I say. "I love when people aren't afraid to call others out on their bullshit. This is why I've always sucked at socializing. There are all these unwritten rules about how to act around new people, and I've never understood that. But you showed me exactly where we stood that night, and I felt like I could just be myself around you because you'd already seen me at my worst."

He smiles, and there's nothing sly or sardonic about it. Then he gives a light laugh, shaking his head slightly. "I never know what to expect with you."

"What do you mean?"

"You rarely laughed or smiled when I first met you. You do more now, but it feels hard-won. I'm secretly impressed with myself when I can make you laugh." He says. "You speak matter of factly, without saying what you think people want to hear. You tell jokes with a straight face and that's somehow funnier than the actual joke you're telling. I can never tell what you're thinking, and that makes me nervous. You make me nervous. You're just...so unlike what I first thought." He shakes his head. "I can't believe it took me months to figure you out when now it couldn't be any clearer to me who you are, and that's who you've been the entire time I've known you."

I'm speechless. It feels like he's confessing something, but I can't tell exactly what it is yet.

"God, you're incredible. I thought that about you even when I wasn't sure I liked you." He continues. "CEO of Seidel Computers at twenty-five, and so beautiful it physically hurts to look at you." My face heats at his words. He thinks I'm beautiful. My heart is skipping beats. "You scared me. When you said you were falling for me I was terrified, because there's no way I can possibly live up to you." I shake my head, about to voice my disagreement when he says, "Especially not after everything I said to you. Every bad thought I ever had about you couldn't be further from the truth."

"You only thought those things because I never corrected you." I tell him. "I chose to be mad at you for it instead. I don't resent you for that. You weren't the one afraid to voice your true feelings, or to ask the questions other people would never dare to. I'm a hard person to get to open up, but you made it so easy. I never knew it could be that easy. I've never actively wanted to share intimate details about my life with someone, but I want to with you. And I want to know everything there is to know about you." I take in a deep breath. "Even if we never see each other after tonight. I want to know."

He grins from ear to ear, and even though it's pitch black outside I could swear the sun is shining. "Then we'd better get started, because we have a lot of ground to cover."

We spend the night talking, eventually moving to the couch to get more comfortable. I tell him how I met Chastity and he tells me how he and Jane got to be so close. Another pot of coffee is brewed, and we finish it off faster than the first. I'm wired on caffeine and Marcus, my eyes trained on his the whole night in fear of missing a single moment. At around one in the morning, we arrive at our first lull.

"Hm. What else?" Marcus asks.

I think for a moment. "Oh! Cookies."

"What?" His brows crease as I rise from the couch and make a run for the kitchen. I pick up my phone from the bar and return back to him just as quickly.

"Alex told me about this place that delivers fresh baked cook-ies." I tell him as I look up the phone number.   "What?" He repeats. "It's one in the morning."

"I know." I nod. "They close at three."

"Wait a minute, you're telling me there's a midnight bakery in town that delivers cookies to your door, and no one told me about it?" He shakes his head, a curl springing free from the top of his head as he does so. "Amazing."

"I thought so." I grin and reach a hand up to his hair to fix it, running the strands between my fingers. His eyes shut as he leans his head closer to my touch. The light casts flecks of gold and bronze on top, contrasting the dark, chocolatey notes underneath. Anyone who thinks brown hair is boring just isn't paying attention. I could lose time like this, straightening the locks through tight fingers and watching them form perfect curls when they escape my grasp.

He rests a hand on my cheek, titling my jaw down until I meet his molten eyes. There's no disguising the desire in his gaze, but it's confirmed when his thumb brushes the edge of my bottom lip. If he kisses me again, I won't make it. The thought comes unbidden, and I halt before I can lean into him. His eyes regain focus as if he can sense my hesitation, but I don't want him to ask me what's wrong.

I kiss him before he has the chance. He stiffens, but after a moment he opens up to me. I shiver when his tongue slides against mine, aching to press him closer. I have to cast all thoughts of tomorrow aside. Tomorrow does not exist in this moment - only Marcus. I'll deal with the emotional fallout later.

His hands trail down my body, stopping at my hips. Somehow I've crawled on top of him, his waist between my knees, and I have no memory of forming this new position. Of how needy he makes me. My lips trail down his jaw, down his neck, until I'm clawing at the fabric of his shirt for more skin. Distantly, I think to ask him if I'm moving too fast when I feel cool air on my back and realize he's pulled up the hem of my sweater to my chest. I waste no time raising my arms to lift it over my head and cast it aside to the floor before joining our lips together again.

"Your turn." I say against his lips as I pull him up to a sitting position.

I tug his shirt up and over his head, and it falls to the floor with my own. Now that we're skin to skin, the enormity of what we're about to do hits me. But then -

He's gotten the power back somehow, kissing me until he's pushed my back against the sofa cushions. I'm pinned down beneath his weight, and reminded of a dream I had of him months ago. Even back then, somewhere deep in my subconscious, I wanted him. I lose myself in his touch all over again, my hands gripped in his hair as his kisses trail lower. Down my jaw, the hollow of my throat, to the top of my breasts. Oh, god.

"Wait-" I manage just as his hands find the clasp of my bra. He stops as soon as the word is out, lifting himself off of me and making room for me to sit up. "I haven't been on the pill in over a year." I blurt. "I really didn't think this would happen when I invited you over. I'm not prepared-"

"Crap. I didn't think about that either." He says. "Should we - we should probably stop." But I hear the unspoken question in his voice.

"Yeah." I nod, but I'm already closing the distance between us. "We should stop."

"You know," His voice is pitched low, husky in a way I've never heard from him before. "There are other things we could-"

He's cut off from finishing his thought by the doorbell. What the hell? We're shocked still for a moment before I remember the cookie order. I let out a groan when the doorbell rings again, reluctantly raising myself from the couch and reaching for my sweater. "To be continued." I tell him as I head for the door.

"Order for Da-" The delivery guy cuts himself off, reading the label with squinted eyes. He's handsome in a pretty boy type of way, like Marcus, only more clean cut. His hair is styled back away from his face, making his cheekbones more pronounced. He can't be much older than twenty, and I think he must be a student at the University. More likely, a frat boy. "I'm sorry, I can't-"

"Dacia." I supply, holding out my hand for the wrapped baked goods. "Do you have a condom?" He chokes, nearly dropping the box, but I catch it just in time. "Hey, watch it, man."

"What? I don't-"

"Oh, come on." I cut off his startled reply. "I thought all guys kept one on hand. You know, just in case." I shrug easily as he gapes at me.

"I-I guess I might have one." I watch impatiently as he pulls out his wallet and retrieves one. He holds it out, and I exchange the wrapped foil in his hand for a folded fifty.

"You're a good man." I clap him on the shoulder before slamming the door in his face.

Marcus is lounging on the cushions when I return, hair ruffled and still shirtless. I take my time walking back to him, enjoying the view a little too much. How did I never notice how muscular his arms are? My eyes roam down his sculpted shoulders, down his lean chest to the decipherable bulge in his jeans. My skin heats, about to unravel all over again.

"You're wearing my shirt."

There's heat in his gaze. It's making me walk faster. I look down at myself when I reach the couch, surprised to find that I am indeed wearing his white henley. In my rush to open the door, I didn't notice I'd grabbed his shirt by mistake.

"Must have grabbed it by accident." I say, lifting it over my head along with my bra as I sit back in his lap, my knees straddling his hips. "That better?" He lets out a groan, pulling me closer until our skin makes contact.

"Mm," He kisses my neck, his hands circling my waist. "I don't want to get used to seeing you in my clothes. It's giving me ideas I shouldn't have."

"Oh?" It's comes out as a moan.

"Lazy Sunday mornings, breakfast in bed." His words vibrate against my collarbone. "You wearing my shirt and nothing else, for the rest of the day." A shiver runs down my back as his hands reach the waistband of my pants. He snaps the button open and the zipper goes down with it. I let out a gasp as his hand dips low in my panties. Yes, yes, oh god, yes-

An unintelligible sound escapes my throat. My hands are clawing at his shoulders to keep me upright, because my knees are having trouble keeping me steady. His fingers find the spot I need him most, working in circles. I bite down on his shoulder to keep from screaming out at the pleasure. My thighs clench around him as I find release.

"Oh, god. I'm never gonna get enough of this, am I?" I sigh. He chuckles against the curve of my neck.

"Are you religious?"

My brows crease at his question. "Not at all. Why do you ask?"

"No real reason. Just that you seem to call out to god a lot." He's sliding my pants off my legs, crouching down until his head hovers between my open legs. "You should try calling out my name instead. Just a suggestion."

There's that crooked grin again, his eyes sparkling as I'm stunned speechless for two reasons: this new, highly indecent position and his cheek.

"Marcus. Shut up." He chuckles before kissing his way down my stomach, my hips, my -

"Oh, go-" The word catches in my throat as he pushes the fabric of my underwear aside. He halts his movements, waiting. "Marcus."

"Good girl." He chuckles darkly. I'm about to call him a very unflattering name when his tongue slides down my center, and then up to my clit. I let out a gasp, hands curling into fists in his hair. I can't get enough of him. I'm arching my back and burying his head into me for more. Whoever taught him how to do this is a saint. It isn't long before another orgasm has me shaking underneath him, even sooner than the first one.

"Did you already-" I'm nodding before he can finish the question. Then I bend down to retrieve the condom from the pocket of my slacks, and his eyes widen in shock when I hand it to him. "Where did this come from?"

"The delivery guy. Thank the lord for horny college students." I pull myself up from the couch and reach for his arm, pulling him up with me. "Bedroom. Now, please."

We don't bother with the lights as we stumble onto my bed, kissing with renewed fervor. I find the button of his jeans and I'm embarrassingly eager as I pull them off him.

"Dacia," His hands cup my cheeks, smoothing the wild hair back from my face. "You know I have to ask. Are you sure you want to do this when-" He doesn't have to finish the question. My horny brain fog clears for the moment as I look up at him.

The pale moonlight through my window lets me see his expression, his eyes creased in concern, the frown marring his lips.

"Yes. I'm sure." I nod, even though my heart is pounding for an altogether different reason. "I don't want to regret not letting myself have as much of you as I can." Even if it undoes me. Even if I'll always wonder what we could've been if our situation was different. "Are you sure?" I parrot the question back to him, because I don't want him to have any doubts about this, either.

He nods without hesitation, and then his lips are on me again. It's a different kiss this time, a sadness tinged to it, maybe only for the sudden pressure filling my chest. Then I pull him on top of me, our bodies tangling together. My hands run down his back, nails digging into his shoulders in anticipation as he puts the condom on himself. The pressure in my chest doesn't alleviate when he enters me, only grows bigger somehow. I'm hyperaware of each second, of each thrust, of each gasp of air that leaves my throat.

"Marcus." His name leaves my mouth in a sigh. I'm close, but not as close as I sense he is. As if he knows, he puts his hand between my legs, fingers working where I need him. I shut my eyes, focusing on the feel of him until anything resembling a coherent thought leaves my brain. "Marcus."

"Dacia," My name is a huff of breath against my neck, warm and enveloping. The pressure builds low in my belly, no emotional torment to distract me from this moment. "Dacia, open your eyes."

I do, and for a moment I'm undone all over again. Until he let's out a groan as he comes, his body shaking all around me, and buries his face in my neck. I'm close to follow, his arms wrapped around me tightly as I do. Then he falls onto me, crushing me with his body weight. But it's a nice feeling, the pressure of his body. It eases the emotion threatening to choke the back of my throat with tears. My arms wrap around his back for more of his weight.

He plants a kiss on the side of my head before nuzzling his face in the crook of my shoulder. Tears sting my eyes, and I furiously blink them away before they have a chance to fall. I won't allow myself to feel sad while we're still together. There'll be more than enough time after this.

We fall asleep in each other's arms.

I don't wear his shirt in the morning. We dress in our clothes from last night, no sound but the rustle of fabric as we turn our backs on each other for some semblance of modesty. It doesn't matter that all forms of modesty were thrown out last night, have been thrown out for almost as long as we've known each other.

"Last night was..." He lets out a choked laugh. "Fun, to say the least. A good last hoorah." His voice wavers as if he's nervous, maybe of saying the wrong thing or not knowing what the right thing to say is after a night like last night. I'm not feeling as sensitive as I was after we had sex, so I let him off the hook.

"Out with a bang, as they say." I turn my head to shoot him a sardonic smirk. He shakes his head, smiling sadly. "What time are you leaving?"

"We have enough time for breakfast."

"How 'bout just coffee?" I ask. "I haven't been to the grocery store in weeks."

He nods, and we make our way into the kitchen. I start the coffeepot and find the box of cookies we forgot about last night, and we end the night the same way it began: the two of us sitting across from each other, mugs of coffee in hand, a goodbye looming on the horizon. We don't talk very much, and I'm almost grateful we don't have to suffer through a whole meal like this.

Almost, but not quite.

I walk him to his car when we've drained our mugs. He holds my hand the entire way, fingers intertwined.

"I guess this is it." He says. I give a half nod, half shrug. He opens his mouth to speak, but nothing comes out. I force myself to let go of his hand.

"What is it?"

His eyes are as glassy as mine feel. "Nothing. Just...I'm really gonna miss you."

"I'm really gonna miss you, too." I force myself to smile, because it's how I want him to remember me. "Hey. Kiss me before you go."

He steps forward, his hands reaching up to cup my cheeks. For a moment we just stare at each other, and I take in every detail of his face. His skin as brown as his morning coffee, his light-colored eyes, his head of curls I love so much. This man I know without a shadow of a doubt I could fall in love with, if given half a chance. That's a scary thing to know about someone you're not sure you'll ever see again.

Then he leans forward until our lips meet. The kiss doesn't last long. There's no heat behind it. I don't think either of us could take it otherwise, but my heart still aches when he pulls away from me.

And then he's climbing into his car, and I watch as it shakes to life as he turns the ignition. He backs out of the parking spot, looks up once to wave goodbye, and then pulls forward and out of view.

Once I'm back inside, I finally let out the emotion that's been building in my chest all night. It's the hardest I've cried in months.

CHAPTER 21

A month in my new place has passed, and I've yet to finish unpacking. This isn't like me. Austin wasn't supposed to be like this. A Nordic sea of new beginnings surround me, but I can't help how hollow I feel.

When I was younger, I used to dream of living in a high rise overlooking the River North's tall, sparkling buildings and the body of water below. As I grew older, that dream turned into an obsession. I would scour through listings every night, admiring the sleek appliances and modern decor. I would bookmark furniture on Pottery Barn and create whole Pinterest boards dedicated to interior decorating. I envisioned myself into a poshly decorated high rise each night before bed until it made cameos in my dreams. But after I got my MBA and my dad got sick, I had to hold off on searching for the apartment of my dreams. I told myself it would be the perfect gift to myself for when I was publicly named CEO. That was before the looming doubts started circling in, telling me I'd never be good enough to fill the role.

I haven't thought about that particular dream in months. Maybe I didn't allow myself to because I no longer felt worthy of it.

The apartment I've chosen now is a cozy villa in a gated community, just fifteen minutes from downtown. Bare white walls surround me in the living room. The far wall is stacked with boxes I haven't touched since the day I moved in. I occupy my first free weekend by looking up high rise listings in downtown Austin, and only one appears. It won't be available for very long, but maybe a year from now another one will be. If everything goes according to plan, that is.

But I still have doubts, because some things never change.

"So, when are you gonna unpack all this stuff?" My brother walks the length of my living room, eyeing the stacks of boxes with undisguised judgement. He tries to step closer to them, but I block his path. He's been here all of ten minutes and he's already getting on my nerves. Not that I'd have it any other way. His hair touches his shoulders now, but the length weighs down his natural waves. Add in the cargo shorts, Birkenstock sandals and unwashed hair, he looks more like Jesus than a junior in college.

"I'm taking my time." I cross my arms over my chest. "Hell, I'm only here for three more months so maybe I won't unpack them at all."

"That's no better than living out of a suitcase, Dacia." He tries to step past me, but when I block him again he lets out a sigh. "You gotta let me help you unpack. It's bad enough you forced me to come down here for Christmas, but if I have to stare at your wall of boxes for two weeks, I'm gonna go crazy."

"Haven't you heard? Christmas is cancelled this year." I turn my back on him as I head into the kitchen. "What do you want to eat tonight? I don't have much, but we could always go to HEB later if you're up for it." He doesn't answer me, and when I turn around I find him slumped on the couch, his face buried in his hands. "Jorge?"

I take in a breath, my heart pounding faster. He doesn't answer for ages, and anxiety creeps up my spine as I anticipate his reply. Is he feeling worse than I thought? Or is he just exhausted from the trip down here? Finally, he raises his head and I can see his brown eyes are shiny with tears.

"Nothing is ever going to be the same anymore, is it?" He wipes his nose with the back of his hand. His voice breaks on the last word, and my own heart breaks to hear it. "I've been dreading this, you know. I always do. First birthday, first holiday, first monumental moment without him."

"I know." I sit next to him on the couch and wrap an arm around his shoulders. Then I let out a long breath as he leans into me. "I have been too."

"I'm not like you. I can't be so cavalier about everything changing." He pulls away from my hold to look up at me. "I knew what our Thanksgiving would look like if I came down here. Amelia and Nana would try to overcompensate with food and cheer, and I'd just feel even worse about dad not being here. But I didn't think Christmas would be like..." He looks around the living room, and start to I see it through his eyes. The large expanse of empty space, not even a TV to fill the empty corners. He shakes his head. "I'm sorry. I know you probably have it worse."

I'm not sure why it surprises me to hear him say that, but I snap my head back to look at him. "What makes you say that?"

"Are you kidding me?" He lets out a humorless laugh, a hollow sound. "You're the adult between the two of us. I can't imagine what this has been like for you on top of the stress you have to go through at work. It's no wonder you got so good at compartmentalizing."

"I'm not as good at that as you think." I confess. "And I really missed you at Thanksgiving. Amelia's a good cook and all, but her stuffing isn't half as good as dad's was." He smiles lightly at that. "Maybe you're right, though. I am getting a little tired of staring at all these boxes."

"Yeah?" He asks.

"Yeah." I nod. "Maybe you could even help me liven the place up a little. Make it look more like an actual holiday is coming up next week."

"You sure it won't make us feel more depressed that dad won't be here to see it?" His brows crease, and he lets out another sigh. "I don't even remember what we did last year for Christmas. How bad is that?"

"It was nothing special." I remind him. "Dad slept half the day, and woke up later that night when I made hot chocolate. We caught the end of It's a Wonderful Life on cable and then he went back to sleep. I don't think we even put up the tree." That was around the time his sickness got worse and he became too weak to work. Mr. Banks had taken over by then, and my father was too exhausted to complain about it.

Jorge shakes his head in retrospective disappointment. "It sucks that that was his last Christmas. I know he was more concerned about work, but still. We should've made it - I don't know. More special than that."

"It's not like we could do our regular traditions. He was in no condition to make tamales, even with both our help." I say. "Amelia didn't even get drunk on that spiked eggnog she usually makes every year and force us into Christmas-themed karaoke."

"No wonder I hardly remember it." Jorge says. "But come to think of it, I do remember Nana bringing her nasty fruitcake, even though we never eat it."

"That she did." I nod solemnly. "And she probably will again this year."

"At least we can count on some things to never change." Jorge laughs. Then, his smile falls as the weight of this time of year settles on us once again. "I can't believe it's almost been an entire year already. It feels like it just happened."

He's right. Exactly three weeks from now, it'll be a year since our father died.

"I know." I let out another breath. "I can't believe how fast time flies sometimes. Come on, let's go." I get up from the couch, tired of the pity party we're throwing for ourselves.

"Go where?" His brows crease in question.

"Target, of course."

Five hours and enough string lights to cause a fire hazard later, my living room is unrecognizable. We did not get a small tree, despite my insistence at the store. Jorge let an employee talk him into buying a twelve foot Christmas tree and about four hundred dollars worth of decorations. The tree stands in the corner near the window, so those looking out can see when its lit up. Jorge hung up two sets of colorful string lights on the living room walls. Giant red bows are tied to the light fixtures hanging above the kitchen bar. Red and white striped stockings are hung up near the tree despite there only being two of us. A chestnut scented candle burns on the coffee table as we survey the work we've done. We're both covered in tinsel and glitter by the time we're finished.

"Not too shabby, huh?" Jorge asks.

"It'll do." I shrug. "You better help me take down all this stuff before you leave."

"Let's not worry about what will or won't happen after the holidays," He says, and I glower at him. "Now we have to decide what we're going to make for Christmas dinner."

"How bout we focus on what we're going to eat for dinner now first. I'm starving."

We pick up food from Chipotle and return to my apartment. Once we're seated at the kitchen with our burrito bowls, I say, "How 'bout we just order tamales from the Barrera's restaurant?" I suggest.

"I guess." Jorge says. "Do you think we can make them home-made next year? I promise to help!"

"We'll see." I tell him. "You could always convince Amelia to help you out next year. You could teach her the recipe." He shrugs as I pick up my phone. "I'll call Chastity and see what we can manage."

I move to my bedroom to call Chastity. She answers on the first ring. "Hey! I've been meaning call you."

"You've probably been busy. Don't worry about it," I tell her. "I'm actually calling to see if your parents have any kind of delivery or catering service for tamales."

"Say no more. I will hand deliver two dozen to you myself on the twenty-third." She says. "I need an excuse to visit you in Austin, anyway."

"Have I ever told you you're the best friend a girl could have?"

"I don't seem to recall." She laughs. "You know I got you covered. Is Jorge there, too?"

"Yup. Just arrived this afternoon." I tell her.

"I'll see if I can get Christian up for a visit, too. It'll be nice for them to see each other again."

"Sounds good." I tell her. "I'll see you soon."

On the morning of the twenty-third, Nana Wilhelmina and Amelia arrive at my doorstep. Nana comments on the decorations and Amelia exclaims over Jorge's presence before telling him he needs a haircut. Jorge just shakes his head, but his mouth is curled up in a grin.

"Where can I put this?" My grandmother indicates the annual fruitcake in her hands.

"Fridge is right in there." I point her to the kitchen.

"Oh," She heads that way, then suddenly stops and turns. "Please tell me there's no pig head this year." I roll my eyes. She says this every year. Making tamales was my mother's favorite holiday tradition, and the classic recipe calls for pork from a pig's head. The first year my grandmother came over to visit us when I was five, she noticed a large covering in the fridge and, because she's too nosy for her own good, unwrapped it to find quite a scare. She's never let us live it down since.

"You're in the clear, Nana." I tell her, and she nods before turning back. I look back at Amelia. "You have good timing. Chastity's arriving with food soon."

"Oh, yay!" She says. "I haven't seen her in forever. It'll be nice to catch up."

"Is she bringing Christian?" Jorge calls from the hallway. He steps into the living room still wearing his pajamas, his hair mussed from sleep.

"I'm sure she's convinced him." I tell him.

Sure enough, Chastity and Christian arrive not too long after, and it's a full house in my apartment. Jorge and Christian have taken over the living room to play video games (Christian went out of his way to bring his game counsel from home), and Nana and Amelia have taken over the kitchen to bake Christmas cookies. Chastity and I are in my room catching up on everything.

Well, almost everything.

"You really haven't been dating a single person in Dallas?" I ask her. "I can hardly believe it."

She rolls her eyes and shoves my arm playfully. "I thought after everything with Jane it'd be good for me to take some time for myself. Try to get over her before jumping into something new again. I don't know, even the thought of dating someone else right now sounds exhausting."

"Mm." I nod thoughtfully. "Do you still think she was the one for you?"

"I clearly don't know anything." Chastity shakes her head. "I guess I just wish we'd had more time to figure it out, you know?"

"Yeah. I get it." For a brief moment, I consider telling her about everything with Marcus. It'd be good to finally get everything off my chest once and for all, but wouldn't it be selfish of me considering everything she's been through with Jane? Chastity might fall in love too quickly, but I've never seen her this heartbroken before. I can tell in her strained smile that she's trying to make it look like she's unaffected, but she can't hide her feelings from me. I don't want to make this all about me, so I decide to bite my tongue. "Did you ever see her in Dallas?"

"No." She sighs. "I chickened out and stood her up. I'm pathetic."

"Chas," I admonish. "If you want her back, just say so. Stop hiding from your true feelings. That's my thing."

She lets out a surprise chuckle. "You're right. This isn't like me at all. I've just never been this scared before."

"You could always ask your parents if the San Antonio restaurant needs any permanent help." I tell her. "You wouldn't be moving back for her. You'd be doing it for you, and seeing where your relationship goes along the way."

"Do you really think I should?" She asks.

I put a hand on her shoulder in a firm grip. "No more asking for my opinion. Do what you know in your heart you want to do, and do it unapologetically."

Her eyes widen. "That is not the kind of advice I've come to expect from you. The Dacia I know would tell me to snap out of this funk and move on with my life. Where'd that Dacia go?"

"Wow, you really think I'm that harsh?" She shrugs, and I have to scoff. "I just hate seeing you so unhappy, Chas. If you're holding yourself back because of something I or your brother said, please do yourself a favor and stop listening to us. We're kinda stupid when it comes to other people's feelings."

"That's true." She smiles sadly. "How do you know I'm unhappy?"

"Because I know you. And I will always support you, no matter what you choose to do."

She pulls me into her arms, and I let her gladly. "Thank you, Dacia."

Later that night, I find Christian nursing a cup of coffee at the kitchen bar. Chastity and Amelia are fast asleep in my room, and I didn't want to wake them with my restlessness. I wonder if there's something on his mind keeping him awake. There's something on mine I'm fighting hard not to face. "Can't sleep?" I ask him.

"Not really." He says as I take the seat across from him. "So, I hear you might be a full-time Texan soon."

"Not as soon as you'd think. And it might not even happen." I admit. "The board could still vote no."

"I bet they won't. As much as you might hate it, Texas looks good on you." The side of his mouth turns up in a crooked grin, and the sight of it brings me back to freshmen year of college when we first met. He had to know about the massive crush I had on him back then, but now I can only recall the feeling through memory. Funny how much time can do.

"That's what everyone keeps trying to tell me." I shrug. "Maybe they're right."

"Maybe." He agrees, and we fall into companionable silence for a moment. "Hey, tell me something." My brows crease in question. "How come it was you and Anthony and not you and me?" The question throws me off guard that I don't respond for a full minute. "Sorry, I shouldn't have asked. I know you always loved him."

"I didn't." I admit. "I thought I did, but I realize now it was just me falling into what's comfortable. You were the one I wanted to be with at first."

He looks up with surprise. "Why didn't you ever tell me?"

"I was too scared. Surprise, surprise." I laugh humorlessly. "But I don't have any regrets. Your friendship means a lot to me, especially your friendship with Jorge. If we got together and it didn't work out, it could've ruined what we have now."

"You're probably right." He nods. "But a part of me still regrets never trying. Is that crazy?"

"No, you're not crazy. I used to have that regret, too."

"But you don't anymore? Ah, let me guess. Because of Marcus." I don't respond for so long I'm in danger of giving myself away. "You can't even deny it, can you?"

"How did you-"

"Amelia mentioned him in passing. When I asked her how she knew him, she was deceptively quiet and I put two and two together." He says. "Something happen between you guys recently?"

"Yeah, kind of." I admit. "But it doesn't matter. We'll probably never see each other again."

"Hmm. You really believe that?" I'm not sure where to begin to answer that question. "Listen, I can't even imagine how you guys started up whatever you have. But I know you, so I know it had to have been less than easy."

"Understatement." I grumble.

"It'd be so much easier if we were in love, wouldn't it?" He says and surprises me all over again. "Chastity would become your sister and Jorge would be the little brother I always wanted.

We'd move into a highrise downtown, like you always wanted. Have kids. I'd open up a trendy restaurant of my own to support us and you wouldn't have to work with your shitty board members anymore. It's a nice picture." I let myself imagine it for a moment. He's right. It is a nice picture. But...

"But Chastity is already like your sister," He continues. "And Jorge is already a brother to me. We don't need to be married for that. And I'm willing to bet you'd rather live in that highrise by yourself and I'm not even sure I want kids. My parents will never let me become their competition and you will never, ever give up your career, no matter how many assholes you have to put up with on a daily basis." He shrugs. "I don't think you like what's comfortable nearly as much as you think you do."

I shouldn't be surprised by how well he knows me, but that last part can't possibly be true. I don't just like what's comfortable, I live for comfortable.

"When it comes to the people in my life, I do." I counter. "Work isn't even that different, if you think about it. It's been in my family for years, and I've been with Seidel for years. Starting over would be devastating."

"We both know there are plenty of tech companies that would love to poach you from Seidel. Sure, you wouldn't be as high up as CEO, but you would be comfortable. You choose to stay at Seidel, not for your family, not for the shitty men you work with, but because you want to. You just said yourself that it'd be devastating if you left. Why?"

"Because-" I start and stop myself. He's right. The tension leaves my body and I sag in my chair. "Because no one thinks

I can succeed. Not even me, sometimes. I'd like to show us all up in one fell swoop so I can burry my doubts once and for all."

"It hasn't been easy though, has it?" He smiles knowingly.

"Okay, but that's different from the people in my life." I say. "I have all the friends I need with you and Chastity. I was with Anthony for four years before I realized I was better on my own. What do you have to say to that?"

"You do remember how you and Chastity became friends, don't you?" When I stare at him blankly, he continues. "She hated you! I mean, she also begrudgingly respected you because you were scary, but that respect turned into lifelong friendship. You can't tell me that was easy, either."

"We were stuck in a cramped dorm room together. We were bound to bond sooner or later."

"I never bonded with my freshman roommate." He says. "He's out there in the world somewhere and I could care less to find out what he's up to. Point for me. And maybe it'd be good for you to air this out once and for all: why did you break up with Anthony?"

"You know why."

"Do I?" He smiles knowingly again. "Let's see if I can remember your exact words. You said-"

"I liked the time we spent apart long distance more than I liked the time we spent together." I repeat from memory, and then I cringe. "God, I still can't believe I broke up with him that way."

"Long distance should've been hard for you. Almost devastating, if you really loved him the way you thought you did. But it was easy, and you didn't like that."

"So apparently I like making life hard for myself." I say. "No wonder things never seem to go my way. Thanks for the lesson."

"Anytime." He yawns. "Okay, I think I'm finally ready for bed. I've got a long drive back tomorrow." I leave him to the couch and return to my bedroom, where Chastity and Amelia are still fast asleep. But my mind turns over everything he said, wondering how I could possibly live in a world where Christian is right.

Chastity and Christian leave early the next morning. Amelia and Nana stay with me until New Years before returning back to San Marcos. It's the smallest our holidays have ever been, but it's also nice not making a huge deal of it. Jorge goes back to school in two weeks, and decides to stay with me in Austin for that time.

"Are you sure you'll be okay by yourself?" I ask for the thousandth time the night before I'm due back at the office. "I know you've sworn off ever working for Seidel, but you could always do a one-week intern stint and see if you might change your mind."

"No, thank you." He says. "I think I'm gonna spend my time exploring the city, check out a couple live gigs. You know, fun things college kids are supposed to be doing on their breaks from school."

"Suit yourself." I say. "Just know if your whole starving artist thing doesn't pan out, we'll always be happy to have you in the office."

"No way. My acting career is totally gonna take off after I graduate." I roll my eyes before leaving to get ready for bed.

The next morning, I'm starting to feel more like myself when I get to the office. The building isn't nearly as extravagant as HQ in Chicago, but a contrasting red brick with tall glass windows that look over downtown. The floor plan was remodeled sometime after my father was promoted, now with an open work area, glass desks that give the elusion of more space, and lots of windows to let light in. Much more inviting than the stuffy cubicles that preceded it.

My office is on the second floor balcony overlooking the work area, right across from Mrs. Henderson's office. It'll become my permanent office, if all goes as planned. I've gone ahead and taped new pictures of my family to the monitor. There's one we took of all of us on the twenty-third before Chastity and Christian left, some individual ones of Amelia, Jorge, and Nana. I even stalked Marcus's Instagram page and printed a picture of him from 2018 at Cloud Gate in Chicago, because I couldn't resist. It's taped face-up under the corner of my glass desk. A home that could've been in a home that used to be.

There's a knock at my door, and then Mrs. Henderson enters my office. She asks how my break was, and we settle into idle small talk before she briefs me for the week's goals. The day goes by in a chaotic blur. I don't have time to check my phone until lunch, but when I do I have to do a double take.

I have three missed texts from Marcus.

CHAPTER 22

Almost two months have passed since the last time we saw each other. Two months of pretending I'm okay with goodbye, but something as simple as his name flashing across my lock screen feels like a punch to the gut. A reminder of what could've been.

I don't read his messages. I can't. I can't make myself, not right now.

Working through lunch isn't the helpful distraction I think it will be, so I log off and decide to go for a walk to clear my head. The winters here are more like a suggestion - the air is icy as it hits my skin, but once I leave the shady cover of trees when I cross the street, the sun warms my back through my coat. I shrug it off when I reach a Starbucks, the heater blasting high enough to be suffocating. I will never understand what goes through people's minds down here when the weather turns. The snow melts as it touches the ground, but that doesn't stop their central heating from working overtime.

This was my idea, I remind myself. I didn't want my last interaction with Marcus to be through a missed text, but now

I have three of them sitting on my phone. Has he changed his mind? Have I changed mine?

When I return to the office, an intern's copy error on an email sent to HQ takes up the rest of my work day and for the time being, I forget all about the missed texts. It isn't until I get home for dinner that I unconsciously check my phone and see that three has turned into eight missed alerts. A few are texts from Amelia and two are a missed call and voicemail from Marcus. A sense of dread crawls up my spine, but I'm not sure why. He wouldn't repeatedly contact me like this if he didn't have something important to say. I should read his texts, get the inevitable over with. But...

I let out a groan before throwing my phone back into my purse. I'm a wimp with a million buts, the most important but being that saying goodbye the first time was ten times harder than I anticipated, and I don't even want to consider what a second one will do to me.

See, I can only be good at compartmentalizing when the past stays past. Nostalgia has been historically detrimental to my mental health, so it's better for my sanity to focus on what's right in front of me. Work and Jorge, until my brother goes back to New York. Then work again and reading for pleasure on the weekends, until the next time I see Amelia or Nana or Chastity or Christian and I remember how much I missed them.

This is how I talk myself into ignoring Marcus's messages until the next morning. But by then even more appear, and dread builds in the pit of my stomach when my eye catches on a single word - a name.

I know we're technically not supposed to contact each other, but I need to talk to you.

If I could ask anyone else, I would. But this is too important.

Please, Dacia.

It's about Sarah. Please call or text me back or I'll have to come up there myself.

Okay, you're giving me no choice. I'm in Austin, on my way to your office.

Shit shit shit -

I throw on the first presentable work clothes I find in my closet and rush out the door without brushing my teeth. I don't even say goodbye to my brother on my way out the door. When I get in my car, I dial his number from the bluetooth screen, but he doesn't pick up. Is he really in Austin? Am I really about to see Marcus again?

The office is eerily quiet when I arrive. Everyone is typing away at their computers, focused on work while inside I'm imploding. What has Sarah done to warrant Marcus to come up here in the middle of the week? Christian's words from months ago ring in my head incessantly. He has brothers who were Jorge's age when she-

I take the stairs to my office two at a time, cursing myself for ignoring his texts out of fear or spite or whatever my stupid, emotional self was thinking. He's not there when I reach my office, and the sudden thought that I could be too late halts me in my tracks. It's an illogical thought, but it gets stuck on my mind. Not even twenty-four hours have passed since his first message, but -

What if I could've stopped her sooner? Why didn't I trust him all those months ago when she first forced her way into his life? If I could've prevented this, whatever she did -

I dial his number again, but it goes straight to voicemail. I'm cursing under my breath again when a knock sounds on my door. I turn around, and there he is. Marcus.

He's dressed in jeans and a blue V-neck, his hair even more disheveled than usual. His chest rises and falls as if trying to catch his breath, and I wonder if he's been running around trying to find me like I've been trying to find him.

"I'm so sorry I didn't text you back." I cross the room to him in two quick strides. "What happened? What did she do?"

"Nothing, thankfully." He tells me, shutting the door behind him. "But she could have. I caught Luke texting her over the holidays and gave him the lecture of a lifetime. He swears all they've done is talk, but if it wasn't for you it could've been much worse. You have no idea how much I owe you for telling me the truth."

I let out a relieved breath. "Thank god."

I pull him into a hug, because on top of seeing him for the first time in weeks and worrying that something was wrong, I'm overwhelmed by the need to touch him. To hold him. To make sure he's really here and that everything's really okay. His arms wrap around my back as I sink into his chest, secure. Safe. The spicy scent of his cologne fills my nostrils, and I allow myself to breathe him in. To settle into the solid warmth of his body like it's the only home I've ever known. God, I missed him so much more than I'm willing to admit.

After a long moment I never want to end, I pull away as a thought occurs to me.

"Wait. If nothing happened, then why are you here?"

Worry lines appear on his forehead as his brows crease. "I have kind of a huge favor to ask. I understand if you say no, but this is too important not to ask. Otherwise I never would've bothered reaching out."

"Okay." I say. "What is it?"

"There's going to be a trial against Sarah." He says. "A family member of the plaintiff contacted Luke through Twitter. They're looking for potential victims to testify against her." I don't say a word, because suddenly I know why he's here. "Luke showed me the messages. Their lawyers don't think his story is strong enough to hold weight in court. Then they asked if he knew anyone else Sarah was in contact with, anyone she might've hurt. We didn't give them your brother's name because I wanted to talk to you about it first."

Seven years have passed since I ran Sarah out of town the first time. I never once considered that an opportunity like this would arise one day. But the fact that we didn't handle what happened to Jorge in the right way weighs on me now more than ever. I ran her out of Chicago just so she could go and destroy someone else's family. I'm almost as responsible for that as Sarah is.

I want nothing more than to see her get the end she deserves, but this isn't my choice to make.

"I have to ask my brother." I say. "I have no idea what he'll say."

"I understand." He tells me. "But can you do it soon? I want to give them an answer as soon as possible."

"He's staying with me until he goes back to school." I tell him. "I'll talk to him tonight."

"Okay." He says. "I'm staying in town with Jane for awhile. Call me when he has an answer." He hesitates for a moment, as if about to say something else.

"What is it?" I ask.

"Nothing." He shakes his head. "I should let you get to work." He turns around and heads out of the office. We wave goodbye, and then he's walking down the narrow hallway to the elevator. I watch his back as he leaves, half hoping he'll turn around and give any sort of indication of how he's feeling. But he never does, and then he's gone.

Jorge is in the living room putting on his shoes when I get back to the apartment. He looks up as I enter and flashes his hundred-watt smile, looking so much like our father I nearly gasp.

"Hey!" His face is too bright, too happy for me to disrupt the good mood he's in. I have to tell him soon, but do I have to tell him right now? "How was work?"

"Good." I answer, hoping he doesn't hear the waver in my voice. "Where are you headed?"

"The 360 bridge." He says. "I thought it'd be nice to watch the sunset there. Do you wanna come with?"

"No, you go ahead." I sigh. "I'm exhausted. I think I'll stay in for the night."

"Cool." He says. "In that case, can I borrow your car?"

"I better get it back in one piece." I toss him my keys. "Go have fun." While you still can. When he leaves, I plop down on the couch with a sigh. I don't know how to ask my little brother to relive everything we went through with Sarah in front of a courtroom. In front of jurors analyzing every word out of his mouth. In front of a lawyer who will twist his story to work in his client's favor. In front of Sarah herself.

As if of their own accord, my fingers dial Marcus's number on my phone. He answers on the first ring.

"Hey." There's surprise in his tone. "I didn't expect to hear from you so soon."

"I don't have an answer. I couldn't even get myself to tell him anything." I'm not sure why I called him to tell him this. I'm not sure why I called him at all. Only that seeing him again today opened a floodgate of emotions I haven't had the courage to sift through for an entire month. Once that realization hits, I say, "Never mind. It's stupid. I'll call you after I talk to him."

"Wait-" He stops me before I can hang up. "Do you want to talk about it?" I don't say anything. "We can meet up somewhere and-"

"I don't have my car." I tell him. "You can come over here if you want. Jorge's out adventuring the city." He agrees, and I text him the address. Fifteen minutes pass before there's a knock at my door.

"That was fast." I say.

"I'm not staying far from here." He tells me. I walk toward the couch, and we sit down beside each other. "You sounded conflicted earlier." He says.

"I guess." I cross my arms over my chest. "I'm not very good at this."

"At what?" His brows furrow.

"Talking out my feelings. We've been through this." I say, waving a hand dismissively. "I'm more of an internal person."

"I remember. You're a sentient AI who only goes to Amelia when you need to cry." His mouth quirks up at the side, but it's not quite a smile. "So, why haven't you gone to her about this yet?"

I shrug. "I don't know. She'd be the perfect person to talk through this with. She was the only one I ever talked to about Sarah. Before you, I mean."

"Right." He nods. "What do you think she'd say?"

"I don't know." I look down at my hands. "She'd be pissed, I can tell you that much. She flipped out when I told her about seeing Sarah in San Antonio. I think..." I let out a frustrated sigh. "This is an impossible situation to think through logically. I'm a problem solver - Amelia, too. We have to be to work for Seidel. I'm constantly assessing situations without letting my emotions cloud my judgement. Until my dad died and my anxiety spun out of control, but that's not what-" I shake my head, flustered. Then I take in a breath and continue. "Anyway. This whole situation with Sarah is rife with emotion. This has been an emotional year in general." I let out a humorless laugh. "And I'm a terrible sister. Jorge and I don't talk about what she did. I don't ask, and he's never talked to me about it once in seven years."

He moves as if to wrap his arm around my shoulders, but hesitates at the last second before taking my hand in his instead. The warmth of his touch is comforting, and I find myself wishing he'd wrapped me in his arms instead. But I understand his hesitation, that uncertainty of what we are and what's acceptable to do for the other. I catch the emotion flashing in his eyes, but I can't look him in the face. It's too much. I'm barely keeping myself together, and if I look at him I'll completely break.

"Hey," He tilts my chin up to meet his gaze, and that does it. The tears stinging my eyes begin to fall. "I'm sure that's not true. Give yourself more credit than that." I start to shake my head, but he cups my cheeks with his hands to stop the motion. His thumbs wipe away the wetness on my cheeks. "You're allowed to have feelings about this, okay? I can't even begin to imagine what this past year has been like for you, and I know I didn't make it any easier. Come here."

And then my wish is granted when I'm pulled into the comfort of his arms. I sink into him, my snot and tears seeping into his shirt as I let myself cry. He doesn't mind. He just squeezes tighter, until I find myself breathing easier once I've let the emotion out of my system.

"He's my baby brother." I finally say. My voice comes out warbled, another sob threatening to burst free. "I didn't protect him the way I should have. And I still can't."

He pulls back a bit to look at my face. "You don't have any idea what he'll say about this?"

I shake my head. "I don't have a clue. Maybe if I did, maybe if we talked more about what happened to him, I would. I don't want to sway him either way, but I also don't want Sarah to ever have the chance to pull this shit again." I let out a long breath. "We did everything wrong when we found out what she was doing. I mean, she was my best friend for four fucking years and

I never knew. She watched him grow up and it just makes me so sick to my stomach that-" I have to stop myself there before I'm tempted to break my hand through a wall. Marcus doesn't say a word, listening as I unload seven years worth of baggage on him. "I despise her. I'd wish she was dead, but that's not enough. Nothing ever will be, and I highly doubt whatever a judge rules will come close to being enough. But there's not a damn thing I can do about it."

He smooths the hair back from my tear-stained cheeks as I take in another breath. When I look up at him again, his eyes threaten to undo me all over again. "I just don't want to see Jorge get hurt again." I say. "She's done enough to us."

"But he deserves to know." Marcus tells me. "He's an adult now. You might be surprised by what he has to say."

"I know." I nod. "And I will tell him. It's just...a lot to process."

"I'm sorry I had to spring this up on you out of the blue." He says. "But honestly, I'm glad to have an excuse to see you again. Is that terrible?"

"Yes." I say, but I'm smiling. Despite everything, my heart feels full at his admission. "I wish it were under different circumstances, but I'm glad I got to see you again, too."

"I'm here if you need me." He says. "You don't have to go through all this Sarah stuff alone. But if you don't want me-"

"I do." I say quickly. "As long as you want to be here. I don't want you to feel like you have an obligation to me."

"Are you kidding?" He takes my hand and intertwines his fingers through mine. "We're beyond all that now. I want to be here for you in any way I can be."

Our eyes meet and lock. Awareness spreads over my body as I find myself inching closer, the memory of his lips closing over mine making my head spin. He's leaning toward me, eyes hazy as they flick down to my mouth. I don't care about what this will mean or the confusing web of emotions I'll be left with in the aftermath. We're both here, and so is whatever this thing is between us. We can't seem to shake it.

But we're interrupted when the front door cracks open. I spring apart from him as Jorge walks through the door, eyeing the two of us with surprise.

"Oh. Hi." Jorge says. Then he looks at me, eyes creasing in concern when he sees my red eyes and tear-stained cheeks. I square my shoulders and clear my throat of phlegm to regain some dignity. Instead of commenting on what I'd prefer my brother not have seen, he cracks a joke at my expense. "You haven't been at the office very long yet, sis. I didn't know you could make friends that fast."

My tears have never dried up faster. I scowl, and it deepens when Marcus says, "She can't. We actually met over the summer."

My brother laughs. "That explains it, then. I'm Jorge." He holds out his hand, and Marcus shakes it.

"Marcus." He introduces. "You must be the brother she goes on and on about."

"Oh, god. Nothing embarrassing, I hope." Just everything, I think to myself, but I don't say a word.

"Just that you make the best croissants she's ever had." Marcus says, smiling easily.

"Oh, that's just her dopey way of saying she loves me because she can't express her emotions." Jorge rolls his eyes, but a flicker of concern returns to his eyes when he looks at me. Then, he shrugs. "I just make the pillsbury kind."

"Hey!" I kick at my brother's shoe, and he takes a step back from me. "I can express myself plenty."

"You've known her for half a year." He tells Marcus. "What do you think? Is my sister a robot?" But there's a curious glint in my brother's eye when he looks at him, as if trying to decipher how much the man knows.

"More like an AI." He looks back at me with a grin. I hide mine behind a hand. Marcus chuckles before turning back to my brother. "She's not that bad."

"Wow, you must really like her to lie like that." I kick at Jorge again, and he stumbles away. "Easy! You're gonna make me trip!"

"That's the point." I get one last kick in before he moves away.

"Is anyone else starving?" Jorge asks. "I'd like to hear some embarrassing stories of Dacia from summer. I've already heard a few from Christian and Chastity, but I'm sure there are tons more."

I roll my eyes as Marcus says, "Happy to oblige. We also spent some time in San Marcos, so I have plenty."

Jorge claps a hand on Marcus's shoulder. "I like you already, buddy."

CHAPTER 23

We're sitting in a booth at Hopdoddy's waiting for our burgers to arrive when Marcus asks, "Want to hear how Dacia and I met?" There's a wicked glint in his eyes when he looks at me, and then back at my brother.

"Oh, god." I cover my face with a hand.

The burger joint was dead when we arrived, but now that we're seated a line to order has formed. Jorge sits across from Marcus and I, leaning forward in interest with his arms folded in front of him. He meets Marcus's eyes with unmasked excitement.

"Yes, very much." Jorge nods enthusiastically.

"It was at a wedding," Marcus explains. "There was a large group of us and we were introducing ourselves, making small talk-"

"Oof, Dacia never was very good at the small talk." Jorge notes. I roll my eyes and Marcus continues.

"So we're all there talking about our mundane jobs, and then Chastity tells us that Dacia is running Seidel Computers. I've never felt like more of a peasant in my life. Meanwhile, Dacia is looking around like she'd rather be anywhere else." Jorge laughs. "Seriously, her head was turning right and left for a quick exit."

"You're not wrong." Though I'm surprised again by how much he seemed to notice back then.

"My sister hates attention." Jorge says. "She's basically the opposite of Chastity, which is how I'm guessing she got caught in that situation to begin with."

"Mhmm." I nod. "I wouldn't have even been at that wedding if it wasn't up to her."

"The bride was her cousin, right?" Marcus asks. When I nod, he says, "I almost wasn't at that wedding, either. I got some pretty bad news the night before, but I couldn't drop out of the wedding party so last minute."

"Oh," I feel my brows crease as I wonder what news he's talking about. But he diverts the subject by returning to his story before I can ask.

"Just think how different our lives would be if you weren't there to insult me and I wasn't sitting in the perfect spot to eavesdrop."

"Wait, what?" Jorge looks back at me. "You'd barely just met the guy! What did you say about him?"

"I'll set the scene." Marcus says. "I was sitting at a table with my best friend, Jesse, minding my own business when-"

"Do we really need to rehash this again?"

"Don't listen to Dacia. Go on." Jorge rubs his hands in antic- ipation, like a maniacal Disney villain.

"So we're just talking about our plans after the wedding when we hear Chastity's voice behind us, and she's talking about me to Dacia." Marcus explains. "I guess Chastity wanted to set us up, so she's talking me up, saying how adorable I am, and how she'd ask Jane if I'd be interested in her."

"Can we not?" I cover my face with both hands.

"And what do you think Dacia said?" He asks Jorge.

"She shot you down hard, huh?" Jorge asks. "Shit, and you had to hear it! I'm so sorry man. My sister has no mercy, so I know whatever she said had to have been cold."

"She did shut me down." Marcus says, putting a hand to his heart as he looks over at me. "In the most brutal way possible."

"Which I already apologized for." I remind him.

"You apologized to someone?" Jorge gasps. Then he turns to Marcus. "She never apologizes. Even after she dropped my Nintendo 3DS down a flight of stairs when she was helping me move into my dorm freshman year."

"I bought you a new one." I roll my eyes.

"I had a game plugged into that one!" He counters. "I lost half a year of progress on it!"

"Maybe you should find a hobby less sensitive to an accidental fall down a flight of stairs." I say. "Maybe try opening up a book every once in awhile, huh?"

"If the roles were reversed and that had been your laptop, you never would've forgiven me."

"You can't compare a gaming counsel to a computer! I work on my laptop. If you dropped it down the stairs, you'd have endangered my entire career."

"You see?" Jorge turns back to Marcus. "You're more likely to get an honest to god miracle than an apology from Dacia."

"Then I guess I should consider myself lucky." He shoots me a smile, and I can't help but return it. Our food arrives, but not before I catch Jorge looking back and forth between us like he knows exactly what's going on. We continue catching Jorge up with everything that's happened since Marcus and I met (almost everything, anyway), and before I can stop them, they start making plans to hang out again.

"We should do this again! How long are you in the city for?" Jorge asks.

"Just until the end of the week." Marcus says. "My sister has a gig downtown this weekend, and she actually might be looking to move up here if she can afford it."

My head snaps up to face him. Does Chastity know that?

"Sounds cool! Maybe we can all go out and support her." Jorge says.

"Oh, Dacia probably doesn't want to do that. Bars aren't really her scene." But he's looking at me with undisguised hope in his eyes.

Jorge opens his mouth, probably to say something along the lines of, "Anywhere outside the office and her bedroom 'aren't really her scene,'", but I cut him off before he can.

"Of course I would." I tell Marcus. "Just text me the time and place and we'll be there."

We part ways when I drop Marcus off at the Air B&B he's staying at, and then all is silent. I pull out of the parking lot and onto the highway, and then outside my apartment. Maybe I was wrong earlier, and my brother hasn't picked up on anything between Marcus and I. I'm about to breathe a sigh of relief when he says, "So when are you gonna tell him?"

"Tell him what?" I ask, a note of caution in my tone.

"That you looooove him." He teases. I let out a groan. "I'm a little surprised, sis. I've been picturing you with Christian for so long-"

"Excuse me?"

"Like you didn't know." He rolls his eyes. "When you broke things off with Anthony, he wanted to ask you out. He claims he didn't because you guys are always in different cities or whatever. I really liked him for you, but it looks like he's finally got some competition."

"You don't have to say 'finally' like that."

"Oh, I think I do." He laughs. Then he lets out a long sigh. "Actually, if I'm being honest, I just thought it'd be nice to call Christian my brother. I really look up to him, you know?"

"There's a scary thought." I say.

"He's more understanding than you think." He says, and I'm reminded that Christian knows about Sarah, too. That my brother felt more comfortable talking to him about what happened than me. He confirms my thinking when he says, "I love you and all, but there are things I feel like I can go to him for that I can't with you."

"Like Sarah?" He looks up at me in surprise. "There's something I haven't told you about this summer that I've been scared to. I ran into her in San Antonio."

"Oh." He looks away from me. "How is she?"

"Like I know or care." I scoff. He flinches at my tone and a flash of guilt goes through me. This is why he feels like he can't talk to me. "I don't know." I say more softly. "Look, I know I haven't been the most understanding about this in the past. But that's just because I love you, and I can't stand to think how badly she must've hurt you. I trusted her when I shouldn't have, and-"

"I know." He says. "I didn't know how bad it must've looked to you back then. But in hindsight, I get it now." He pauses. I don't say a word, letting him gather his thoughts. "I know you think she hurt me in some kind of unspeakable way, but it wasn't an obvious kind of hurt. I'd always had a crush on her, and to have those feelings returned was...exhilarating, to say the least. I thought I was so cool, and I couldn't wait to tell everyone about us. But she never failed to remind me that we had to be a secret. She could be..." He takes in a breath. "She could be scary when I didn't do what she wanted. Looking back on how everything went down, I realized that she liked the control she had over me more than she actually liked me."

I look away so he can't see the tears welling in my eyes. My hands grip the steering wheel so hard my knuckles turn white. I could kill her. She doesn't deserve to walk away from this unscathed, and I could kick myself all over again for letting her.

"I started seeing a therapist at school." Jorge says, surprising me. "Not talking about it for so many years was weighing on me in ways I didn't even realize until I got to college. We don't just talk about Sarah. We talk about school, acting, when I'm feeling overwhelmed. It might be the best thing I've ever done for myself."

"I'm glad." I tell him. "Truly."

"Yeah. So you really ran into her in San Antonio?" He asks. "You didn't kill her, did you?"

I shake my head. "I'm calling it a missed opportunity." Then I take in a breath before I say, "Especially since you're not the only one she's made to be a victim."

His eyes widen. "What? How do you know that?"

I explain everything then, about confessing to Marcus everything that happened, and about Marcus catching his younger brother texting Sarah, to finding out about the trial against her. He takes everything in, looking down at his feet. When I finish, he looks up at me with an unreadable expression.

"This is why you were crying earlier, isn't it?" The question catches me off guard that I have no choice but to nod. His shoulders slump in defeat. "Shit, Dacia. Shit-"

"Don't worry about me." I reach for his hand. "It's not your job to worry about how I'm feeling or what I want. Put all that aside for now-"

"Do you want me to testify against her?" He asks.

"Don't think about what I want." I repeat. "What do you want?"

He's silent for so long I'm not sure he's going to reply. I'm about to tell him to take his time, that he doesn't need to answer right away, when he says, "I'll do it."

I sit back in my seat. "You don't need to answer now-"

"I'll do it." His voice holds more conviction this time. "It's my fault she had the chance to do this again. If I'd said something earlier, right after this happened-"

"It's not your fault." I tell him. "She was manipulating you-"

"And I still could've said something after she was gone!" He exclaims. "Instead I was too ashamed to admit the truth to myself. I didn't want to believe her love was abuse, and look where that got me. Look where that got someone else." He shakes his head, eyes watery. "You wanted to report her, and we didn't. We could've prevented this-"

"Stop." I put my hands on his shoulders in a firm grip. "This isn't your fault, and you shouldn't do this solely because you feel guilty. Take a breath." He does as I say. "Good. Now, you're going to sleep on this decision. If you still feel the same way in the morning, then I'll tell Marcus. But if you change your mind, for whatever reason, I won't judge you for it and neither will he. I want you to really think about what you're getting into, and if you're truly ready for it. Do you understand?"

He nods. "I don't think I'll change my mind, but I understand."

"Okay." I nod. "We'll talk about this again tomorrow. And hey," I stop him before he can open the passenger door. "I'm glad you felt like you could finally open up to me."

"Me, too." He says, smiling sadly.

CHAPTER 24

The next day after work, I return home with the express purpose of talking to my brother about his decision. But when I get there, I open the front door to find Marcus and Jorge playing a card game. They acknowledge me with a head nod and a grumbled "hey" before turning back to their game. Marcus lays down a red five in the middle of the table and yells "uno!"

"Dammit!" Jorge yells. With exaggerated caution, he changes the color with a blue five. Marcus lays down his last card, a blue seven and fist-pumps the air. Jorge scowls to himself, crossing his arms over his chest.

"Better luck next time." Marcus says, then he turns back to me. "Hey, Dacia."

"Hey," I look between the two of them, not sure if I like the male bonding going on without me in my living room. "I didn't know you two had...plans."

"I found him in my Instagram suggestions." Jorge says. "I messaged him this morning and we've been hanging out all day."

"Well, not all day." Marcus says when he sees my expression. "We really just got lunch and played Uno."

"And watched six episodes of a show on Netflix." Jorge says.

"Yeah, unemployment life is clearly working out great for me." Marcus laughs bitterly.

"What are you talking about?" I ask him. "I thought you were going back to your old job."

"They didn't take me back." He says. "I was replaced a lot quicker than I thought I'd be." He shrugs, but his shoulders are tense. "There's a reason for everything, I guess."

I consider asking him how he's going to go back to school, but stop myself for fear of depressing him more. I'd gladly sign him a check if I thought he'd actually take it. I know how much the prospect of teaching means to him, and it's all I want for him.

"So, when are we hitting the bars?" I roll my eyes at my brother. When I turn my head to glare at him, he says, "What? You can't say anything now that I'm of age."

"How 'bout we look at books instead?" I counter, turning to Marcus. "I can show you around my favorite indie bookstore in town." Jorge mimes snoring. I shove him off the barstool with my foot, and he just barely catches himself before falling completely.

"That actually sounds really great." Marcus tells me. "You up for it, Jorge?"

"Nah, I'd rather stay here and sleep." He says. "But you two go ahead!"

I roll my eyes at his transparency. "Whatever. Enjoy your nap." I look to Marcus. "Shall we?" He nods, and I lead him the way to my parked car. "Come to think of it, I don't actually know what kinds of books you like."

"Mostly middle-grade. I like finding books to recommend to my future students. But I like to think I read from across all genres. Thrillers are another favorite of mine."

"That's really cool." I tell him. "I just read whatever I can get my hands on when I'm not busy with work. Sometimes, even when I am." I shrug, and he smiles. "It's just nice to have that escape when you need it, you know?"

"I can definitely relate." He says. "None of my siblings read. I mean, Jane reads poetry sometimes but she's not really big on prose. My parents thought I would grow up to be some kinda super genius or something because I read so much. I didn't have the heart to tell them fiction books can't do all that." He laughs.

"My family doesn't it get it either." I tell him. "Well, my mom did before she died. When I was growing up, she would pass along her favorite books for me to read, a lot of Isabelle Allende and Gabriel García Márquez. She tried to do the same with Jorge, but it never took."

"That must've been hard." Marcus says. "To lose both parents so young."

"There's nothing I can do about it." Which isn't to say I'm not still hit with waves of sadness, sometimes. A twinge in my chest makes it hard to breath, but I press on anyway. "Sometimes I wish I didn't have to grow up so fast, or inherit Seidel at twenty-five. I'm sure to some people it must seem incredible, but there's also an incredible amount of stress with that kind of position. The pressure got to me after my dad died, which was the reason I came to San Antonio in the first place. I was so ashamed of myself for for failing, but I was the only one who seemed to think of it that way."

"I remember that. You had a panic attack" He says. "And they're right not to call it a failure. I can't imagine what that must've been like for you. You'd just lost your dad. It's okay to give yourself a break when you need one. It doesn't make you any less capable of fulfilling your job."

"Yeah, and I get that now." I tell him. "Took me a lot longer than it should have, but I've always learned my lessons the hard way." I give a hollow chuckle, but my smile is real. The truth is, I'm thankful to be in a much healthier state of mind now. "Okay, enough about me and my shame. You're way too perfect for me to be looking this bad in front of you."

"Are you kidding?" He shakes his head. "That couldn't be further from the truth. I'm not perfect."

"Oh, come on. You're the one going into a noble profession. I'm just a shady business woman about to inherit an evil, money-hungry corporate machine." He shakes his head again. "What is it?"

"Since we're confessing our secret shames, I guess I should tell you it's my own fault I haven't graduated yet."

"What do you mean?" My brows furrow.

"I changed my major after two years." He explains. "Even though I knew what I wanted to do more than anything was teach elementary, I got a lot of flack for it. My brothers made fun of me, and so did most of my friends. Well, my guy friends, anyway. It affected me a lot more than I'd like to admit." He shakes his head. "When I moved to Austin for college, I registered as a biology major. I don't know why, sine I hate science. I just did it because everyone I knew was doing it and thought I should, too. In theory becoming a doctor sounded good, but I could never quite picture myself doing it. You'd think that would've been my first clue." He rolls his eyes. "The dumbest mistake I've ever made. I came out of my second year with a 1.2 GPA."

"Oh my god." I say. "What happened?"

"I almost dropped out. But when I moved back home, I transferred to UTSA because my parents wouldn't let me quit." He says. "After Jane bypassed college, they were hellbent on me getting a higher education. That's when I realized I should've just listened to myself and majored in Education in the first place. I would be a teacher by now." He sighs. "My parents helped with tuition for the first two years, but our budget is really tight."

"Five kids will do that." I say sympathetically.

"Exactly. And I thought I had it covered until I realized last year that financial aid wouldn't cover my student teaching semester. That's the bad news I got before the wedding. I was devastated. Since then, I've looked into just about everything that could help, but I've had no luck. I can't get any scholarships because my GPA is too low. The state test doesn't mean a thing if I don't have a bachelor's degree. I've already taken out two student loans, and if I take out a third I'm afraid I'll never be able to pay it back. I'll just be caught in this endless cycle of debt and live with my parents forever."

"God, that's rough." I sympathize, my heart pulling for him.

"I only have one more semester left." His eyes shut. "It's my own fault, and I know that. Once I came back home and switched majors, it was like everything clicked into place for me. No matter what anyone thought, I knew I was finally making the right choice for myself. But in some ways I feel like I'm disappointing my younger self."

"What do you mean?"

"I had all these big dreams, like move as far away from my crazy family as possible, for one." He laughs softly. "Explore the world more. I'm happy where I am, don't get me wrong. I love my family, and I love that I'm there to help them out when I can. But for the last couple years, it feels like I settled before my life could even begin. I've only travelled out of Texas once, and that's because a friend from college paid for me. My family could never afford plane tickets or cross-country road trips with five kids. I always felt so stuck, but now that I'm older I don't even think about that kind of stuff. Its like it doesn't even concern me anymore."

"You got comfortable." I say. "I know the feeling. Not in the same way, but I know."

"That's exactly it." He nods. "Somewhere along the line, I forgot to want more for myself. Maybe because the only thing I want right now - to finish my goddamn degree - isn't working out like I thought it would." He lets out a sigh. "Maybe the Henderson's can hire me again, or refer me to another family until Fall semester."

"You'll find a way." I tell him.

He looks over at me with narrowed eyes. "Come on. You're supposed to tell me the truth."

"I am." I tell him. "I'd give you the money right now if I thought you'd take it."

"No, don't." He shakes his head. "I'm not looking for a pity handout-"

"It's not pity." I tell him. "And it's not a bad thing to accept help when you need it. Isn't that what you just told me?"

"I appreciate the thought. Really." He says. "But I'd feel too weird accepting it."

"I know that." I say. "So I'm going to help you come up with a better solution." I park my car outside the bookstore. "Come on."

"I don't think you're going to find anything." Marcus says once we're inside the bookstore. "I've looked enough times to know."

"We'll see." I stop beside the door and open up the email app on my phone and compose a message to Nana and Mr. Banks Marcus tries to look over my shoulder, but I angle my phone away from him. "Why don't you get a head start and look around?"

Marcus's eyes narrow. "Why are you trying to get rid of me?"

"Stop being paranoid and skedaddle." He rolls his eyes, but does as I say. Once I finish typing out an email, I send it and follow Marcus through the shelves.

"That was fast." He says. "I take it you didn't find anything?"

"We'll see." I say. "Which section should we browse first?"

"Dacia, what did you do?"

I look him right in the eye. "Absolutely nothing."

"How am I just finding out now that you're a terrible liar?" But he shakes his head and laughs. "Come on. The YA section is calling my name." We spend the next few hours wandering the bookstore, pointing out which ones we've read and which ones are on our lists. The books we love and the books we hate. I leave the store with a small stack under my arm, because I can't be stopped from not buying at least one book at a bookstore. When we get back in my car, I hand him one from my stack.

"What's this?" His fingers trace the embossed title, Sadie.

"One of my favorites I think you'll like." I tell him. "I bawled like a baby at the end. And you know me, I don't cry."

"I'll start it tonight." He shoots me a smile. "Thank you."

As soon as I get back to my apartment, I call Chastity. She answers on the first ring with a squeal. "Dacia! This is a surprise. What's up, girl?"

"Oh, nothing much." I lie.

She can tell right away. "Out with it."

"Twice in one day." I say more to myself. "Do you have any plans this weekend?"

"I have a meeting with a local retailer on Friday. She has the cutest clothes, all plus-sized. I'll send you her Insta-"

"What about Saturday?" I cut her off with a note of impatience. My leg is shaking in anticipation. If Marcus still thinks this was my fault, then I need to fix it. A second loose end to tie up before we say goodbye for good. "Do you have anything going on?"

"I don't think so?" There's a note of suspicion in her voice. "Dacia, just tell me what you want to tell me."

"Okay." I sit up on the couch as if readying myself. "If you want another chance with Jane, come to Austin on Saturday." She's silent for so long I start to think she's hung up. "Chas?"

"I'm here." Her voice wavers. "How do you know she's in Austin? Did you run into her, or-"

"I just do." I'll explain everything to her soon. I'm long overdue to. I can hardly believe I've gone this long without telling her about Marcus. "This could be your last chance to tell her once and for all how you feel. Take it if you want it."

I hear her breathing quicken through the static. Then, she says, "Okay. Okay, I will."

CHAPTER 25

When Saturday morning comes, the early sunlight wakes me up before nine. I'll finally have the day free to hang out with my brother. I kick the sheets off of me and start getting ready for the day before heading to Jorge's room. He's still asleep, the covers flung over his head. I tackle him on the bed and he flinches awake before seeing it's me, and then he lets out a groan.

"Dacia, it's too early." He mumbles.

"You don't even know what time it is."

He checks his phone on the nightstand before exclaiming, "It's not even nine yet!"

"Too bad. Come on, I'm bored!" I pull the covers off him and shake his shoulders until he sits up. "You have to spend time with me before you leave for school and forget all about me."

"Can you brush your teeth first? You're blowing morning breath in my face."

I blow a deliberate gust of air in his face before leaving his room, dodging the pillow he throws at me on my way out the door. A few minutes later, he's fully dressed and cranky as hell.

We head to a breakfast cafe downtown, where we're seated at an iron garden table outside. I still haven't talked to him about his decision, but now I'm not so sure a public space is the place to do it. However, I'm saved from having to bring up the topic myself.

"I already told Marcus I'd do it, by the way." He says. "The day he came over to play Uno."

"Oh." I say, surprised. "Why didn't you tell me?"

"I was afraid you'd try to talk me out of it." He says. "I think you were wrong, by the way. I do have on obligation to step forward and tell my story, if it will stop Sarah from doing something like this again. I know not everyone in my position will feel that way, and it's their right to do or not do whatever makes them comfortable, but this isn't about them. Plus, I need to do this for myself, too. I think it'll help me finally move forward from all of this."

"I understand." I tell him. "And I never would've tried to talk you out of it. I just wanted to make sure you made this decision with a clear head."

"I did." He says. "You're a great sister, Dacia."

"I know." I shrug easily, and he shakes his head with a laugh.

When our food comes, we shift to lighter topics and it's the best I've felt with my brother in years.

Later that night, we get ready to see Jane play at a dive bar on Sixth Street. We're sitting front row and center, drinks in hand. I attempt to covertly send Chastity a text asking where she is without Marcus or Jorge seeing. As Jane is introduced onstage, I break away from the crowd to look around and find Chastity emerging through the entrance. We lock eyes and she gives a small smile.

"You okay?" I turn around to find Marcus at my shoulder.

"Yeah. I just...need to throw this away." I show him the damp napkin crumpled in my hand before throwing it in the metal trash bin next to us. He gives me a look like he knows I'm lying, but doesn't say anything. When he offers me his hand, I take it and let him lead me through the crowd back to where Jorge is sitting. It's a simple gesture, but my heart is racing. He's heading back to San Antonio tomorrow morning, and I'm not ready for another goodbye.

This is the first time I've ever heard Jane sing, and I have to admit she's better than I thought she'd be. Her voice is low and throaty, a sultry quality I never knew her voice had. I'm not a music person, but it's always amazed me how much emotion certain songs can evoke in me. Her second song is about lost love, and maybe it's because Marcus is standing right next to me, but it hits me hard. When she sings the line, "the timing's never right, but I swear I'm right about this", I look up at him. As if he can feel my eyes on him, he turns his head and looks down at me.

He smiles sadly, like he knows exactly what I'm thinking. The weight in my chest is so heavy I can hardly breathe. I lean into his shoulder and he wraps his arm around my waist. I soak in the warmth of him while I still can.

I lose myself in Jane's voice until she stumbles on the last chorus. Her eyes dart away from the crowd and back to her guitar, and in that quick instance she recovers. I'm sure most people didn't notice the slight catch in her voice or the shock in her eyes at whatever - whoever - she saw.

I turn around and catch Chastity's eye right away. She waves, then moves her finger back and forth between Marcus and I as if to ask what's going on with us. Her wide eyes scream, "What the heck is going on and why didn't you tell me!?", and I smile back sheepishly. She shakes her head at me but she's smiling ear to ear, because at the end of the day Chastity Barrera will always be happy for me.

Once the set closes, Chastity moves forward to the edge of the stage to greet (read: bombard) Jane. No matter what happens, I'm proud of my friend for finally putting herself out there again. If Chastity can have a happy ending with Jane, then that's enough for me.

"Was that Chastity?" Marcus eyes the stage with concern, but there's the barest suggestion of an amused grin on his lips. Then he turns back to me. "Did you invite her?"

"Guilty." I shrug.

He shakes his head, but his smile grows wider. "Wow. This can't possibly end well."

"I don't know." I look back at the stage, at Chastity and Jane's heads bent close together. At Chastity's thumb stroking Jane's bare shoulder in small circles. "I wouldn't count them out just yet."

"Maybe." He relents. "Are you heading back?"

"As soon as I find Jorge." I notice his empty chair with a scoff. He must've left to give us a final moment alone together. "Thanks for inviting us."

"Of course." He pulls me into his arms and I squeeze back with all my strength. "Can I swing by in the morning to say goodbye?"

"Of course." I nod into his chest, not ready to pull away yet. But sooner than I'd like, I don't have a choice. We spot Jorge near the exit and say a quick goodnight. I force myself not to look back as I walk away, but I cave when I reach the door. Marcus is standing closer to the stage, in quick reach should his sister need a getaway. He doesn't look back at me, and I turn around before I have the chance to catch his eye.

If Jorge can sense something wrong, he doesn't say anything. Once I've showered and gotten ready for bed, I begin to think maybe this will all be for the best. This year is going to be insane for me work-wise. It's better that Marcus and I part ways now, before we can hurt each other even more in the long run.

That's what I try to fool myself into believing, but I'm not nearly convincing enough. Because I know without a shadow of a doubt that Marcus is it for me. I'm not sure when I knew for sure, but I know now that if I'm meant to settle down and start a life with someone, there's no one else for me but him. I don't want anyone else, and I don't want to want anyone else down the line. I'll be fine by myself if I have to be. I really will. I've never had trouble envisioning myself as a powerful business woman who takes no shit and is unafraid to live alone for the rest of her life. A woman who doesn't need her other half, because all of her is all she needs. I believed it before I met Marcus, and I still believe that now.

But wants and needs are different, and all I want is Marcus. If there's any chance he feels the way I feel for him...there's no way

I'd let the opportunity to be with him slip by, no matter what we had to do to be together.

Midnight turns to three AM, and I still can't sleep. My body is drained, but my thoughts won't stop spinning in senseless circles. I can't take this unbearable sense of loss when he was never mine to begin with. But there were moments when it felt like he was mine, though they never lasted nearly as long as I wanted. I reach for my phone and hover over his name in my text messages. Dignity no longer knows my name when I start typing out a message asking him to meet me, but I'm interrupted mid-sentence with an incoming call.

From Marcus.

CHAPTER 26

His voice is low, an unreadable quality to it when I answer the phone. "I'm sorry to be calling so late, but I can't sleep. Did I wake you?"

"No." I tell him. "I can't sleep either."

"Oh." He says. "Can we talk in person? There's something I-"

"Yes." I interrupt. "You can come over."

Ten minutes later, he texts that he's here. I pad barefoot to the door and there he is, the silver moon's light outlining him in the doorway. Emotions cross his features faster than I can read them, and then he squares his shoulders and his face becomes unreadable once more as he steps over the threshold. My brother is asleep, so I lead him to the balcony so we can talk in private. There isn't any furniture, so we sit on the wood paneling and face each other. Marcus leans his back against the railing with a sigh.

"I'm normally not this crazy." Marcus gives an awkward laugh. "I was driving around in circles all night before I finally had the courage to call you."

"Don't worry about it. I did the same to you not too long ago." I remind him. "What's on your mind?"

I watch his chest rise and fall as he takes in a breath, as that unreadable mask melts away and his eyes soften. "I just...I keep thinking about our last night together. What we thought was our last night together. Now that I'm going back home, I keep thinking about what's going to happen with us. Or, what's not going to happen. If we'd become this unfinished thing we were so afraid of becoming in San Marcos. But we're always going to be unfinished if I don't admit how I really feel about you."

A rush of air reaches my lungs. I hold it in place, as if suspended in time.

"Dacia, I...I never expected to fall for you as hard as I have. And if I'm being honest with myself, the reason I kept holding myself back is because I'm scared this won't last. You're not going to be in Austin for much longer, and I might never move out of the town I grew up in. Having you just to lose you is such a terrifying thought, but what's more terrifying to me now is letting you walk away without knowing how much I care about you. Even if you don't feel the same way I do anymore-"

"I do." I interrupt. "God, Marcus, of course I do. I'm not just falling in love with you, I'm in love with you. I'm so in love with you I can barely imagine a time when I wasn't. That's been obvious, hasn't it?"

"Obvious?" He chokes out a laugh. "Dacia, if that were obvious I would've been here a lot sooner. Come here." I crawl forward on my hands and knees and he meets me halfway. It's a relief when I'm in his arms again, when his lips are on mine.

All the passion our last kiss lacked has returned with full force, and it just feels right. Like I'm finally right where I belong.

"Dacia," He says against my lips. "Dacia, I love you."

The words make my heart melt. I haven't yet known him a year, but it feels like I've been waiting centuries for those words to come out of his mouth. I place my hands against his cheeks, fingers curling through his hair as I look into his eyes.

"I don't know what's going to happen in the future." He continues. "I just know I want you in mine. I don't want to go home without fighting for us. People say long distance never works, but maybe those people just didn't want their relationship as much as they think they did."

"I used to say that." I tell him. "And you're right. It didn't work because the relationship wasn't working to begin with. Long distance is hard. It's one of the hardest things a relationship can go through. You have to be willing to put in the work every single day. I never thought anyone would make me want to work that hard ever again." I push the hair back from his face and look into his light brown eyes. "But you do."

His smile is brilliant, a happiness that has no words. I lean my face closer, so close I could almost kiss him again. His hands shift from my shoulders down my back.

"It'll only be for a year." I say. "And then the board will vote to move HQ here in Austin. Now I have an even greater incentive to make sure they say yes."

He chuckles lightly. "I like being your greater incentive."

"Words every man lives to hear." I smile against his lips. "This will be good for us. We'll have one year to get our shit together. I'll prove to myself once and for all that I'm the CEO Seidel needs, and you'll finally get your degree. Fall semester will come and go before you know it."

"I can only hope." He looks away. "Guess I'll have to bite the bullet and take out another loan."

"No you won't." I shake my head, turning his head back to face me. I try to hold back my smile, but it keeps bursting free. "You're gonna be just fine, Marcus."

He narrows his eyes in suspicion. "Dacia. What did you do?"

"Nothing at all." My voice takes on a teasing quality. "But you might want to check your email in the next few weeks."

"Dacia-"

"I don't want to ruin the surprise." I say in a rush. "You know I'm a bad liar now, don't make me ruin it. It's a good one."

"You're too much for me." He says near my ear before planting a kiss there. His arms wrap around my back tighter, pulling me flush against him. "I don't know what I did to deserve you, but I'll be counting my blessings every night."

We spend the entire night talking, wrapped in each other's arms until the sun rises above our heads. When he leaves, I ask him twice to make sure Jane will be the one driving them home. He assures me that she will, and that he'll have a nap in the backseat. I nod in approval before sending him off with a kiss goodbye. The kiss is an indecent one in full view of anyone looking outside their window, but the goodbye is far from permanent.

Later in the day, I catch the date on my phone. January 13th. An entire year has passed since the day my father died. I knew my life would never be the same after that day, but I never could've imagined everything and everyone that would come into my life. Or that I would be just fine, this soon.

EPILOGUE

Eleven Months Later

The light bounces off the top of the Alamo Dome in the early morning sunlight as Chastity and I make our way up the ramp. Damn her for making me wear heels. We have to stop twice for me to adjust the strap where it won't dig into my skin. Of course, I have no such luck. A balmy breeze cools the sweat on my forehead, and I'm convinced that no amount of time will ever make me get used to seventy degree weather in the middle of December.

Inside, we force our way through sweaty crowds of people to the top row where the Galindo's are already seated. They exclaim greetings in a way that makes me feel right at home, even though I know they're mostly aimed at Chastity. She and Jane have been going strong for a couple of months now. Even though they've dated for less time than Marcus and I since they got back together, Chastity has a closer relationship with the Galindo's than I do. Luke is the only one who expresses outward like for me, and I'm betting its only because he's hoping for an internship. (He's mentioned a new hobby for disassembling computer parts in passing more than once. It remains unclear if he knows how to put them back together.) I'm hoping once Marcus and I are settled in our place in Austin, I'll have ample time to correct that.

The graduation ceremony lasts no shorter than three hours, but it goes by fast. I cheer as loud as my voice can carry when Marcus crosses the stage, his bright, smiling face filling the double screens for everyone to see. It isn't long before we're all filed outside and taking turns capturing photos with Marcus.

"Alright, time for the next location." Marcus says once we've finished.

"Can we stop for lunch first?" Isaac asks him. "We're starving. That ceremony lasted forever. You make me not wanna graduate."

"Yah!" Mrs. Galindo hits his shoulder with her purse. "Don't say that! You're next in line to graduate college."

"Hope it doesn't take you six years like me." Marcus smiles sarcastically.

"Better late than never." I tell him, hugging his arm. He shifts so it rests around my shoulders and kisses the top of my head.

After lunch, we head to the UTSA Main Campus so Marcus can take more graduation pictures. I remember asking him a few months ago why he waited so long to take them.

"I actually took a bunch of them before I got the FASFA news." He explained. "I can't even express to you how much of an idiot I felt like. The next time I put on a cap and gown, I want it to be minutes before I walk across that stage."

Which brings us here, on the stone steps of Marcus's college campus. I've got a long list of monuments Marcus wants pictures in front of, and we have the entire day to take them. The University Center is closed, as are most of the buildings when we arrive. We try walking through the John Peace Library ("It'll take us to the Sombrilla faster this way"), but end up having to walk around it to get to the center of campus. But when we get there, Marcus is disheartened to find the fountain, number one on the list, shut off.

"Wow, this day really isn't going the way I thought it would." He rubs the back of his neck. "My family's gonna get here any minute now."

"It's fine. There are plenty of other sites to get pictures with." I point to the giant Roadrunner statue (next up on the list) on a raised platform ten feet from us. "Let's get one with the bird."

I grab a wooden chair from the Sombrilla's seating area and carry it to the statue for Marcus to use to climb on top of the bird. After I've taken a few pictures of him, I zoom into the last picture taken when a flash of gold catches my eye and I realize something. Then I look up at the building behind us.

"Huh." The side of my mouth quirks up in a grin. "You didn't tell me this was it."

"Oh, yeah. That's right." He looks up at the gold lettering above the entrance. "I didn't have any classes on campus, so I completely forgot about it. That used to be the MS building before your incredibly generous donation to my higher education."

"MS?" I ask him.

"Sorry. Multidisciplinary Studies."

We turn back to look at the building. The Dacia García building looks much like the two buildings it sits beside. The pol-
ished lettering stands out garishly against the faded grey stone.

"Does that mean everyone calls it the DG now?" I nudge him
with an elbow. He rolls his eyes, but I can tell he's amused. "And
hey, that donation wasn't only for you. It was just made because
of you."

A whopping quarter of a million dollars for the Education
program to start a scholarship program specifically for education majors during their Student-Teaching semester. I made
sure the GPA requirement only applied to classes taken while in
the Teacher Certification program, making Marcus the perfect
candidate to apply.

The Galindo's find us outside the DG (when in Rome, and all
that), and we explore the campus for more landmarks to take
pictures of Marcus in front of.

We have Marcus's graduation dinner at Margianno's later that
night, and it's a full affair. Jesse, Amelia, and Alex come down
from San Marcos for it. We stay here for hours, just catching
up and laughing about nothing and basking in each other's
company.

The night ends with me at Marcus's house for the very first
time. It's a modest two story brown stucco with four bedrooms
(the three youngest are crammed into the master bedroom together until Jane and Marcus move out). Marcus gives me the
grand tour before stopping at his bedroom. Before we go in, his
parents hug me goodnight before retiring to their bedroom, and
think I may actually be making more progress with them than I
thought.

"Here's where the magic happens." He opens his door with a flourish, but it's anticlimactic. Other than his corner bookshelf and made bed, its entirely packed with moving boxes. But I rush forward to his bookshelf with excitement in every step. I told him to pack his books last so I could look into his soul before they're moved into my - our - apartment next week.

"Rick Riordan, Rick Riordan, Rick Riordan Presents," I count off the top two shelves, which turn out to be a dedicated shrine to the master of Greek myths for kids, as well as his publishing imprint. The entire third shelf is dedicated to the Magic Tree House series and Vashti Harrison books. "Wow, you weren't kidding about the middle-grade."

"They're not just for kids." He assures me. "Well, what's the verdict?"

I count off the titles on the bottom half of his shelves, where lots of Riley Sager, Alex North, and Ruth Ware reside. The book I gave him nearly a year ago sits at the very top of his shelf next to a framed photo of the two of us at Times Square. The trip was Jorge's idea and though it only lasted a weekend, it was a lot of fun.

"Half child, half adult." I tell him as I stand up. "Just as I always suspected."

"No shame in loving what you love." He says. "Now you get to help me pack up the books." He smiles slyly and I let out a groan. "I can't believe I'm finally moving out of this place."

"No regrets, I hope."

"Not a single one." He tells me. "Now, lets hope I can find a job up there. Might be harder in the middle of the school year."

"There's no rush. The board hasn't even voted yet." But that didn't stop me from signing a year lease on a highrise in downtown Austin. I can only hope my final report was enough to convince them, but from the updates Mr. Banks has been sending, it's looking more and more likely the vote will land in our favor.

"They're gonna say yes. They'd be crazy not to." His arms wrap around my middle and he nuzzles his face into the crook of my neck. There isn't a set of four walls in the whole world that could possibly feel more like home to me than when I'm wrapped in Marcus's arms.

We wake early in the morning to beat traffic, Marcus's belongings divided between our two cars. Chastity and Jane will be driving up his U-Haul next week. An hour on the road passes quickly, and then we're standing in front of our new home. Marcus cranes his neck as he looks up and lets out a low whistle.

"I don't even have a job yet, but I can already tell this is wildly out of my price range."

"It's only for a year." I remind him. "We can always downsize later. It's not exactly a child-friendly place."

Good god. I clamp my mouth shut as we head inside, cringing at the slip. It's way too soon to be bringing up kids. As if he can sense the tension radiating off me, he wraps an arm around my shoulders and kisses the top of my head.

"Whatever you want." He says. I deflate as I lean into him. "You're cute when you're nervous."

"Shut up." But I can't help the smile that spreads across my face.

Marcus lets out another low whistle when we reach the suite. Floor to ceiling windows take up the north wall, facing out toward downtown. Its the first thing we see as soon as we enter, and it takes my breath away each time.

"Wow." Marcus breathes. "That's-"

"Incredible." I agree. "I have to live in my dream apartment at least once in my life. I've been dreaming of this place since I was sixteen."

"I see." He nods solemnly. "And has it lived up to your ten-year expectations?"

I look out the window again, the glittering lights of cars and steel and glass buildings and blue, blue sky. Then I look back up at Marcus.

"Yeah." I nod. I reach for his hand, intertwining our fingers. "For the first time in a long time, I have everything I could ever want and more."

www.ingramcontent.com/pod-product-compliance
Lightning Source LLC
Chambersburg PA
CBHW071725190726
48292CB00003B/617